POWER

of an

INNOCENT

MIND

LILLIAN BLACK

TATE PUBLISHING
AND ENTERPRISES, LLC

Published by Tate Publishing & Enterprises, LLC
127 E. Trade Center Terrace | Mustang, Oklahoma 73064 USA
1.888.361.9473 | www.tatepublishing.com

Tate Publishing is committed to excellence in the publishing industry. The company reflects the philosophy established by the founders, based on Psalm 68:11,
"The Lord gave the word and great was the company of those who published it."

Book design copyright © 2015 by Tate Publishing, LLC. All rights reserved.
Cover design by Samson Lim
Interior design by Angelo Moralde

Published in the United States of America

ISBN: 978-1-63449-863-0
Fiction / Thrillers / Supernatural
15.09.18

To God the Father, God the Son, and God the Holy Spirit.

Acknowledgments

I would like to acknowledge the following people for their contributions to my life through the teaching of the word of God: Pastor Chris Oyakhilome, for the undiluted word of God you have taught me throughout the years. Rev. Ken Oyakhilome, for the blessings and prayers you have pronounced upon my life. Pastor Aloy, Pastor Agatha, and Pastor Shola, for the teachings you bestowed upon me throughout the years I was with you. Mama Ruth Wilcox, for your support and love. My sister, Bessie Kolobe Magama, for your support, encouragement, and unfailing love. My sister, Mmoni Mgumba, for all the support you rendered unto me. And finally, my two children, my son Mathiba Chibiya, and my daughter Samantha Chibiya for the inspiration you provide me with daily.

Introduction

When they were faced with the greatest evil creature, everyone—including the Kings and soldiers—ran for their lives, except Princess Grace. She confronted the evil creature without fear or hesitation. She believed God's word without struggling, and she believed that because of the spirit of Christ in her, nothing can harm her. She knew that whatever she asked of the Father in heaven, He would always give it to her because the Word says so. Read on and enjoy the wonderful work that King Wisdom and his daughter, Princess Grace, did for the Kingdom of Heaven. You will find love, soul, winning, romance, riches, and glamour throughout this book.

Personal Note from the Author

This book is a gift from God to both myself, the author, and all those who will read it. I was unfamiliar with the concept of writing a book; all I had was the calling to win souls for Christ.

Recently God spoke to me and told me to write a book. The first thing I said was, "How can I write a book when I don't even know where to start?" An encouraging voice said, "Yes, you can." Just as the voice promised, the words started flowing. This entire book was written through the inspiration of the Holy Spirit.

This is the lesson in line with the word of God; with God, nothing is impossible. We can do all things through Christ who strengthen us. *The Power of an Innocent Mind* shows us that by being single-minded with God, you can do what the Word says you can do. Read the Word and what it says you should do as a saved Christian. Live your life in Christ every moment of your life—as a young child, teenager, or a young or old adult—everywhere you go you will see miracles and wonders follow you.

1

King Wisdom was the first son of King Luther and Queen Rosemary of Netherlands. He had two brothers and one sister. At the age of seven, he was sent to an all boys' boarding school. The school was one of the most expensive schools in the world. Most of the world's Royals and the rich sent their sons to this school. This boarding school was where, at the age of nine, the young Prince gave his life to Christ. He loved reading the Bible and especially enjoyed the stories of King David. He read about how God said David was a man after his heart. That challenged him a great deal. One day, he told some of his friends that when he grew up, he was going to do mighty things for God, just like King David had in the Bible. Prince Wisdom claimed he would do even greater things than King David had. He told his friends that God would say of him, "King Wisdom is a man after my heart and knows how to put a smile on my face."

His friends laughed when they heard him speak this way and they told him he was dreaming. "Keep on with your wild dreams," they said. At school, they used to make fun of the Prince, saying things like, "What kind of a name is Wisdom?" He answered them with confidence and said, "It means the wisdom of God. That's who I am. So watch out, guys, because all your intelligence combined cannot match the wisdom I have, for I am wisdom itself."

At the age of twenty-one, the Prince joined the army as part of his Royal duties. He retired from the army at the age of twenty-nine. The summer after he left the army, he came home and his father, the King, suggested that the King and Queen host a ball so that the Prince might meet and select his future Queen. This was in accordance with family and cultural custom. Despite the fact that the future King was more interested in the young lady who comes to the palace to visit her father, Lord Paul, he agreed to his father's plan. Whenever she came to the palace and her father was busy with the King, the young lady would study the Bible. She sometimes went to the garden and sketched in the book she usually carried. The Prince never knew what she was sketching, for he never wanted to bother her or ask.

But one day, he screwed up his courage and approached the young lady while she was sketching in the garden. "Good afternoon, Lady Fiona," he said. "You are Lady Fiona, are you not?"

She stood up, shocked that the Prince knew her name. "Yes, my Prince, I am," she said.

He told her that he frequently saw her sketching and asked if he could see what she was working on.

"No, please, my Prince, it is really nothing, and besides, you will laugh at me," she said, embarrassed.

The Prince promised not to laugh and the young lady handed the book to him slowly. The Prince looked at the sketch she was working on, and he was shocked at what he saw. He asked her if she would let him show it to his mother, the Queen. She hesitated a bit, but finally agreed. The future King ran to his mother's chambers and told the butler that he wanted to see his mother. The butler went to the head lady and told him that the future King wanted to see his mother. The head lady went to inform the Queen. Within five minutes, the Prince was ushered into the Queen's chamber.

The Queen was happy to see her son. "What brings the future King to my chamber?" she asked him.

"Mother," he said, "I want to show you something and I want your opinion on it, please." He showed her the sketch Lady Fiona was working on, and the Queen was amazed at what she saw.

She was quiet for a moment before saying, "Son, this is the most beautiful sketch of a ball gown I have ever seen. Is that what you want me to wear for your ball dance?" Before he could answer, she said, "Let me get my dressmaker to start working on it right away."

Prince Wisdom asked the Queen to accompany him on a walk in the garden to visit Lady Fiona. When they arrived at the place where Lady Fiona was sitting, Prince Wisdom introduced Lady Fiona to the Queen.

The Queen said, "I know Lady Fiona, the only daughter of Lord Paul and Lady Faith."

Prince Wisdom said, "Mother, I asked her if I could see what she was sketching and she said it was nothing. I promised not to laugh at her, and she showed it to me. I was amazed when I saw it, just like you were and I asked her if I could show it to you to get your opinion."

The Queen was surprised that this young girl had such unique gifts and that she was so shy about it. The Queen moved closer to Lady Fiona and looked straight into her eyes for a moment without saying a word. She took Lady Fiona by the hand and said, "Never take the gift that God gave you so lightly, child. You have a very unusual talent. Use it." The Queen asked Lady Fiona if she had ever made a gown out of one of her sketches.

Lady Fiona said, "Yes, your majesty. I've made seven for my mother and several more for myself."

The Queen said, "If you didn't have anyone in mind when you made this sketch, I would like you to make it for me."

Lady Fiona fell to her knees in front of the Queen and said, "Your majesty, the truth is that I made this sketch with you in mind. I was imagining you coming down the stairs, all eyes on you, wearing it for the Prince's ball. But I thought it was just a teenager's silly dream."

The Queen pulled Lady Fiona to her feet, hugged her, and said, "You will be highly rewarded for this. Go and start working on my ball gown. You have only three weeks to finish it, Lady Fiona."

Prince Wisdom stared at the two women the entire time they were talking. When Lady Fiona started to walk away, he was amazed at how gracefully and elegantly she walked. He had never seen a woman walk with elegance and grace like that. It was hard to imagine that this young woman was only eighteen. The Prince said to himself, *What a strange thing. This young lady has the fear of God, beauty, grace, and intelligence, and that is all I need in my future wife.*

Suddenly, the Queen clapped her hands twice in front of his face and said, "Penny for your thoughts, my Prince. I can see that you have already found your bride."

The Prince said in a low voice, "She is too young to be my wife. Besides, she has the whole world at her feet. What will she do with an old man like me?"

"Never put age between you and your happiness," the Queen said. "Age is just a number. What you need is a bride who is full of wisdom and knows how to carry herself in the palace and in public. It looks like you, my son, have found her. Don't be a fool and let her pass you by."

Prince Wisdom smiled at his mother and said, "Are you calling the future King a fool? Are you aware you can lose your life for that, woman?"

The Queen laughed and said, "Well, future King, don't forget who is on the throne now. You are standing in front of her majesty, the most powerful woman in the world. What she says goes."

They laughed together.

⅄❁

After one week, the Queen sent for Prince Wisdom to accompany her to Lord Paul's castle for her gown fitting. Their arrival at the castle was unexpected as they had not sent a message ahead of time to say they were coming. Lady Faith met them and welcomed them into her home and took them to the family room. "Can I offer you some tea," Lady Faith asked her visitors.

"Yes, Lady Faith, I hear you have the best tea in your garden," the Queen answered. Lady Faith told her staff to give the Queen and the Prince the best tea available and to use the best tea sets.

The Queen turned to Lady Faith and said, "I am here to see Lady Fiona, in case she needs me for fitting. I thought she may be afraid to call on me for a fitting so I came to her."

The Queen had two things in mind: one, to see how Lady Fiona carried herself when she was not in the palace, and two, for Prince Wisdom to have an opportunity to see Lady Fiona again. Lady Faith knew about the clothes her daughter was making for the Queen because the day Lady Fiona came back from the palace after meeting the Queen and the Prince, she was burbling with excitement. She told, her mother how blessed she was to be making a dress for the Queen. She ran around looking for materials for she wanted everything to be perfect for the Queen. Since then, she had locked herself in her room and chained herself to her work station, dedicating all her time to the Queen's gown.

Lady Faith excused herself to check on Lady Fiona. She soon came back to inform the Queen that Lady Fiona would be with her and the Prince shortly. Lady Fiona's chamber was huge. As she was an only child, her parents had spared no expense and had spoiled her. The decorations in her chamber were breathtaking. Upon seeing Lady Fiona's chamber, the Queen remarked at the beauty of the room. "She did all the decorations herself," Lady Faith said.

"She truly has an eye for beauty," the Queen said.

When they arrived at Lady Fiona's work station, the Queen said, "Well, Lady Fiona, you have a beautiful place here."

Lady Fiona thanked her and escorted her to the fitting room. She called upon her ladies to help the Queen with the fitting. She then came and called Prince Wisdom into another fitting room. The Prince was surprised as he was not expecting anything for himself. Lady Fiona handed him a beautiful suit and coat made out of fine black and creamy white silk material. He was happy to see that she had thought of him.

Both the Queen and the Prince were amazed at the quality of work Lady Fiona had accomplished in just one week. Both their clothes fit them so well, and transformed them into a fairy Queen and Prince. To them, the garments looked finished, but Lady Fiona said there was still a lot of work to be done. They thanked her and both Lady Fiona and Lady Faith escorted the Queen, the Prince, and their company to their transport. Lady Fiona informed them their outfits would be ready in a week's time. She thanked them both for coming and for giving her the opportunity to make their clothes. They thanked her again, hugged her, and left.

On their way home, the Queen asked Prince Wisdom what he thought of the experience. He told his mother that he was very impressed by the work Lady Fiona had done so far and that he found her chamber beautiful. He looked at his mother and said, "Mother, name one quality this girl is missing. I am lost for words. I don't know how to describe her, except to say she is unique in every aspect of her life."

The Queen said, "Yes, her place is really beautiful and very clean, and the young lady has good taste and talent." The Queen asked her son if he had any feelings for Lady Fiona. Prince Wisdom laughed and told his mother that he had anticipated the question and wasn't surprised. He decided not to answer the Queen. She did not press her son for more detail. Both the Queen and the Prince spent the rest of the journey home quiet, in deep thought about Lady Fiona.

Lady Fiona was not used to anyone praising her as she had never done any work for anyone except her father, mother, close relatives, and their workers. Her work for them was unexpected. In a week's time, Lady Fiona took the garments for the Prince and Queen to the palace. Upon arrival, Lady Fiona found the Queen with the King and Prince Wisdom. There, she showed them what she had brought. The King was so impressed with what he saw that he asked Lady Fiona to name her price. She looked at King Luther and said, "I have what I want already, your majesty. My greatest desire was to make clothes for her majesty."

Lady Fiona's eyes met the Prince's and she looked away quickly. Prince Wisdom also looked down, shyly. The King thought he noticed something in the glance between the two but he could not determine what it was. The King excused himself and left to visit Lord Paul. He asked Lord Paul how he would feel if the Prince was to ask for the hand of Lady Fiona in marriage. "It will be an honor, sir," Lord Paul assured the King.

The King said, "I am not certain that it is Lady Fiona my son has set his sights on. But," he continued, "I hope it is."

2

It was a custom that on the day of the ball, all Princesses and Ladies of high society came from all over the world looking like beautiful garden flowers. The media was busy taking pictures and trying to determine which woman Prince Wisdom would choose for his bride. All the women were so beautiful and it was quite a difficult task to choose the best looking and best dressed among them. The speculating came to a halt when the Prince and Queen arrived.

The Queen made her entrance with the Prince on her arm. She arrived after everyone else, guaranteeing herself a grand entrance. The entire party came to a standstill and everyone looked to the top of the stairs where the Queen and the Prince were standing. The Queen looked radiant and the Prince was very handsome. Together, they were breathtaking. Everybody wondered who designed the gown for the Queen and where the Prince had gotten his attire. The Queen's ball gown was so unique and very beautiful. It fitted her perfectly. The Prince was also wearing a very elegantly tailor-made suit that fitted him perfectly along with a coat that exactly matched the suit. They looked as though they had stepped right out of a fairy tale story or a movie. Photographers took pictures of them as they descended the staircase. Reporters asked the Queen who had designed her gown. "It's a secret," the Queen said smiling, "But before the night is over, you'll know." Ladies began lining up to dance with the Prince.

Lady Fiona was nowhere to be found. The Queen and the Prince both looked everywhere for her. Finally, the Queen asked

Lady Faith where Lady Fiona was. "She was right behind us," Lady Faith said. "She should be here shortly."

Unbeknownst to her parents, Lady Fiona had tripped and fallen while she tried to get into her transport to the ball; She had damaged her gown and was forced to change it. She had no choice but to wear the gown she had made for herself before she'd begun work on the Queen's gown. The gown was very beautiful but Lady Fiona worried that it might draw attention away from the Queen. She wanted the Queen to receive all the praise that night. But as it was her only other ball gown, she had no choice.

There was commotion at the entrance and people pushed each other to see what the fuss was about. All of a sudden, the butler announced the arrival of Lady Fiona, beautiful daughter of Lord Paul and Lady Faith.

For a moment, nobody could speak. Lady Fiona was radiant in her gown. The gown shimmered in white and gold with a train, like a wedding dress. She wore matching slippers of gold and white. Her hair was pinned on top of her head and decorated with white and gold ribbons, which made her look a little bit older than her age. She had completed the elegant look with white and gold earrings. Her makeup was understated and had been professionally applied. She was a beauty beyond description. Most of the Princesses who had attended in hopes of being chosen by the Prince as the future Queen knew immediately upon seeing Lady Fiona that she had stolen the Prince's heart. They saw the look in the Prince's eyes and knew that Lady Fiona was everything a man could want in a woman.

For a moment, Prince Wisdom became wary and asked her mother, "What will I do with a goddess like her, mother?" He answered himself and said, "I will be afraid to touch her and definitely won't be able to perform any of my duties as I will be drawn to look at her at all times."

"She deserves a King and you, my son, are the future King," the Queen said.

The King walked toward her and said, "Lady Fiona, you have truly stolen every young man's heart, including us old fools." They both laughed at the King's joke. "Welcome, Lady Fiona," he said.

The Queen greeted Lady Fiona. "Your gown and slippers are the most beautiful I have ever seen. How did you find slippers that matched so well?" the Queen asked.

Lady Fiona answered the Queen in a very low voice, "It is an inexpensive trick, my Queen. I sewed the cover of the slippers out of extra fabric and glued it to an ordinary slipper." She went on, "Your majesty, I did not intend to wear this gown because I wanted you to be the center of attention tonight, but I slipped and fell on my way here and had to go back and change. This was the only gown I had that was fitting for the occasion."

"You see, Lady Fiona, God knew this was your night; so he corrected the mistake you were about to make in time, so that you can be the star of the night," the Queen said. "I still love my gown, so don't feel guilty. I have also enjoyed my arrival because you were not here yet. Thank God you came after me," the Queen smiled. They both laughed.

At that moment, the Prince arrived. Extending his hand, he said, "Lady Fiona, may I have this dance?" Lady Fiona did not speak, only nodded "yes." The guests quietly left the dance floor so that the Prince and Lady Fiona had it all to themselves. As the dance ended, Prince Wisdom dropped to one knee and removed a ring from his pocket. It had belonged to his great grandmother. "Lady Fiona, daughter of Lord Paul and Lady Faith," the Prince said, "Will you please marry me?"

Lady Fiona trembled, for she could not control her feelings for this man. She knew without a doubt that she was in love with him. She answered in a small, trembling voice, "Yes, yes, I will marry you, my Prince."

The family came forward first to congratulate them. Lady Faith hugged her daughter with tears in her eyes. Her grandmother came and kissed her on the forehead and said, "I knew all along that you were going to be a Queen. Grandchild, you couldn't have chosen a better King or kingdom. I am so proud of you. But please don't forget who has been watching over you all your life. Don't ever be too busy to give Him praise every morning and night." Lady Fiona promised her grandmother that she would not forget to praise the Lord every morning and evening.

The Queen came and gave Lady Fiona a hug and said, "I can't wait for you to be my daughter-in-law and to be my decorator and designer. My son chose well. I am so proud of him, and I am a blessed woman among blessed women to have a daughter like you."

She then called upon the journalist who had asked her who had designed her gown. "You asked about my designer earlier? I am happy to introduce her. This is Lady Fiona, my designer and future daughter-in-law." The journalist took a picture of them both and asked Lady Fiona if he could interview her later. She promised him that they would set a time and place for an interview.

Prince Wisdom came forward and said, "I hate to break the unity, but can I have a dance with my future wife please?"

Immediately, the King spoke up from behind him and said, "Not yet, young man. Let me welcome Lady Fiona and congratulate her first before you keep her to yourself." He took Lady Fiona by the hand, kissed it, and said, "Welcome to your kingdom, future Queen. There is no one else I would have my son choose as his wife. You were made for this family." The King turned and looked at his son and congratulated him. "You have done well for yourself, my son, and for this family." The King continued, "You have made an excellent choice for the Kingdom as well." Then, with a loud voice, he declared, "Let the celebration begin! Eat and drink as much as you want for this is a great day indeed!"

The celebration lasted well into the night as the guests had so many things to celebrate. Not only had the Prince returned from the army, but he had chosen the future Queen and proposed to her on the spot! Prince Wisdom and Lady Fiona danced and danced all night long. Finally, after so much dancing, they stepped outside for a breath of fresh air and a walk in the garden. Flushed from dancing and excitement, they were giddy and wide-eyed.

Prince Wisdom turned to Lady Fiona and said, "You are the one God chose to help me achieve God's will. I don't know yet how but when the time comes, I know you will help me."

"Anything for the one who created heaven and earth," Lady Fiona replied.

Both the Prince and Lady Fiona felt so happy that they were both faithful, God-fearing people. Each had dreamed of finding a like-minded partner.

><!--flower--> ✻

The following day, Prince Wisdom sent a message that he would be coming to see Lady Fiona so that they might discuss their wedding date. The Prince was not able to sleep the night before as he was very excited and spent the evening counting down the hours and minutes until he would again see Lady Fiona. The Queen would be in charge of planning the wedding and, as expected, she invited Lady Faith to help her.

The Prince arrived at Lord Paul's castle. This time, Lord Paul was home. They had tea together before the Prince took Lady Fiona out for a ride to discuss their wedding date. Lord Paul said to the Prince, "I know my daughter is in the right hands. Thank you for honoring my family, Prince Wisdom."

"The honor, sir," the Prince said, "is all mine."

Lord Paul blessed the Prince.

Prince Wisdom and Lady Fiona left the castle and discussed their choices for their wedding date. The Prince told Lady Fiona that, by right, they were supposed to be engaged for six months or more before marriage, but that he could not wait for six months. "I also think that six months is too long to wait," Lady Fiona said. "It is too long to be without you." They agreed to tell their families that they wished to be married in three months. Both the Prince and Lady Fiona prayed that the elders would accept their proposal for a faster wedding date. The Prince and Lady Fiona both knew that, for a royal family, three months is a very short time to make wedding preparations. They knew that everyone available would have to help and that the entire kingdom would be very busy for the next three months.

"When I asked you to marry me," Prince Wisdom said to Lady Fiona, "I was praying that you would say yes. I was very nervous."

"I thought Kings never got nervous," Lady Fiona said.

Prince Wisdom laughed. "Not when it comes to matters of women. There is a certain power women possess which can't be explained." The Prince looked down, shyly. "I also worried that you would turn me down because I am too old for you."

Lady Fiona said, "And I thought you would not consider me because you might feel that I am too young! But only God knows what your presence did to me. I knew I was in love with you the day you found me in the garden."

"And I knew I was in love with you long before that. I knew the first time I saw you visiting your father, the day I arrived home from the army," Prince Wisdom said, taking her hand in his. "Whenever you and your father talked and laughed in the garden, I watched you from my window."

Lady Fiona blushed.

The two talked about what they would wear for their wedding and where they would go for their honeymoon. Lady Fiona told Prince Wisdom that she would like to make her own wedding dress as she had started one a few years ago.

Prince Wisdom laughed. "You've really been making your wedding dress for years?" he asked?

Lady Fiona nodded yes.

"Is it a gown fit to marry a Prince?" the Prince asked, smiling.

"It is. And it's almost finished. I will need only a few weeks to finish some details," Lady Fiona said. They were both happy with that. Lady Fiona knew she had a lot of work to do in the next three months, for she intended to make gowns for her mother, the Queen, Prince Wisdom's sister, (Princess Catherine) and her grandmother.

Over the next few weeks, Lady Fiona spent a great deal of time making sketches for the gowns she wanted to make. She spent even more time looking for materials with which to make the gowns. She ran into a problem for whenever she went out, photographers and reporters followed her everywhere. It slowed her down and she quickly fell behind schedule. Finally she decided to call the store owners and ask them to bring several choices of materials to her, so that she could choose without interruption. Lady Fiona's was so busy making all of the dresses that some nights, she didn't go to bed but instead worked through the night.

After six weeks, Lady Fiona had finished her work and surprised first her mother and then her grandmother by giving them their gowns to wear for the wedding. They both adored the gowns. Lady Fiona then traveled to the palace to give the Queen and Princess Catherine their gowns. They were happy and shocked at the same time as they had not been expecting such beautiful, handmade gowns. The Queen's gown was so beautiful that she became worried. "I don't want to look more beautiful than the bride," she said to her future daughter-in-law.

"You need not worry, my Queen," Lady Fiona said, "My gown is even more beautiful than this one."

Her future sister-in-law, Princess Catherine unwrapped hers and she told them that she had never had a gown as beautiful as that one in her whole life. She made them slippers to match their gowns. Queen Rosemary was so touched with the work Lady Fiona had done for them and she told her so. They thanked her and told her that if she ever needed anything, she should not hesitate to let them know.

⤳❀

Three months later, the wedding took place at the palace. The whole town was invited. The VIPs were given special seats and were afforded the best places to eat and sit. The King owned a hotel nearby called Kings Hotel that was reserved for only Kings and Lords. The hotel had 70 king's suites, 104 presidential suites, and 340 VIP suites. All the lords, ladies, and VIPs stayed there. This was a very expensive hotel. The furniture in the hotel was the best, extremely classy, elegant, and expensive. Some stayed at the palace and some in the King's guesthouses. More than nine thousand guests attended the wedding. Guests came from all over the world.

The wedding itself took place in the King's Hall and in the garden. After the ceremony, where they exchanged vows, the Prince and his wife went to the main gate of the palace to salute the multitudes of people who had come to be outside the palace gate for the wedding. The Prince and his new wife thanked them for coming.

Lady Fiona asked permission to do something unusual; to throw her bouquet at the main gate where the townspeople were gathered in support. When Lady Fiona announced her intention to toss her bouquet to the townspeople, they fell in love with her even more. They appreciated that she acknowledged the ordinary people and wanted to do something special for them. They said she was the people's future Queen indeed. The bouquet was caught by a very small girl named Liberty. Liberty was drinking from her bottle when the bouquet fell right next to her. She dropped her bottle, picked up the bouquet, and took a bit bite. Her mother laughed and took the bouquet from her hands.

Princess Fiona and the Prince Wisdom laughed when they saw what happened. Princess Fiona went to the small girl who was about three months old and thanked her for catching the bouquet and kissed her. "Was she hurt?" she asked the girl's mother.

"No, she's not harmed, Your Majesty," Liberty's mother said. The small girl laughed like she understood what they were saying. Both Princess Fiona and Prince Wisdom remarked at the beauty of the child and her mother.

"What are your names?" Princess Fiona asked.

"My name is Mmoni," the mother said. She was a beautiful black woman with a lovely accent. "And this is Liberty." She gestured towards the little girl. Princess Fiona and Prince Wisdom shook hands with Mmoni. Everybody laughed. "I will keep this bouquet safe for her until she is grown up your majesties," Mmoni said. "She's only three months old."

Good food and drinks were sent out for the townspeople.

A lot of money was spent on the wedding. Some said it was over a hundred million Euros, some said it was close to half a billion. Lord Paul was one of the richest men on earth, and the King and his family were even richer. Lord Paul owned mines and hotels all over his country as well as overseas. In addition, many Kings, Lords and Prime Ministers of other countries gave wedding gifts of money, gold, diamonds, and silver.

In addition to her beautiful wedding dress, Lady Fiona designed and made a beautiful suit for Prince Wisdom to change into after the wedding ceremony. Most of the gifts beside money were expensive and tasteful materials like silk from all over the world; for the guests knew that Lady Fiona was known for making beautiful clothes and that it was her passion.

Years after the wedding, radio stations, newspapers, and television shows were still talking about the wedding dress and referring to it as the wedding gown of the century. What made it even more spectacular was the fact that the bride had made it herself. People said after they saw what she wore for the Prince's ball; they wondered who would make a dress grander than that one for the wedding. But the wedding dress was one of a kind and very beautiful, simple yet expensive, made out of pearls with a trail of shells. They made small whistling sounds when the Princess walked.

After the wedding, Lady Fiona's wedding gown was taken to a museum to be displayed along with the slippers and accessories she wore that day. Until today, no gown had been made like that one. The fashion experts suggested that the gown would sell for 150 million Euros. A name and a legacy were created by Princess Fiona, who never set foot in design school. When she was interviewed about the wedding gown, she told the media that she had started designing the gown when she was fifteen. She began sewing it when she was seventeen, and she finished it two months after the proposal. She told the media that she had known since she was young that she was going to marry a Prince but did not know which one. Her grandmother had always told her that she would marry a Prince as well. She kept the Bible verse Hebrews 11:1 close to her heart. "Now faith is the substance of things hoped for, the evidence of things not seen" (NKJV). Faith was why she took time to design a wedding gown fit for a royal wedding. The reporters asked her where she went to learn how to design. She told them it was a natural gift from God. She had never gone to school to learn design. She had started drawing designs at the age of seven and at the age of nine, her mother bought her a sewing machine and materials. That was when she became serious about designing every day. She always wanted to do something much nicer than what she had done the day before. Finally, she started making clothes for herself and her family. Later, she made clothes for their workers.

Nine months after the wedding, Lady Fiona gave birth to a son, Prince Hope. A year later, she gave birth to Princess Sasha. The King and Queen went overseas for a visit after the fifth celebration of Princess Sasha's birthday. It was the first time Prince Wisdom and Lady Fiona were left alone with the responsibilities of the Kingdom. On their way back, the King and Queen's plane crashed. The news of the death of the King and the Queen was devastating to the entire kingdom. The Kingdom mourned the King and the Queen for six months. At the end of the six months of mourning, King Wisdom told Queen Fiona to look for something she will like to do, aside from her duties as Queen. "You have not been yourself since my parents' death," King Wisdom said to his wife.

"They loved me and welcomed me into their family," Queen Fiona said sadly. "But do you think I might open a design school; So that I might share my talent with others?" The King was pleased with the idea. Together, they built a design school for the Queen in one of the lands owned by the Royal family. The Queen taught decorating and design. People came from all over the world to attend the school. The school was a very big success for Queen Fiona. Every year, the Royal family gave free scholarships for hundred children in their country to attend Queen Fiona's school.

The first two years, Queen Fiona was spending most of her time at the school as a way of escaping from the memories of her in-law's death. Whenever she was at the palace, the pain was too much for her. When she was at the school—and she was busy with the children and schoolwork—she didn't feel as much pain. Lady Faith had to talk to her to remind her that she had children and a husband who loved her and they were also hurting and in need of her comfort.

Every year, King Wisdom celebrated Queen Fiona's birthday in style. He was always thanking God for the days with his family and his kingdom on Earth. He was also grateful for the way the Queen raised their children. He used to say, "Every day is a celebration for me for what God is doing in my life." His love for Queen Fiona grew day by day and he used to tell her that he couldn't imagine life without her for he loved her with all his being.

The King was aware that his parents' death had affected his wife a great deal and he wanted to give her as much time as she needed to mourn them. Lady Fiona felt the same for him. King Wisdom thanked God every day for their love for he believed it was the work of God.

The students at the Queen's school planned to surprise Queen Fiona with a birthday party and a gift from all of them. The Queen cared for her students and they loved her a great deal.

Since the palace was huge, the King told his siblings after the death of their parents, that if they still wanted to live in the palace after marriage they were welcome to. The King also offered to build each of them a beautiful castle if they preferred not to live at the palace. That was the same reason he said he did not want Lord Paul's castle to leave the family. One of his children would take over the castle when the comes. The King wanted his generation to know where their great Queen came from.

King Wisdom was committed to God first, then his family and his country Netherlands. He was the one who led his siblings and his parents to Christ when he came back from school. He could never get out of his chamber in the morning without a prayer. And even as a King, with all the duties overwhelming him, he always created time for God and his family. That was why after the death of his parents he immediately resumed the role of father figure to his siblings without struggle. They all respected him. He gave the west wing of the palace to his siblings because he wanted them to be free; the east wing, which was the biggest in the palace, the King used with his children. The South and North Wings were for their visitors. Three times a week he met with all his siblings and family to take fellowship together. He always encouraged them to be strong in the Lord. He explained to them that a wise man or woman sought the kingdom of heaven first and God would take care of the rest for them.

King Wisdom still remembered his promise, that he was going to do something great for God. He was always searching for ways to please God. He usually said, "As long as I am alive, my duty is to put a smile=on God's face. I want Him to smile whenever He looks at my life."

His father used to tell him, "Take it easy, son. God knows you love him. That is why you made all of us accept him as our Lord and personal savior. That is a big gift to God because when you give God a King, you gave him his kingdom as well. You want to please God, keep on praising him. You have even turned the palace into a place of worship. How much more can you give? You are only human." His father would smile and say, "If someone would have told me that one day I would have a temple in the palace, I would have thought that person was mad. Now look, you took my great room and turned it into a temple."

King Wisdom knew that his father didn't understand the burning desire in his heart to please God. He told his father that he loved Jesus more than anything on earth. His father would just shake his head. He did not know what got into his son's head.

After Lady Fiona's marriage to Prince Wisdom, the Princess noticed that her husband always left their bed at 11:30 p.m. and came back at 12:30 a.m. One night as the Prince was getting ready to leave, the Princess woke up and asked where he was going. "I have turned one of the palace rooms into a temple. I am going there to pray," he told her.

"May I join you?" the Princess asked.

From that night on, they had been praying together. Prince Wisdom explained to his wife that he liked to enter every new day with a prayer. That was why he prayed every day at midnight. "It's a good habit to have," the Queen said. "I like it."

One night after the midnight prayer, the King told his wife that he would like to do something very special to honor God. "I would like for us to start praying about it so that we can know what we can do."

The Queen agreed.

They decided to start praying every morning and evening with their children until the King received his request from God. After a few weeks, the King invited the palace staff to join them in their Bible study and prayer routine, for he had already led them into the kingdom of God. It became a culture of the palace and continued on. Lady Faith joined them in their worship when she came to the palace to visit her grandchildren. After she realized that they prayed every morning and evening, she made a point to be at the palace at the time of prayer. Lord Paul never missed any of the prayers. Queen Fiona's grandmother wanted to come, but she felt it was too much of a walk twice a day, so she joined them only in the evening.

After the Queen's fortieth birthday, which she celebrated together with her grandmother—as they shared the same birthday—the King told his wife that he finally knew what he wanted to do to honor God. He said, "First, I want the whole palace to go on a special prayer."

The Queen said, "Talk to me, my King," as he had been quiet for a few minutes, thinking.

He said, "I want to give God a child, who will only know God in her life." He told her "I want to bring that child on earth in a prayer and worship atmosphere and raise her to worship and praise God in a way no one has ever done." The King continued, "I want this child to live for God and God alone." The King explained his plan to the Queen and she was moved. He said the only thing the child would know when he or she grew up was God. He then called his King's men and told them his plan. They prayed for forty days, and then they chose the place where everyone would meet for prayer every day; the palace temple.

King Wisdom started preparing for the child before it was conceived. He spoke to his King's men to select God-fearing men and women to study each book of the Bible. The first man was Prince Lawrence, the King's brother. He was given the book of Hebrews. Princess Catherine, the book of Ephesians, Lord Paul took the book of Proverbs, Prince Hope the book of Romans, Princess Sasha the book of Esther, the King himself took the book of Revelation, and the Queen, Psalms, and so on. At the end of the week, they would meet together with the King and Queen and they would be asked questions about their assigned books to check the level of their knowledge and understanding. The King prayed for his wife and touched her belly during every midnight prayer. The King and the King's men engaged in a great deal of fasting. The first fast lasted for forty days, and every week thereafter, they fasted for three days. They all met in the palace temple in the morning of the fast and left at the end of the third day of fasting. During fasting, they shared the books they were studying, and prayed and sang to the Lord. Every one of them was always looking forward to the three-day fast, for they had a wonderful time with the Lord.

Meanwhile, after the announcement was made to select God-fearing men and women to pray for the child who the King wanted to dedicate to God completely, the country heard about it, and they decided that they would also go to the gates of the palace every morning to join in prayer. It became a tradition for the country. Prayer and worship were occurring continuously in the palace. The King loved the book of Psalms so he had special psalms he used to praise God with. He spent hours by himself using the book of Psalms to praise God. The peace in that country was the kind of peace that surpasses man's understanding. There was prosperity in that country. The news about King Wisdom and his plans travelled over the continent. There were those in other countries who condemned the whole thing, but the King was not moved. The most important thing was that his country was one-hundred percent behind their King. They acted as one voice and one mind; even if they didn't, he would still do what he believed was right in the eyes of God.

On the seventh month of the prayers, the Queen announced to the King that she was pregnant. The King announced the Queen's pregnancy to the prayer group he had selected. There was so much joy, but this time they celebrated with the Lord. The people sang praises to God for three days of fasting and thanked God for his goodness and mercy which endures with them forever. The King told his prayer group that no one should talk about the Queen being pregnant yet. This time, the King selected some men and women of the Bible study group and prayer group to go to the Queen's chamber every morning to pray with her before she left her chamber. On the third month of the Queen's pregnancy, the announcement was made to the multitudes gathered outside the gates. There was so much joy in every part of the country. The news travelled fast. Some people started bringing gifts for the child.

3

The child was born right on time and the Queen had an easy delivery. The labor pains started at eleven thirty at night and by twelve midnight, the child was born. The baby was a girl and she weighed 9.5 pounds at birth. The King named her Princess Grace (the grace of God). He said, "The grace of God is upon this child and upon the palace." She was born with long, thick red hair and eyes as green as emeralds. "It can't be a coincidence that the child was born during prayer hour," the King said to the Queen.

As the King had promised God, from her first day in the world there was prayer by her bedside every morning, afternoon, and evening. The King read the book of Hebrews and Proverbs for Princess Grace before she could talk or understand the words. By the time she was five-years-old, she knew the books of Hebrews, Proverbs and the Lord's Prayer by heart. Children's books were made for her for those Bible books. At times, actors would visit the palace to act out Bible stories for the young Princess. She enjoyed herself a great deal. Whenever she saw her tutors coming, she ran to meet them and asked them to start telling her the Bible stories. She could never get enough of hearing them. She was never happy when her tutors left. She used to cry when they left, but the King had a talk with her at the age of three to tell her that crying was not a good behavior. She apologized to her father and stopped crying, even if she didn't want the tutors to leave.

At the age of five, the King ordered that Princess Grace should proceed to the books of Romans by Prince Lawrence and Princess Catherine, the book of Ephesians. By now, the Princess was eager to learn by herself. They gave her children's books for

Romans and Ephesians, which, from time to time the Princess would read by herself. She would call these men and women to ask them questions concerning these books. She was moved to her own chamber at the age of two. During every hour, there was someone reading the Bible with her, actors entertaining her, or a group of people praying with the young Princess.

Everyone in the palace was surprised by the Princess behavior. From time to time, she would come up with good suggestions for her tutors and would often ask them if they prayed before coming to her chamber. She would also tell them to make sure they prayed before preparing for her teaching. When they arrived at her chamber, she would stand up and start worshiping and praising God. When she finished, she asked everyone to pray. She began leading them in prayer without anyone telling her to. She observed what was going on in her chamber as she grew up and started doing it without anyone asking her to. Sometimes, her tutors would say that they felt like they were the ones going for lessons with the Princess, because the kind of questions she asked were very deep. But the King reminded them that he gave them seven months before the Princess was conceived and nine months before she was born to study and prepare. He also reminded them that each one of them was studying only one book but the Princess was studying all of the books as they were given to her and she was only five-years-old.

There was something about Princess Grace that no one could explain. She loved people and was very peaceful, yet most people were uncomfortable around her. She was bold and polite. The only language or games she knew were from the Bible and prayer. For her sixth birthday, the King gave her an adult Bible. She was so happy, she ran around showing it to everyone. She went to her mother and said, "Mother, now I can praise the Lord with psalms the whole day and night! I can read more books by myself." Her mother reminded her to rest at night and that she needed to sleep in order to grow to be a big girl. The Princess agreed with her mother. She went on, "Oh, Mama, I can read Matthews; I can read Genesis, the beginning of the world. Oh, Mama, how wonderful this is!"

But the King told her that there were certain books in the Bible she should not read until she reached a certain age. She was still very excited and said, "Yes, Papa, I will not read the ones you said I shouldn't read yet."

Her father told her that he would write down the books of the Bible that she could read now and that he would keep adding to the list as time goes on. It was settled. The Queen looked at her daughter and smiled for she reminded her of herself when she was young. She would get excited just the same way. She remembered the day her own mother bought her a sewing machine, she couldn't sleep out of excitement.

Princess Grace was very obedient. She always did as she was told. She often told people around her when she saw them doing something they were not supposed to do that the penalty for disobedience was spiritual death. She explained that there was nothing as bad as being dead spiritually while you were still alive physically, because in the spiritual world you are a zombie. She would go on and tell them never to allow themselves to die spiritually while they were still physically alive, because that was the worst punishment anyone could endure. On Princess Grace's sixth birthday celebration, one of the children choked while eating a piece of fruit. People ran to the child and started applying first aid. The Princess told them to stop in a firm voice. She looked at the child and said, "Fruit! Out of him!" The child coughed the fruit out. That was the first time she exercised her faith in front of the people. After commanding the fruit to come out, she didn't stop. She continued to tell people about the gift of the Bible like it was not a big deal that she just commanded the fruit to come out without touching the child.

After the celebration, the King took the young Princess out to see the city and surrounding areas. They went first to the King's

Hotel and the zoo. Then they went to the hospital and the hospital officials took the Princess on a tour to the children's ward. There she met the young Elisa who had been badly burned from head to toe and was wrapped up in bandages. Princess Grace asked the nurse what had happened to Elisa and why she was covered. The nurse explained to the young Princess that Elisa came from a very poor family. They could not afford electricity or gas, so during the winter, they used a big tank to boil water so the family could have a warm bath. One day, Elisa was sitting by the fire, eating her breakfast when one of the stones supporting the tank holding the boiling water broke into pieces. The water rushed out of the tank and burned little Elisa.

When the nurse finished telling the Princess the story, Princess Grace asked the nurse to remove Elisa's bandages. "I can only remove the bandages on a doctor's orders," the nurse said.

The King then stepped in and said, "Nurse, please do as she says." Hospital officials told the nurse to do as the King asked even though they didn't agree with him.

The nurse's hands trembled as she told herself that this young Princess didn't know anything and her father should not be supporting her on matters like this. "But," she thought to herself, "He is the King. I must do as he asks."

The nurse carefully removed the bandages. She thought Princess Grace would run away when she saw Elisa without the bandages, but Princess Grace stepped forward, looked at Elisa, and said, "Elisa, this is the day the Lord has made for you. You shall rejoice in it." She lifted her small hand toward the little girl and said in a firm voice, "Elisa, be healed and be whole in the name of Jesus!"

Immediately, in front of everyone, the wounds in Elisa's body began to heal and the new skin started covering her body. The hospital officials were shocked and afraid of this small Princess. The nurse looked at Elisa with great shock. She turned her attention to the Princess and passed out.

The King was so happy and said, "Now, Princess Grace, let's go to the temple and give God thanks." The Princess asked if Elisa could come with them. The King spoke to the authorities to release Elisa and to inform Elisa's parents that they had taken Elisa with them. He extended an invitation for Elisa's family to follow them to the palace temple.

On the way to the temple, the Princess expressed her desire to keep Elisa at the palace. The King agreed that she could stay, on one condition. The King said that they would have to ask permission from Elisa's parents and if they said yes, she could stay at the palace. The Princess asked the King what she would call Elisa if she stayed at the palace. "She will be your friend," the King said.

The Princess was surprised that her father had said that. "Father, what about God? God is my friend before I was born, and I don't want to offend him by giving someone his place."

The King explained to the young Princess that God would always be her number one friend and that no one could take his place. He gave her an example of her and her siblings. "You are my child, but Prince Hope and Princess Sasha are also my children. None of you can replace the other." The King explained, "God is the same way. He is too big and too powerful to be replaced. He will forever be your friend, even up to the end. And his friendship cannot be compared to that of a human being; So God will not be equal with Elisa." The Princess was quiet. It was too much for her to swallow and she knew she would have to talk to God about it when she was alone in her chambers.

The King, Princess Grace, and Elisa arrived at the temple and talked for some time with the minister. The minister told Princess Grace that he had a gift for her.

"I love gifts," she said.

He handed her a gold chain with a cross of Jesus. Princess Grace was overjoyed. She held the minister for a while with tears in her eyes and said, "Thank you. Thank you, sir." She fell to her knees and thanked God for the wonderful gift. She asked the minister to help her put the chain on her neck and told him she would never remove it. They then proceeded to go to the temple for prayer.

Elisa's family had just arrived. They were full of joy and thanked Princess Grace for what she had done. The Princess then told them to give thanks to God for He used her to do His good works. "Elisa also had faith," the Princess said. "All I did was to obey." Elisa's family talked with the King for some time and told him how they were dealing with a lot of stress with what had happened to Elisa.

"I don't think I can ever forgive myself for what happened to Elisa," Elisa's mother said. The King told her that it was meant to happen, and there was nothing she could have done to avoid it. Then the King told them about Princess Grace's request that Elisa should stay at the palace with them.

"Only if you agree to it," the King said.

"Yes, your majesty. It will be an honor for our own child to stay with your family," Elisa's father said.

Princess Grace ran to Elisa's mother and father and held on to them tightly for a long time. She didn't care that they looked dirty and very poor. They were dressed in dirty rags. It was as if Princess Grace did not see the difference between herself and the poor family. This touched their hearts even more. For this Princess to hold them when many people in their city avoided them when they saw them coming because they looked dirty and poor, meant so much.

Princess Grace sent a message to the palace to prepare an honorable chamber for Elisa close to hers. The King ordered one of his men to arrange tutors for Elisa. He invited Elisa's father and mother to come with them to the palace for few hours. They praised the Lord before they left, and to everybody's surprise, Elisa sang to God, thanking Him for all He had done for her. For a small child like she was, she had a beautiful and powerful voice. She asked if she could dance for God. Of course everyone said yes. It was a joy to watch her dance. The King fell in love with her even more.

When they arrived at the palace, Elisa saw a basket full of fruits, and she asked if she could have some. "Help yourself, my dear child," the King said. She climbed on top of the table and grabbed one fruit then another and another. She took bites from each one, not sure which one to eat first. She took a bite into the banana, then the apple, then the pear. She was so happy that she forgot she was with other people. She sat down on top of the table in front of the basket and ate. Princess Grace came to Elisa. "Don't spoil your appetite! Soon we'll be eating dinner," she said. The Princess extended her hand and helped Elisa down from the table.

The King asked the palace staff to prepare food for Elisa and her parents. Within thirty minutes they were eating. The King called on Lord Paul and they met for an hour. When they came out, they informed Elisa's parents that the builders would come to where they live to build a house for them and all their children. The children should also go to school on Monday as the school fees had already been taken care of. Then Lord Paul presented them with a check for five-hundred-thousand Euros. The King ordered the staff to load the transport with food, drinks, clean water, clothes, and furniture for Elisa's family. He then offered Elisa's father a job at his hotel. Elisa's family was overjoyed. They had more than one testimony in one day. This was a miracle they had never expected. They had been praying for Elisa's father to get a job with a construction company. Now he was going to work in the hotel and they had the kind of money that can support them for the rest of their lives. The King was building a house for them. It was difficult for them to take it all in and they started to cry.

"It's okay to cry," the King said. "You have struggled all your lives. But that time is over now." He told Elisa's father that a driver would come to take him shopping for the clothes he would need for work at the hotel and one of the palace staff would come with him to help him choose the right clothes. Elisa's mother asked the King what they should do with the check. The King told them the staff member will go with them to the bank and help them open a bank account tomorrow.

✂❀

Over the next six months, Elisa was busy with the tutors from morning to night learning how to carry herself, table manners, how to walk, and how to read and write. She was also being taught Princess Grace's favorite Bible books. Princes Grace could not spend time with her until she completed her orientation. At the end of six months, no one could believe that this was the same little girl who had come in with no shoes and running to snatch the fruit from the table. She was now a lady. She knew the book of Hebrews by heart. Princess Grace was also teaching her the ways of faith and how to speak like a child of God.

Elisa's parents were invited to come and see her. They were also looking much better. Elisa's father was now working at the hotel and going through some tutoring too. He told Elisa that he could now read and write and he worked in the office doing photocopying. After he graduated, he would be promoted to hotel clerk. He couldn't stop telling Elisa all the good things that had happened to them and how their lives had changed. "We're the envy of the town," Elisa's father said.

Elisa's mother was busy at home since they now had a big house that has eight bedrooms and good furniture to take care of. She cooked for Elisa's siblings while they were at school. She told Elisa that she went to shop for clothes for her and her family every month and that every week the King sent a supply of food and toys for the children. "People who never spoke to us before visit us all the time now. We always have extra to spare for other families in need," she said. The most shocking thing was the visit from the mayor who wanted to see how he could help them.

Elisa was very happy to hear all that. Elisa's mother was looking beautiful and people were surprised at the beauty that had been hiding under all the dirty rags. She was so beautiful that many heads turned when she passed by.

What people didn't know was that the King had ordered warm water and food to be provided for less advantaged people after hearing about what had happened to Elisa. He could not sleep after hearing the story of how Elisa's poverty led to her injury. He didn't know there were such poor people in his country. For that, he told Lord Paul that they had to work on improving the lives of those people. The King approved free school for everyone in the Kingdom.

Princess Grace also didn't sleep that night after hearing how Elisa had been burned. She didn't know that there were people who couldn't afford warm water and food and couldn't send their children to school even if they wanted to.

The people of that town changed the name of the town after all the blessings from the Royal family. They renamed the town "Blessed City." The construction in that town started immediately. There was warm water in every home, food supplies every month, and free school for all. Most people employed at the construction sites were the townspeople.

Once a month, the King would take Elisa to visit her family and there would be many people waiting in the road and outside Elisa's home to get pictures of the Royal family and Miss Elisa. Miss Elisa was now a celebrity. Elisa was always happy to visit her siblings and her family's new house.

One afternoon, Princess Sasha, Princess Grace, and Elisa were studying the book of Esther in the Bible when they noticed people running toward the side of the staff quarters. The chief cook came running toward Princess Grace. "Would you please come with me, Princess Grace?" he asked her. She followed him with Princess Sasha and Miss Elisa close behind. They arrived at the staff quarters and a twenty-two-year-old member of the kitchen staff was lying on the floor with white foam coming out her mouth. Her whole body was shaking.

Immediately, Princess Grace asked, "What kind of evil is this which entered my father's house?"

The chief cook tried to explain that the young lady had been having these fits since she was young, but the Princess said, "Well, this is my father's house, it cannot happen here." She commanded in a firm voice for the evil to depart and never come back. For the first time ever, the people in the palace saw the Princess angry. She said, "How dare this evil enter my father's house? From today onward no evil will ever enter this house in Jesus' name."

The young lady woke up, the shaking stopped, and the foam coming from her mouth dried up. She was confused. She did not know what was going on. Princess Grace stepped forward and hugged her and said, "It is well. You won't experience that again. And no one in this palace will experience evil attacks. We are sold to the Lord of No sickness." The young lady never got sick again.

The King and Queen of a country called Good Hope came for a visit to arrange the wedding of their daughter Samantha to Prince Lawrence. They brought Princess Grace a gift of a rare bird. The Princess fell in love with this bird. "What kind of bird is this?" she asked.

"It is a parrot," they said. "It can repeat whatever you say and it will remember to say it at all times, as long as you teach it well."

The Princess was happy and said, "Good, for it will be my partner in praising the Lord." Princess Grace taught the parrot bird to say, "Good morning, Lord Jesus" and "Jesus is the Lord of my life." As soon as someone entered Princess Grace's chambers, the bird said, "Good morning, Jesus. Jesus is Lord," and the Princess said, "Amen, Jesus is Lord." She loved this bird. She sometimes took her Bible and sat by the bird cage and read the Bible to the bird. She spoke to the bird as though it understood everything.

When Elisa came to visit Princess Grace at her chambers, the bird would say to Elisa, "Jesus is Lord," and Elisa would say, "I love Jesus." The three of them would sing a song, "I love Jesus" which they wrote themselves. When they danced, the bird would turn around in its cage, making funny noises, and shaking its head up and down. They figured the bird was dancing as well. The three of them had fun in the Lord.

By the time the Princess was nine-years-old, she had the wisdom of an eighty-year-old woman. Her faith and knowledge of the word and the ways of godly life grew stronger and stronger every day. But the amazing thing was her beauty and the grace with which she walked at the age of nine. Many people enjoyed sitting and watching her walk, which she liked doing in the garden, especially when she was praising and worshiping God with the Psalms of David. She also liked going to spend time with her great grandmother, who was 107 but was still very healthy. She walked without assistance and read without glasses. She loved the Lord and they shared stories of Christian life and read the Bible together.

The King liked watching Princess Grace walk in the garden for she reminded him of Queen Fiona. At her early age, she too had walked with grace. He could still remember those memories as if it was yesterday. The feeling he had in the pit of his stomach whenever he saw Queen Fiona only grew. Amazingly, he still felt the same way about her. He believed that he had never loved anybody the way he loved his Queen.

The whole country was talking about Princess Grace's beauty. Her eyes were emerald green and when the sunlight shone on her red hair, it looked like she was engulfed in flames. She had long eyelashes and a long neck which showed off the beauty of the jewelry she wore. She always chose one string of pearls and the gold chain with the cross of Jesus, which the minister gave her, that looked beautiful on her. She was a beauty to behold. Some said she took part of the beauty from her mother, while some said her beauty came from within. Others said her beauty was not of this world and some said it was because of God's word which dwelt in her mightily. Her father was a handsome man. Whatever the excuse was for her beauty, the fact remained that it was rare.

Since Princess Grace had never known anything else in the world except what the Bible said, worship, praises, and prayer, her faith was growing stronger and stronger and she was performing miracles which most people believed to be impossible. Wherever anyone saw her since she was six-years-old, she'd have the Bible with her. She never went outside to play with other children, and it was not because she was forbidden. It was just that she had grown up knowing God's company and enjoyed it a great deal more than playing. She was brought into this world for one purpose, to praise and worship God and to be a vessel for the word of God at all times. That was the wish of her father, and God answered that prayer. That is why King Wisdom was always thanking God for answering his prayers.

It was quite clear that this young girl was going to do great things. Most people were looking forward to seeing what kind of a woman she was going to grow into. Most Kings were already approaching King Wisdom to ask for her hand in marriage for their sons, but the King always told them that he did not have any authority to arrange her life. In short, her life was in God's hands. Whatever God wanted would happen. For the King knew that Princess Grace was a very special child and strong minded too. He knew that when she grew up, she would do what was right. But the King had no doubt about the wisdom in the young lady.

There were rumors that one King in the East was raising a child similar to the way King Wisdom had been raising Princess Grace. This King, after hearing that King Wisdom's kingdom was praying for a child who will love and save the God almight, had a three month old son. He also arranged for people to start teaching this child the Bible before he learned how to speak. After hearing that the child born to King Wisdom and Queen Fiona was a girl, the King had been hoping that King Wisdom would see fit for his son to marry Princess Grace. The boy was also strong in the ways of God and he had already started ministering at an early age. The King was waiting for the right time to visit King Wisdom with his son. He trusted in God to take control of his desire from there.

People called Princess Grace by different names. Some called her Glory, some called her Beauty, some Shining Star, and some Angel. One day, she asked her father what her name really was. The King laughed. "You are who you want to be called," he said.

She said, "No, father, really what is my real name? Who did you say I am when I was born?"

He laughed again and said, "Oh! You mean that. Let me think. What did I say you were?" He put a hand to his chin and looked as if he was thinking.

Princess Grace laughed and said, "Father, you will never pass at the school of lies even if you can study for a hundred years, or the Devil himself comes to teach you, you won't even make it to the first hour."

The King laughed and said, "You can't blame your old man for trying to bring a smile to his beautiful daughter's face. And, young lady, your name is Grace. The Grace of God. Don't you ever forget that as you go on collecting more names."

She looked at her father and said, "Father, do you mean people are still going to call me more names?"

The King told her yes and stopped walking. He turned to his daughter and said, "Some day you will be married and your husband will call you 'honey,' 'baby,' 'sweetheart,' 'sweetie,' 'love,' 'darling,' 'cupcake,' 'wife,' and so on."

This time Princess Grace laughed hysterically. The King fixed his eyes on hers and said, "Then you will have children and they will also give you names like 'mother,' 'mom,' 'mommy,' or 'old lady.' The list keeps on going, young lady."

At this time, she forgot who she was. The Princess fell on the ground laughing so loudly that the staff came out to see what was going on. She could not imagine herself been married and becoming a mother. The King finished by saying, "But you will still be my pumpkin."

The Princess looked at her father and said, "And you will always be my hero, Father."

4

Before Princess Grace's tenth birthday, her father asked her what she wanted for her birthday gift. She paced for some time and said, "Father, I would like to celebrate my birthday in the town where Elisa was born. I would like all the disadvantaged children and their parents to come and celebrate my birthday with me, and for my entire birthday gift to be shared among those children." She stopped for a minute and said, "All the clothes and things that me and Elisa have outgrown or are not using should be given to them as well."

The King said to his daughter, "I will do more than that, pumpkin. I will also ask your brother, sister, mother, cousins, uncles, and aunties to bring out all the things they have outgrown and those they are not using and I too will also bring out some things." He went on to say he would send trucks of vegetables and fruits to be shared among the community.

She looked at her father and said, "Father, one more thing please."

The King said, "Go on, pumpkin."

"May all my tutors come and read to the children? And can the actors also come to perform at the party?"

The father agreed.

The King went back to the palace, called on his leaders, and told them what he had discussed with Princess Grace. He then commanded them to start making preparations and to make sure everything was ready and even better than what the Princess had asked for. He then went back to the garden to meditate on Psalm 33 which was one of his favorites. He knew it by heart and he always praised God using it. Princess Grace also liked praising God with the same Psalm. This was one of the many things they had in common.

The Queen liked praising with Psalm 21. She believed God had always given her husband all of his heart's desires. Princess Sasha also liked praising with Psalm 21 like her mother. The Queen was very close to her first daughter, Princess Sasha.

Prince Hope, the future King, liked praising God with Psalm 15. Prince Hope was also very fond of his baby sister, Princess Grace. Princess Grace also liked praising with Psalms 19 and 63. She also loved praying with Psalm 23.

They selected the town hall as the venue for the party as there was plenty of empty land around it. That way, they knew there would be enough room for overflow. The day of the party, the town hall was decorated and the townspeople were very happy. The streets were also decorated and big screens were set in every corner for those who could not enter the hall to see and hear everything going on inside. Most people came to the town hall to see how they could help. Posters and flyers were sent out to invite the townspeople to the party and some who came to see how they could help became the distributers of the flyers. They invited children and the nearby city people to come and join Princess Grace in celebrating her birthday. Several big tents were erected where most of the gifts and food were stored. Princess Grace's big birthday gifts started arriving before the party. People brought bars of gold, diamonds, and large amounts of cash. She told her father to convert all of her gifts into cash for the townspeople. Some of the money would be used for development of the city and to help the cities which were stricken by poverty. She gave the city council money to help with the development of some charities.

The party started at 10:00 a.m. and ended at 8:00 p.m., many games took place. There were many lines for those who wanted to received clothes, toys, vegetables, and fruits. Many lined up to see the actors performing and so on. No matter how much was given to the people, there was still more clothes, food, vegetables, and fruits remaining. Announcements were made encouraging the people to take more. Children came and took more clothes and toys. Trucks of food kept arriving. Some were from the stores and factory owners who heard what the King was doing and wanted to help. They brought food like rice, cooking oils, drinks, salts, sugar teas, and much more

Princess Grace enjoyed this day even though the crowd was huge and she could not meet everyone who came and wanted to celebrate with her. She was touched by the crowd, to see that all these children and their parents had come to celebrate with her. She learned how to play basketball that day. She found a group of children playing basketball and watched for few minutes before asking them if she could play too. They taught her how to play and she discovered that she had skill. She thanked the children and moved to another group that was playing other games. Children were eager to teach her their games. The Princess was also eager to teach them the word of God and her lifestyle. The more she saw how people lived, the more she appreciated her lifestyle.

At 3:00 p.m., she made an announcement for everyone to come and watch the actors. Not everyone was able to fit in the hall, so most people watched on screens outside. Some watched at home. At the end of the performances, the Princess talked to her guests, first thanking them for coming and then explaining the message the actors were giving. She went on to tell them about the joy she had in her life. The Princess said, "I don't have this joy because I am a Princess, but because I belong to God. My father dedicated me to the Kingdom of heaven before I was born. I also gave my life to Jesus Christ. Why? Because Jesus said, 'Let the little children come to me, and do not hinder them, for the kingdom of heaven belongs to such as these.' With that, my friends, I would like to invite you to know Jesus as your Lord and personal savior and please come forward so that I may lead you."

A big crowd moved forward. It seemed as though everyone came forward together. Princess Grace told them to raise their hands wherever they were. They did as they were told. She said, "I will pray this short prayer with you. All that you need is to believe." She quoted the Bible and said, "For God so loved the world, that he gave his only begotten Son, that whosoever believeth in him should not perish, but have everlasting life (John 3:16, NKJV). Jesus said, 'I am come that they might have life, and that they might have it more abundantly (John 10:10)." Then she invited them to repeat the prayer after her.

Dear Lord Jesus, come into my heart. I know I am a sinner, and I ask for your forgiveness. I believe you died for me and rose from the dead for me. I will trust and follow you as my Lord and Savior all the days of my life. I pray that you guide me to do your will. Amen!

The whole crowd said "Amen" together and the Princess encouraged them to rejoice in the Lord. She instructed them to make joyful noise for there was a big celebration happening in heaven. "The heavens celebrate every time for a soul which comes to Christ, but today this city, this nation has been blessed. The kingdom of God is here today. Let all the saints say hallelujah!" Everyone said "Hallelujah!"

The Princess said, "Come on, dance for the lord, sing to the Lord. This is the day you were born into the new Kingdom of the Father, the kingdom of Almighty God. Mark this day, this time and date into diaries, because it is the day when you received eternal life by faith. That is why it calls for a big celebration."

The King looked at his own daughter in surprise. Every day, this girl surprised him. Her maturity in the ways of God always left him speechless. "Whose child is this?" he jokingly asked his wife.

The Queen laughed and said, "I have been wondering when that question was going to come out of your mouth. It was written all over your face. My King, do you have such a short memory? Have you forgotten that you nourished my womb with prayers and praised God and gave him this child before she was even conceived? You literally baptized her with the word of God, prayers, and worship the moment she was born? Do you want me to go on?"

They both laughed. The King said, "I believe my Lord is pleased with her and with what we have done so far."

The crowd was so big that no one could see the end of it. When they rejoiced after salvation, it was like an earthquake. People rejoiced everywhere. From street to street, some made their way to rooftops, some stood on top of their cars, and some climbed trees. The crowds were so big that one could walk up to 15 miles and still be in the birthday crowd. The crowd sang "I love Jesus," and it was like the whole country was singing. Surely this was a day to remember for these young people. In the future, they would tell their children and grandchildren about this day, when a ten-year-old made a great mark in history both in heaven and earth. In almost every corner, trucks continued to give out food, clothes, and blankets. Truck drivers were fighting for space to park their trucks so that the crowd could come and get food and clothes.

For the first time in history of this town, most families were complaining of not having space to store all that they'd received.

At 5:00 p.m., Miss Elisa ran to the stage and sang happy birthday to Princess Grace. The crowd joined in and sang to her. Even those watching at home were singing. The Princess was so touched by the love they showed her. Princess Grace spoke to her sister Princess Sasha with tears streaming down her face. She told her sister that she wished the day wouldn't end. Princess Sasha told her she had the power to stop the day from ending just like Joshua. Princess Grace smiled at her sister and said, "Not for a selfish reason." Princess Grace believed that nothing was impossible. She believed that the same power Jesus had, she also possessed. She believed that she could stop the sun if she wanted to, but that it would be selfish to do so for her gain. She was so innocent that she believed every word in the Bible and because of that, she was able to do just that.

After the song, Elisa's mother came to the stage and announced that it was time to bring out the cake the city had made for Princess Grace. It was the biggest cake anyone has ever seen. Princess Grace laughed. "This is bigger than most cars. It's even bigger than some trucks!" she said.

"It took over one hundred and fifty bakers seven days to finish it," Elisa's mother said. "They worked twelve hours a day."

Elisa's mother called Princess Grace to the stage to cut the cake. She invited her family to come and join her and to help her cut the cake. They came up to the stage while Elisa stayed behind. Princess Grace called to her, "Elisa, where are you? We are waiting for you."

Elisa was very happy to know that she was considered a member of the family. They cut the cake and were joined by a team of women who helped them cut the cake and distribute it to the crowd.

The schoolchildren had acts hidden up their sleeves. Several bands came to perform. Some of them were quite good. Princess Grace enjoyed the matching bands because they were so colorful and full of energy. The way they played drums and danced at the same time was amazing. They played an old song, "Onward, Christian Soldiers, Marching on to War." They were so breathtaking. The group was so large it seemed that half of the schoolchildren were part of it. There were more than five thousands of them by estimation. Other children were running from all over to join the match. The Princess screamed, "Holy! Holy! Holy! Glory to the living God." Everyone, even the King, joined in. The kids were wonderful. Their smiles were beautiful and their smiles came from within. One person said that it was like the coming of Jesus, which he has never seen. That was the best way to describe that moment of praise.

At 6:00 p.m., Lord Paul proposed a toast to Princes Grace. When he finished, the King came, then the Queen, then Prince Hope, Princess Sasha and many other people including the Mayor. They all thanked Princess Grace for bringing everyone together and for the gifts and the love that she shared with them.

The church minister came to thank Princess Grace and commented on the number of people who have received Christ. He appealed to all the Christians for help in nurturing these people. He encouraged them to come to church so that they could grow. He reminded them that the word of God says Faith comes by hearing the word of God. The minister said, "May I take this opportunity to welcome all those who gave their lives to the Lord, to the Kingdom of God. And to say I am happy we are now one in Christ." The minister also thanked Princess Grace for the good job she has done in reaching out to the lost souls and the gifts she has given to everyone. He invited everyone to come to church on Sunday. He laughed and said "I don't know how we are going to fit, but I have learned something from the young Princess. I should never worry about what is going to happen, but just to do what I am supposed to do. When the Princess invited the whole city to celebrate with her, she never worried about space or anything, but God provided." He went on to say, "Look at the multitude of people, food, and clothes." Just then, somebody began speaking through a loud speak, asking those who needed new furniture to come to the end of the street. The minister smiled and said, "You heard him. Go and help yourself." He went on to say, "I have never seen the hand of God like this since I was born. Can we all pray for our birthday girl and our host?" He called on Princess Grace and they all prayed for her.

He said, "Child, God has given you a big heart and I am very happy to see that you are using it the right way." The Mayor approached the stage and whispered something into the minister's ear. He laughed and said, "Glory to God." He said to the crowd, "Good news, everyone. Tomorrow we will worship at the

National Stadium. The service starts at 10:00 a.m. Our Mayor has just blessed us with the stadium for tomorrow's service."

The following day, the eighty thousand seat stadium was filled to capacity. Extra chairs were brought in and placed on the football field. Any available space was filled until there were one-hundred and twenty thousand people inside the stadium. But the majority of people were still outside. The news reported that the multitudes of people were lining up as far as twenty miles in both directions. It was estimated that there could be over fifteen million people who came for the service. They also estimated that seven million had given their lives to Christ at the birthday party.

Some people had to fly in from out of town. There were big buses that brought people to the stadium from the neighboring cities and towns. Many people remembered how the King had declared fasting in the palace before the Princess was born and how he wanted to dedicate this child to God's kingdom. They were happy to see that the King's wish had truly come to pass. Multitudes of people came to hear the word of God from a ten-year-old and she had led more people to Christ than anyone before her. But what was more amazing was the multitude of people who came as a result of the announcement made the previous evening. That was truly an example of how fast the Word travels. The minister encouraged all the believers to minister to the new people who have just given their lives to Christ. He urged them to show them love and support. He went on to thank Princess Grace for bringing so many new souls into the kingdom of God again. The moment he mentioned Princess Grace's name, the crowd went wild cheering and clapping hands, some beating drums. There was so much joy. The minister said, "Whoa, surely the Princess is the Princess of the people."

The spirit of love and thanksgiving reigned in Netherlands. It spread quickly from city to city. As for Princess Grace, her picture was everywhere. Some people were even making T-shirts with her name on them. Whatever the people could come up with to show their affection for their Princess, they did it. They said that she was the first to lead the whole nation to Christ. They said that she was truly a child of God. Toward the end of the service, the minister called on Princess Grace to come to the pulpit. When she got there, the minister asked her to speak to her guests.

For about five minutes, Princess Grace could not speak because there was so much noise from the crowd, excited to see her. This girl, at the age of ten-years-old, had such great effect on people. She kept on saying, "Thank you, thank you," hoping that the crowd would stop cheering, but they didn't. The King and Queen looked at her with tears of joy streaming down their faces. The minister went to stand by them and said, "My King and my Queen, you have done a wonderful job raising this child. Your father in heaven is pleased with you." They thanked the minister and the crowd stopped cheering after five minutes of pure celebration at seeing Princess Grace.

She thanked them all for coming, even those who could not make it inside. "May I pray for you?" she asked. The crowd cheered again and began clapping. She prayed a very powerful prayer, short but to the point. When she finished, she explained to them how Jesus knew what was going to happen to him. He understood everything about being crucified, being beaten, the crown of thorns, and the mocking, but because of the love he had for the people of this world, He went ahead anyway. "So that whoever believes in him as the son of God should not perish with the Devil but should have everlasting life," the Princess said.

"You see, when you love someone, you can do anything for them, and never dream of hurting them, no matter what bad that person has done. When you see yourself enjoying or laughing at someone who has done something wrong, or who is in trouble for whatever reason, know that you don't have the spirit of Jesus in you. It does not matter whether you go to church every day or you call yourself a Christian. You cannot rejoice on someone's downfall. The spirit of Jesus is love, peace, trust, compassion, mercy, forgiveness, and, don't forget, serving. You see Jesus trusted us when we were still in deep sin; that if he died for us, we would accept him as our savior. That is why he went ahead and died for us, because of the trust he had in us, that we will do the right thing. So why can't you trust your neighbor? When you give him love, he will forsake all the bad he is doing. Love is the best correction, not condemnation. Please, my friends, let's show love to one another and work together to make this nation a better nation. Remember, the Devil comes to steal and to kill. What happens when you condemn someone? You steal their joy, and out of that comes depression. Sometimes they die or live a reckless life because they feel people have given up on them. So you have taken the place of the devil. Jesus was surrounded by thieves and prostitutes and he never saw them as anything less than anyone else. He loved them the same and treated them with compassion. That is the meaning of true love. If you are here and you don't know this Jesus I am talking of and you wish for him to be your father like he is mine and you want to accept him as your lord and personal savior, raise your hands wherever you are so that I can lead you to him."

During the Princess' speech, the crowd was so quiet, listening to every word. Most Christians said they had been hearing the message, but this time it was different and there was a very powerful spirit behind it. The spirit was love. She had explained to them what love was in a clear way. Some said it was because the message was coming from an innocent mind; a child, who was raised to serve God. Some said it was because she had true love within her, so when she spoke of love, she spoke of something she knew well and understood. Some said it was because of the foundation her father made for her, with all the prayers in the palace before she was conceived and when her mother was pregnant with her. God must have poured more of his spirit into her because of her father's desire to please and honor God. There were even rumors that when the Princess walked in the garden, she was having a conversation with God. There were so many stories going on but they were all good stories.

When The Princess saw the multitudes of people with their hands lifted up in the air, she called her father and the minister to come and join her in prayer. Hands were lifted up everywhere. The media reported that over five million people gave their life to Christ that day. When the crowd saw the King approaching the pulpit, they roared with excitement. The media took pictures and recorded every word. The King was an anointed man of God and it proved the love he had for God in the three-minute speech he gave before they all prayed the salvation prayer with the minister and Princess. After the salvation prayer, Princess Grace asked those who were not feeling well either in their bodies or in matters of the heart, to place their right hands on their heads as she prayed the healing prayer for them. People were screaming almost everywhere declaring that they had been healed during the prayer. Some people were even rising from their wheelchairs. Others who were deaf began to hear. Those who could not speak began talking. Everywhere, there were miracles. Family members were crying, seeing their loved ones receiving sight and all kinds of miracles.

5

The effect of Princess Grace's birthday party lived on in Netherlands forever. The whole world was talking about this young and powerful girl. Her teachings were so strong for a child and the compassion she had for people was astounding. Many TV stations invited Princess Grace to come on as their guest, but the young Princess told the father that when the time came, she would, but she did not feel it was the right time yet. Her father teased her and said, "Princess Grace, my people love you more and more and they think you are their Queen. You have more influence on them than either me or the church minister."

Princess Grace laughed and said, "No, father, no one can replace you, they are grateful to you for bringing me into this world and the way you raised me; But most of all, Almighty God is more pleased with you and you have done more than King David. He danced for the Lord. You gave him one of your children to serve him unconditionally and to worship Him. And father, I am grateful that I am the one you chose to do that with and I am also happy that my brother and sister are strong in Christ as well. As for this nation, it is blessed to have you as their King and their spiritual leader. Father, we are highly blessed. We belong to Jesus."

The King stopped and gave her a hug. He said, "You are always correct, my pumpkin. You are growing in wisdom every day. It is always a pleasure to talk to you, pumpkin." The King had tears in his eyes when Princess Grace spoke to him, but he didn't want her to see him cry, for he was moved by the wisdom in her at the age of ten. She could hold a conversation like an adult.

She stopped walking and said, "Father, I would be happy if the whole world would accept our Lord Jesus as their Lord and personal savior, I don't want to leave anyone behind when Jesus comes for us. It is my wish that we all go with the Father. It will be a beautiful day when we meet our Lord in the clouds. Oh father, my spirit is overflowing with joy just thinking of that day."

The King looked at her and said, "Yes, pumpkin, and he will be rewarding us for all the good we have done on this earth." He stopped and looked at her and told her that he was happy he had brought her into the world the way he had. He was even happier that she enjoyed the kind of life that he'd raised her to have. He further told her that he was very proud of her. Princess Grace held his hand and hugged him. She thanked him for everything.

They walked on in silence for a while. When they arrived at the end of the east garden, they set down together without speaking. Their spirits were communicating together. They stared at the river running in front of them and finally, they heard a noise from the rose bushes nearby. When they looked up, they saw a man with a camera in the tree taking pictures. The man fell suddenly.

The King ran to the fallen man and asked him if he was hurt.

"A bit, but it's nothing major," the man said.

"Why do you come to my home like a thief?" the King asked.

"I wanted a good picture and a good story," the journalist said. "I have not made it far as a journalist and I needed something to make me a success."

"All you needed to do was ask," the King said. The King invited the journalist to join them by the riverbank and ask him what he wanted to know.

"I have more questions for Princess Grace, if that's okay," the journalist said. Princess Grace turned towards him and said, "It's okay. Please ask your questions."

The journalist was shocked to see that he was staring into a pair of deep emerald green eyes. He felt like this young lady was seeing through him. She was more beautiful than the pictures he had seen. He could not speak. He just looked at her and started shivering. He could not explain what made him shiver, and he was getting weak in his joints just by looking at her.

The Princess asked him if he was cold. He said that he was not. Finally, Princess Grace asked him if he was finished and he said yes. Princess Grace laughed and said, "But you haven't asked me anything. Can I ask you something then?" He nodded his head yes, for he could not speak. She first asked him his name. He told them that he was called James Wilcox. She then asked him if he was born again. He told Princess Grace that he doesn't know what that meant, but that he thought the answer was no. Within few minutes, the Princess was leading him to Christ. The King was watching their conversation and trying to control his laughter at the fact that this man had come to ask his daughter questions and did not even manage to ask a single question before Princess Grace started speaking about God. The journalist looked like he was about to run for his life.

After the salvation prayer, Princess Grace asked the King if they could invite the journalist inside. The King agreed and there inside the palace, the Princess asked the man to bring out his pad so that she could tell him what the world wanted to know about her. The journalist was surprised that the King did not sit with them. Instead, he left the Princess alone with him, and he asked the King, "Your Majesty, are you leaving her alone with me?"

The King said, "Yes and trust me she can handle ten of you. I am not worried for her, instead I am worried for you." He laughed and said, "Relax, young man."

This proved to this journalist that what he had been hearing about this family was a lie. Because out in the town, they were telling people that the Princess never did anything without the supervision of the King or the Queen. They had made it sound like the Princess acts the way she does because she was forced to by her parents or that she lived the life of a prisoner. Now the King had just left him alone with the Princess and she was about to tell him about her life. The King was not concerned with what she says. The journalist said to himself, "How wrong can people be? In this case; very wrong."

Princess Grace explained to the journalist the nature of her birth which she was so proud of. She spoke about how grateful she was to her parents for raising her like they did. The Princess went on to explain to this man the joy she found in her life. She talked about the friend she had in Christ. The journalist asked the Princess if she ever got lonely.

"What do you mean?" the Princess asked, confused.

The journalist explained to Princess what he meant. She then told him that she had never felt that way. At the end of the interview, this man understood that this girl had a beautiful life and she did not know anything negative. Most of the negative words, she didn't even know. He asked her if she could permit him to take a picture of her at close range.

"Of course," the Princess said. After he took the picture, the Princess called one of the workers and ask the journalist to show him how to use his camera so that they could take a picture together. The journalist was very happy and they took more than one picture together.

"I will carry these pictures with me always," the journalist said.

Princess Grace said, "Then you have to bring me a copy too. Now tell me, do you have any children?"

"Not yet," he said. "But I am engaged to be married someday, I hope to have children." He asked the Princess if he could invite her to his wedding.

She laughed and said, "That would be nice. Could I bring my family along?" The journalist agreed.

Later, he returned to his agency and wrote an article titled, "The Power of an Innocent Mind." The Princess' picture appeared with the article. The journalist had been the first to interview Princess Grace and he was so happy about it. He had great respect for her. He wrote all of that in the article and wrote about how the Princess led him to Christ and how the King left him alone with the Princess. He wrote about the remark the King had made when he asked him if he was leaving the Princess alone with him. He wrote about the beauty of the palace with the ceilings made of gold and the politeness of the King's family and everyone in the palace. He talked about how someone's life can change just by visiting the palace because of the behavior of the people there and how respectful, full of love, and caring everyone was.

Many people asked for extra copies of the newspaper. The printer had to print extra copies to meet the demand, and it resulted in a big promotion for the journalist. The president of the newspaper company called him to his office and announced his promotion. The president also told Mr. James Wilcox that from that day on, he would be covering anything to do with the Royal family. Television stations were inviting him for interviews to hear about the life of the Princess. He answered every question truthfully with a smile. He told them that he was now a friend of the Princess. He went on to explain that she might be young, but that she had the wisdom of an old woman and was sweet like an angel. The King's family was watching the interview on television and laughed when they thought about how nervous he had been around the Princess. Princess Grace asked her mother; why was it that people sometimes got intimidated around her even though she would be friendly to them.

"Sometimes people have the wrong motives and they might be thinking that you see right through them," the Queen told her.

Just then, on television the journalist said, "She has eyes which burn through you and it is like she is seeing everything going on in your mind."

The King's family laughed and said to Princess Grace, "There is your answer."

The journalist told the interviewer that he had gone to the palace to steal a picture of the Princess and create a story himself without talking to the Princess, for he never thought he would be able to meet her. Now he was happy because he had not had to guess. Instead he had written a true story and he was proud of it.

He told them, "At ten-years-old, she is 5'5" and very beautiful. To say that her hair is red is not quite true. Her hair is the color of flame, like yellow mixed with red."

The royal family laughed at his explanation. Then the big question was put to the journalist. The interviewer wanted to know what had given him the boldness to go to the palace. He was sincere when he told them how he was sitting on top of the tree watching the King and Princess Grace taking a stroll in the garden. Then he lost the balance and fell. They were laughing on the television program when they heard this. One of the interviewer said, "Point of correction, while you were spying on them, not watching." But they were touched to hear that the King was not angry with him and was instead concerned that he might be hurt. He was glad to hear that they had invited him inside while the King ordered the security department to make sure that nothing like that happened again for the security of his family and workers.

They asked the journalist, "Besides beauty, what else can you tell us about the Princess Grace?"

"To be honest," the journalist said, "she doesn't look human. She is like a spirit or an angelic being. I have never seen an angel but she looked like an angel." He continued, "There is something about her beyond this life that I can't explain. When you look at her eyes, you feel weak and when she talks, it's like everything stops. Being close to her is like being on fire. Her hair is always flying like there is wind even when there isn't. Yet it shines with volume." The journalist ended his interview by telling them that he had given his life to Christ and that the Princess had led him in salvation prayer. They were amazed and wanted to hear more, but the interview was over.

In almost every home, people were listening to the interview on television and many were not surprised to hear what the journalist was saying. But to Princess Grace, it was not a big deal. She was very happy about the fact that he had given his life to Christ.

She had such an innocent mind that she was not aware that people were celebrating her. She was egger to help people but mostly to lead them to Christ, and she didn't care about what people thought. She asked her mother, "Why do people get lonely? The journalist asked if I ever got lonely."

Her mother explained to her that it was because many people need the company of someone special. The Princess was surprised. "But most people have the most special person within them all the time; God the father God the Holy Spirit and God the son.

The Queen said, "But, baby, not everyone knows how to make them their personal friend and that is where we come in, to teach them."

Princess Grace said, "Then we have a lot of work to do and we need more people to help. Surely we need the grace of God to be able to reach everyone." She stopped and said, "Oh, father, can someone help me in following up with the journalist to make sure he understands his new life in Christ?"

Prince Hope said, "I will do that for you, pumpkin." Princess Grace gave her brother the journalist's number and his name.

Prince Hope took the phone and called the journalist immediately. "Hello, this is Prince Hope. My sister asked me to call you and invite you to lunch on Saturday." The journalist accepted the invitation quickly. Prince Hope asked the journalist for his address so that he could send a driver for him.

When he dropped the phone, Princess Grace said, "I didn't say invite him for lunch, I said follow up!"

"That is the only way I know how to follow up," Prince Hope said. "He is new in Christ he needs to talk to somebody face to face. That kind of fellowship is good for him."

"That is good wisdom," Princess Grace said.

Prince Hope looked at his father with a smile and said, "Don't forget our father's name. Wisdom is in our genes." He said this while giving his younger sister a big hug. He whispered in her ear, "I love you." They all laughed. The head waitress came and announced that it was time for dinner.

On the other side, the journalist was so overjoyed. He called all of his friends and family to tell them that he had been invited to the palace by Prince Hope, the future King. He also called his fiancée who asked if she could come with him. He promised that he would ask. The journalist called Princess Grace to ask if he could bring his future wife to lunch. The Princess was happy with that for she thought that it would mean another soul for the Kingdom of God.

As soon as he hung up the phone with the Princess, the journalist called his fiancée, Samantha, and said, "Get ready, I am taking you for shopping for the dress you are wearing on Saturday for lunch." She screamed with excitement.

Elisa jumped up and said, "Princess Grace what can I do to help with your work? The Princess told her that she would create a program to help the church minister with the follow up of new Christians, and that Elisa could work with her on the follow up. Elisa was so happy that the Princess accepted her offer of help.

Later on that night, Elisa went to the Queen and said, "Mom, can I ask a question?"

The Queen said to her, "Of course, anytime, child."

The first week Elisa arrived at the palace, the Queen told her she could call her whatever she wanted. Elisa said, "Can you be my mom, since my mom is not here?" The Queen agreed and told her she would be happy to be her mother. That is why she calls her "mom." Elisa wanted to know how is it that when the Princess prays for people to be healed, they are healed immediately but when other people pray, the same thing doesn't happen. The Queen explained to Elisa that it was because all the Princess knows is to trust in the father and the faith she has without doubt.

She said "Elisa, Princess Grace sees nothing impossible in Jesus' name and that is what you should do. Know that whenever you call on the name of the Lord, everything is possible."

The next day, the Princess asked her father if she could go to the temple. The King called the driver to take her there whenever she was ready. Princess Grace called for Miss Elisa and told her that they would be going to the temple to discuss with the minister how they could help with the follow up of the new souls.

The minister was happy to see them and offered them a cup of tea, but Elisa asked for a cup of milk. They drank tea with biscuits and when they finished, Princess Grace told the minister of her desire to help with the new souls. The minister was happy and listened carefully to Princess Grace's plan. When she finished, the minister took them to the big hall and asked them if the hall would be of use as a workspace. They all agreed. So every Saturday morning at 10:00 a.m., they would come here and minister to the new souls. Princess Grace stopped and said to the minister, "I have the right person to spread the word." She was thinking of her journalist friend. She called Mr. James Wilcox and asked him if he could come immediately to meet them at the temple. He came at once.

The journalist felt very important to be receiving calls from the Royal Family. He dropped what he was doing and drove to the temple. On his arrival, the Princess greeted him and informed him why she wanted to talk to him. She told him that his part was to spread the word by publishing the information in the newspaper and on the television stations for the new souls to come for fellowship on Saturdays. The first group would be from 10:00 a.m. to 11:00 a.m. And the second group would be from 11:30 to 12:30 p.m.; with the final group from 1:00 to 2:30 p.m. Miss Elisa would be giving the people cards to write down their information and she would keep those cards updated for the church she would find someone to help Miss Elisa with that work. She would also help with calling them and praying with them and checking to see how they were doing. She was excited about this.

She turned to the journalist and said, "Now, Mr. James, can you always come and meet us here for help on Saturday? You know in the kingdom of heaven we have to learn to serve first. That is how we receive our promotions and we need more help."

He looked at her and said, "Yes, and I think I can find us more help."

Princess Grace smiled. "That is a good thing, Mr. James."

Mr. James intended to bring his fiancée with him; for he knew in his mind that when they got to the palace, the Princess was going to lead her to Christ. They set the date for the first Saturday in two weeks so that the hall could be made ready for the meetings. Prince Hope contributed the chairs and stationary to support his younger sister's ministry. The Princess parted with Mr. James and told him that they would talk more tomorrow when he comes for lunch. "I am looking forward to meeting your fiancée," she said.

The next day, Mr. James arrived with his fiancée. She was a well-behaved girl, the daughter of one of the judges. She was an average-looking girl who dressed very simply. Yet she had a very sweet smile. After they had settled down, Princess Grace asked her if she was born again. The girl asked her what that meant. The Princess explained to her about the birth and death of Jesus. She said, "If you have not accepted Him as your Lord and personal savior, you cannot enter the kingdom of heaven."

Mr. James' fiancée was paying rapt attention. She asked the Princess what she should do to accept Jesus as her Lord and personal savior.

"I will introduce you to him," the Princess said. Together, they prayed the salvation prayer. When they had finished, everybody at the table stood up and congratulated her and welcomed her to Jesus' family. She was so happy.

"Where do I go from here?" she asked Princess Grace.

"You do the same for other people," the Princess answered. "Lead them to Christ and you can join us on Saturdays to help at the temple." She was happy to do that.

The lunch was a success and Prince Hope spent time with Mr. James and shared the word of God with him. Princess Grace asked Mr. James who he was going to bring to the temple to help. He pointed at his future wife. Princess Grace told him she had already invited her; he had to find someone else. He laughed at how smart and quick Princess Grace was. Princess Grace joined in and soon everyone was laughing.

The following month, Princess Grace spent more time reading about the prophecy of the messiah, the birth of Jesus, and his crucifixion. Sometimes, she cried as she read about the suffering He endured. When she finished reading, she fell to her knees and thanked Him for all He had done for the world. She had one prayer request every time: "Lord, use me please in the way that pleases you."

One day, the King told her that after they finished praying that it was all right to ask for more from God.

"Like what?" Princess Grace asked him. He told her that she could ask for her heart's desire.

She said, "That is my only heart's desire. I don't want anything else. I just want to be close to Him like never before." She was becoming more and more passionate with God. Sometimes she would scream and say, "I am in love with Jesus." She would look at her father and say, "Dad, I love Jesus more than anyone else; More than my family, and His creation." The King would smile and say, "That is a good thing, pumpkin. It is a very good thing." He would tease her and say, "I thought you loved me more." She would laugh and tell him that after Jesus, came him.

6

The whole world was attracted to King Wisdom's country for many reasons, but mostly, they wanted to meet the young Princess. There was prosperity, peace, and unity throughout the country. The first King to come visit toward Princess Grace's twelfth birthday was from the east of Asia. When he arrived at the airport, he came with three planes. Even King Wisdom was surprised, but he later learned that the other two flights were carrying mostly gifts such as gold bars, silk, and much more. There was a ceremony at the King's airport to welcome this great King from East Asia. King Wisdom, Queen Fiona, and Prince Hope were among the people at the airport for the arrival ceremony. After the ceremony, they were escorted to the King's Hotel. After arriving at the hotel and settling in, the Asian King told King Wisdom that the main purpose of his visit was to see the young Princess Grace whom the whole world was talking about. He went on to tell King Wisdom that he had heard great things about the young Princess. He knew about the mighty things she had done in the name of her God, even though he didn't believe in the same God.

"Which God do you believe in?" King Wisdom asked.

"I believe in Buddha," the Asian King said.

"Would you like to hear about our God?" King Wisdom asked.

"No, not right now," the King replied. King Wisdom did not want to offend his visitor so he changed the subject. He knew the time would come for them to talk about their Gods.

That night, the Queen asked her husband if he thought Princess Grace would be able to lead their visitor to Christ. The

King told his wife that he chose to leave everything in God's hands. "Though I admit, this is a tough one," the King said. After their discussion, the King and Queen prayed. The King had already told Princess Grace that the Asian King was interested in meeting her, and she too was praying. She learned that the King was visiting for a week.

In the morning, Princess Grace told the father that he wanted him to delay the meeting with the King since she would be fasting and would not be able to meet anyone. The King asked her when she would be able to meet him. She said that after three days, she could meet him. Usually, when she was fasting, she would always break her fast in the afternoon. But this time, she was dry fasting for three days with no food or water. For the first time, no one, including her parents could see her for three days. Princess Grace locked herself in her chamber. The King and Queen joined her in fasting, but they broke their fast in the evening,

The next day, the King told the Asian King that his daughter was not available for three days, so they would do other things first so that the King would be free to meet Princess Grace on the fourth day. Princess Grace was praying and praising God in her chamber. On the third day, she received the confirmation from God. Nobody knew why she was fasting but the King and Queen suspected that it had something to do with their visitor.

On the fourth day, Princess Grace told her father to bring the visitor to the palace for lunch to meet with her. King Wisdom did not know what was going on in the Princess's mind and did not want to ask questions. He knew that when the time was right, the Princess would talk to him. But right now he couldn't ask her. The Princess was glowing brightly after her fast. The King felt so much anointing in his daughter that when one passed by her, they felt the power of God. Shivers ran down the spine of all those in the Princess's presence.

At 11:30, the Asian King arrived. He was a very powerful ruler feared throughout the whole of Asia. Most Asian countries wanted to be on friendly terms with him in order to assure themselves protection and his favor. His army was one of the most powerful in the world. The King welcomed him to his home and the two Queens met and talked. After everyone had sat down at the dining table, Princess Grace arrived. Immediately, everyone fell quiet, waiting for her to say something. The visitor King looked at her and began shaking. He tried to say something to the young girl, but words would not come out. King Wisdom and his wife also felt the strong presence of God. It was like they were on a different planet. They all stood up. The waiter pulled out the Princess's chair for her to sit down. After she sat, everyone else sat down. Their behavior indicated their respect for the Princess.

Finally, Princess Grace greeted the King and his wife and told them what a pleasure it was to have them in their home and country. King Wisdom stood up to introduce his visitors to his daughter.

"There's no need, Your Majesty. I know who this is," the Asian King said. "I am truly honored to meet you," he addressed Princess Grace.

They ate lunch and the Princess asked for fruit for she had just broken her fast. After the meal, Princess Grace asked the Asian King if it was all right for him to meet him in the study. The King was happy and the Princess excused herself and led the King to the study. King Wisdom and everyone else were wondering what was happening in the study. The Asian King and Princess Grace were gone for almost an hour.

After an hour, the door opened and King Wisdom could see that the King's eyes were red and the Princess was smiling and holding his hand like a child clinging to her father. The King's arm was around the Princess. King Wisdom could tell that the Asian King was not upset with the Princess. He assumed that the King must be born again. He sometimes worried when his daughter spoke to people for he knew that she only spoke the truth and that can upset some people sometimes.

Everyone sat and stared at the Princess and the Asian King, unable to understand what was happening. They remained standing for about thirty seconds as if they were absorbing something. Finally, Princess Grace looked at the King and said "Should I?"

"It will be an honor," the King said.

"Brothers and sisters in Christ," the Princess said, "please welcome our new brother, King Yusuf!" Everyone stood up and clapped their hands. They forgot about the formalities and rushed to hug him. Even Queen Fiona rushed to hug King Yusuf.

After all the excitement, Queen Fatima asked, "What does this make me? Am I also a sister because my husband is a brother?

"No," the Princess said, "You have to do it for yourself."

King Yusuf asked if he could be given the honor of leading his wife to Jesus. The Princess agreed. The King told his wife in his native language the message of salvation and asked her to pray after him. She did and when she said "Amen," they celebrated again. To everyone's shock, Princess Grace started speaking to King Yusuf in his language. The King was shocked.

"Princess," he said, "I did not know you speak my language. Did I lead her well in Christ?"

"Yes, you did," the Princes said.

The King smiled and said, "You see? I am a good student." They both laughed. King Yusuf asked the Princess where she had learned his language and she told them that for the past three days, God had taught her his language. Her parents never knew what was going on with her.

King Yusuf saw that in their eyes and said in his funny, broken English "She is complicated, isn't she?"

"No, she isn't complicated. But she is a wonder," King Wisdom said. They both laughed.

King Yusuf clapped his hands three times and his guards came rushing in. He told them, "Bring in Princess Grace's gifts." He told King Wisdom that he would need a big room in which to put the gifts. The guards brought in lots of gold bars, jewelry, silk, and dresses made in his country. After they finished bringing in Princess Grace's gifts enough to fit in two five-ton trucks they brought lots of silk for Queen Fiona.

"We heard you are on top of the fashion world, Queen Fiona," the King said. "These are for you and your school."

Queen Fiona thanked him. He brought some gifts for the King, such as more gold, as well as gifts for Prince Hope and Princess Sasha. To everyone's surprise, he offered a final set of gifts to Miss Elisa. She was so happy that this man knew about her and brought gifts for her too. She jumped out of the chair and ran to hug him.

"Thank you, sir," Elisa said. "You knew I was here too!"

"Everyone in the world knows about you," King Yusuf said. "You are King Wisdom's last child."

Elisa laughed and started singing and dancing for King Yusuf. He clapped the hands when she finished and said, "Bravo, bravo, Elisa, my girl!" He went on, "Come, child and give me that warm hug again."

Princess Grace went to him and said, "King Yusuf, you are a good man indeed. You did not try to divide my father's house. I will always honor you for that." She hugged him and thanked him for all he had done.

King Wisdom invited the visitors on a tour of the palace. The palace was very big and very beautiful. It had one-hundred and eight bedrooms, seventeen libraries, fifteen major sitting rooms, study rooms in every chamber, and one-hundred and thirty bathrooms. Some of the chambers had two bathrooms. The ceilings were made out of gold. King Yusuf was impressed. He said "King Wisdom, this is the most beautiful and unique palace I have ever seen. Of course, it is very expensive as well. I have seen wealthy palaces but none as rich as this one."

After two hours of touring the palace, the visitors were tired. They rested in the west wing sitting room where the palace staffs had placed refreshments. King Yusuf was impressed with the staff. He could tell that they were not afraid of their King but were very respectable towards him. He asked King Wisdom, "How do you do it?"

King Wisdom did not understand the question. "Do what?" he asked King Yusuf.

King Yusuf replied, "Your servants are not afraid of you and yet they respect you highly and honor you. How can respect go with honor without fear?"

King Wisdom explained to him how in the creation of God, all men were created equal even if some were more advantaged than others? "They give me the best service and, as their King, father, and employer, I have to take care of them. They know I love them and that I would do anything for them and their families. If it comes to anyone endangering their lives, I would rather give my life for theirs."

King Yusuf was perplexed. "No, they are the ones who are supposed to give their lives for you. You are their King," he said to King Wisdom. King Yusuf told King Wisdom about how his servants could not look him in the eye, for if they did, they would be killed. His servants knew that they were not equal with him. He said that if they could say there were equal to him, it would be considered blasphemy and they would die for that.

King Wisdom then explained to King Yusuf how God had sent his child to die for us; so that whoever believes in him can inherit the kingdom of heaven. He explained to him that there is no servant who can inherit which God meant for his children; Which means that God gave us equal rights as his son. He told King Yusuf that all his workers are brothers and sisters in Christ and that he does not have a servant. If God can't make anyone a servant, who is he, King Yusuf, to make God's child a servant?

After an hour of explanation, King Yusuf began to understand, and said, "I have lots of things to learn from you and even more to change when I get back home." He went on, "And now I see why you are so respected and successful around the world.

Truly, this journey was an eye opener for me." He then leaned over to King Wisdom and said, "Please, may I ask a very deep personal question?"

King Wisdom gave him permission to do so.

King Yusuf told King Wisdom about the rumor going around in their country that God had impregnated his wife which is why young Princess Grace was performing such big miracles, because she has God's blood flowing within her. King Wisdom laughed and told him that it was not true. He had slept with his wife and asked God to take over the life of the child. He explained to King Yusuf that if he explained it now, the King may not understand because he had not yet reached the level of understanding of such big revelation. He promised King Yusuf that he would create time before he left to explain everything to him. King Yusuf agreed.

Just when they were about to leave, the King's brother; Prince Lawrence, arrived. King Wisdom was happy to see him and asked him why he didn't tell him that he was coming.

"I didn't want to disturb you since I heard there were visitors in the palace," the King's brother said. King Wisdom introduced his brother to King Yusuf and Queen Fatima. Both men sat down and to King Yusuf's surprise, King Wisdom immediately began to pray, thanking God for protecting his young brother and bringing him home safely. He then went on to thank God for his visitors and asked for divine protection upon them. He blessed them and their Kingdom. King Yusuf was touched.

It came time for King Yusuf and his party to return to the hotel and he told King Wisdom that he wished to spend more time with Princess Grace before he returned to his country. King Wisdom explained that the Princess teaches the new people in Christ on Saturdays and suggested that King Yusuf attend a class, as he was also new to Christ and he laughed; but King Yusuf took him seriously and agreed. Arrangements were made for King Yusuf and his party for fellowship on Saturday. King Wisdom immediately asked Lord Paul to make arrangement for the hall to be ready to receive the Great King and his people on Saturday. Beautiful chairs were brought in and more security was provided.

Princess Grace called Mr. James Wilcox, the journalist to come on Saturday and to bring his camera. She knew this would help him a great deal with his work. Princess Grace asked King Yusuf if he could allow Mr. James to interview him on Saturday after the fellowship. He told the Princess that it could be done but she should understand that there were certain things he could not talk about until he spoke with his cabinet members first. The Princess told him that she understood. "Even in the Kingdom of heaven, there is order to the way things are done," she said.

King Yusuf was impressed with the wisdom in the young girl. He asked Princess Grace how old she was.

"I will be turning twelve in the next three weeks," she said. King Yusuf could not believe that he was having this conversation with an eleven-year-old girl and that he was even nervous, choosing his words wisely because of the girl's intelligence. In his country, a woman cannot address a man, let alone a King. Now here he was, learning from this young girl. But he realized that there was something within him that liked this. He knew that, in the matter of Jesus Christ, this young girl was an elder and he considered her an expert. She told him that Christianity was a training ground for Champions. Yet she was so relaxed that you could see that she was not trying to be someone whom she is not. King Yusuf told Princess Grace that he would like her to come to his country to teach people about this Jesus who was able to give people more wisdom. Princess Grace told him she would like that very much. She also reminded him that Jesus is his Lord and personal savior and he should never forget that. The King smiled and said, "Yes, teacher, I will not forget."

The next day, Princess Grace was at the temple at seven in the morning as she had to be sure that the temple was ready to receive King Yusuf and his company. She already knew that his people were going to give their lives to Christ. She told Lady Elisa this and Lady Elisa asked her how she knew.

"Because God sent these people to me to be the evangelist of their country; It's just that they don't know it yet," she said.

Lord Paul arrived at eight in the morning and was surprised to find Princess Grace already there. Within five minutes, Princess Sasha arrived too. By eight-thirty, most of the elders of the palace were already there. James the journalist was so happy and had agreed to allow his boss to come with him as his cameraman.

When the guests arrived and saw the way the hall was transformed, they saw that the Royals really knew how to make a place look rich. People started arriving and were surprised to see the decoration, arrangements, and most of the Royal family there. They knew someone important must be coming but they never thought it would be King Yusuf. They knew King Yusuf was visiting their country, but they assumed that it couldn't be him since in his country, the people don't believe in Christ. They knew that King Yusuf was a feared and stubborn King. He had all the powerful weapons on earth and some people thought he was a killer, but his people believed he was their savior. No country dared challenge them in war.

There were tents outside for the overflow and TV screens had already been set up.

At eight-thirty, the palace police and soldiers started arriving with a very heavy Royal escort. At nine o'clock on the dot, the palace vehicles arrived. At nine o'clock, Princess Grace began the prayer and everyone could see what was going on inside thanks to the large screens. The soldiers began arriving and King Wisdom and King Yusuf arrived, followed by their Queens. People from outside started cheering and Princess Grace had to stop for some time to let them take in the excitement. After everyone had been seated, she said, "Brothers and sisters, what do we say to our visitors?"

"We love you!" everyone shouted.

King Yusuf stood up and Princess Grace ran to him with the microphone so that he could speak to the crowd. He said in broken English, "Thank you. I am happy to be in the country of Jesus Christ; and one day my country will be the country of Jesus Christ too!"

Everybody both inside and outside stood up and made joyful noise for they were not expecting those words from him. They knew that it meant that Princess Grace had spent some time with him.

During the teachings, King Yusuf paid attention and told his personal assistant to record everything word for word and to observe everything. He whispered to King Wisdom, "Is it not strange that great Kings sit here receiving lessons from a child? This young girl has more knowledge in things of Christ than we Kings."

King Wisdom smiled and told King Yusuf that if he lived around Princess Grace, he would get used to it and would see nothing wrong with it. Toward the end of the fellowship, Princess Grace made an alter call. King Yusuf spoke something in his language. All of his people stood up and he stood up too to support them. There was a lot of joyful noise from the people when they saw this. Mr. James was busy taking pictures and recording everything. At the end of the fellowship, Princess Grace usually asked one of the new souls to give them a closing prayer. She announced that it was time for closing and asked if there was anyone among the new souls who would like to give a closing prayer. King Yusuf stood up fast before anyone else could and began to pray. To everyone's surprise, he prayed in tongues.

King Wisdom remembered seeing King Yusuf's eyes red as though he had been crying when he came out of the study with Princess Grace. He realized that he had just received the Holy Spirit.

James didn't know that Princess Grace had arranged an interview for him. He was surprised when, at the end of the fellowship, Princess Grace told him to go to the visitor's room to interview King Yusuf. With much excitement; he called his boss and cameraman to follow.

The interview with King Yusuf was a success. James was given an opportunity to take pictures of both Kings together and even more pictures of the Kings with their wives. King Yusuf requested a picture with Princess Grace. He said he wanted to show it to his people back home. They left Princess Grace at the temple as she still had more classes to conduct that day. King Yusuf invited Princess Grace for dinner at the hotel, which she accepted.

At the hotel, they discussed inviting Princess Grace to King Yusuf's country and finalized it with King Wisdom. It was going to be Princess Grace's thirteenth or fourteenth birthday gift.

The day King Yusuf returned to his country, King Wisdom and Queen Fiona went to the hotel early in the morning to join the King and Queen for breakfast. After breakfast, trucks started arriving. King Wisdom surprised King Yusuf with gifts. Queen Fiona has also made dresses for Queen Fatima and royal outfits for the King. She had even made some in the style of their clothes back in their country. Queen Fatima was so grateful and could not believe how Queen Fiona had done this in such a short time. She told her that she loved the clothes and would wear all of them. Of course they were designed for the Queen and were very beautiful.

King Wisdom's country was rich in minerals and he brought some of those to King Yusuf. They included a big polished diamond from his mines. The other truck was full of Bibles and children's Christian books. King Wisdom told King Yusuf to give them to the people he was going to bring to Christ. There was another package from Princes Grace for all the people who gave their lives to Christ at the fellowship. It was also Bibles and more gospel materials as well as some CDs of her teaching.

King Yusuf remarked that he came loaded with goods and he was going back loaded with goods as well. The two Kings proceeded to the transportation after fellowshipping together. King Yusuf was disappointed that Princess Grace hadn't come to bid him farewell but he understood that she had a lot to do. The bodyguards opened the door for King Yusuf to get inside the car. As he sat inside, he looked beside him. Princess Grace sat there, laughing like the child she was. The King laughed. "Angel, you surprised me. I thought you wouldn't make it to come and see me off."

"I wouldn't miss saying goodbye to you," Princess Grace said.

On their way to the airport, Princess Grace moved closer to King Yusuf and held his hand. She rested her head on his shoulder and slept. King Yusuf was moved by this, to know that this young girl could be a child too, and that she felt comfortable enough with him to rest her head on his shoulder and take a nap. Since he'd arrived, he had been seeing her busy in the work of God. He'd never seen her having personal time or even playing with her siblings. He loved it and he whispered to King Wisdom, "Look, she is sleeping and she is comfortable around me."

King Wisdom smiled and said "Of course she is. You have the same spirit now. When you came, you had a different spirit and she could sense that. Now we all belong to the same Kingdom which is higher than mine and yours." The two Kings shared the word of God until the Princess remarked on something King Yusuf said; alerting them to the fact that she was awake. She told King Yusuf to create time for God and to put Him first in whatever he does and God would show His greatness in his life.

King Yusuf said, "Yes, teacher I will. You too will hear of the great works I do in the name of your God."

Princess Grace said, "No, *our* God."

The King replied, "Yes, Angel, *our* God. When you come, you will find temples in every corner of the streets.

She said, "It will be churches, not temples." He asked her what the difference was. She told him that he wouldn't understand it even if he tried, but as he grows in the Kingdom of heaven, he will understand without anybody explaining to him. She said, "However, you will have churches and Pastors. Pastors will be guiding people and teaching them like I do." He asked the Princess if she was a Pastor. She said that she was an evangelist and that one day she would be ordained.

King Yusuf asked her what her wish was. "What do you wish to be ordained as?" he asked.

"It's what God wants me to be," she answered. "Whatever He chooses will make me happy."

King Yusuf wanted to know why the Pastor at the temple was called "minister." The Princess told him that the minister at the church was not a Pastor, but that a Pastor is also a minister.

He said, "So are you saying the Pastor is more senior?"

The Princess said, "You could say that. It's a debatable subject. A Pastor has more responsibilities, as he is a Pastor, a minister, and an administrator. Yet a minister is a minister and an administrator, but he is not a Pastor."

King Yusuf asked the Princess if she had learned all of that in school.

"No, I just know," she said.

"Your life is a mystery to me, Princess," the King said.

"It's unique, thanks to my parents," the Princess said. "I wouldn't change my life for anything else on earth."

They arrived at the airport and King Yusuf thanked Princess Grace again for all the teachings and for introducing him to Jesus Christ. She hugged him and said, "We will meet again in your country." He walked to the plane with King Wisdom and the Queens following behind. They bid each other farewell and left. King Yusuf noticed that there was a much bigger crowd when he left than there had been when he'd arrived and many people were holding his picture. Music was playing and bands were marching.

King Yusuf waved to the crowed with a big smile and said, "Farewell, brothers and sisters!"

The crowd laughed and said, "Farewell, brother!"

James sold over two million pictures that day and people still wanted more even though the King had gone. King Wisdom and his family bought some pictures as well. James planned to donate some of the money to the Princess's project of soul winning. He had called Princess Grace and told her about his plan. The Princess was grateful and happy for him. He was still celebrating his success when he received a call from the palace; the King was requesting his audience. He was told to be at the King's hall at 10:00 a.m. the next day. It occurred to James that perhaps King Wisdom was not happy that James had taken King Yusuf's picture and had sold it without royal permission. But he just wanted to do something special for King Yusuf with his countrymen that did not involve the palace.

Being called to the palace could be disturbing; especially when you know you had taken certain matters into your own hands which could put you in trouble. It was known all over the country that although King Wisdom was a loving King and father, he was also firm when it came to the law of his country. The King also told the Queen to bring Elisa to the King's hall.

The next day, James was at the palace by eight-thirty. Even though it was cold he was sweating. He realized that he was afraid. He had called his boss the night before to tell him that he had been summoned to the palace and that he suspected he was in big trouble because of what he had done. His boss was not supportive at all; he told him he had gone too far. That made James feels worse. The meeting was scheduled for 10:00 a.m., but James wanted to get it over with, whatever it was. At 9:30 a.m., he went to the gate and told the soldiers that he was there for a meeting with the King. He knew it would take him at least 15 minutes to reach the meeting place. They checked for his name and gave him the logbook to sign. He was then escorted to the King's Hall. He arrived before the King but there were palace police and soldiers with some of the Lords and all the senior people had been assembled. James became even more afraid. Lord

Paul saw him and asked him "Son, are you okay?" James said he was all right and immediately passed out.

When he woke up, Princess Grace was sitting by the bed he was lying on. She asked him how he was feeling. He then told Princess Grace the truth; that he was so afraid and he believed he was in trouble.

"Why would you think that way?" asked the Princess.

He explained his suspicion to Princess Grace.

She laughed and said, "You are fine. Is that the reason you are shaking so badly? The King is very proud of you for what you did yesterday for King Yusuf and his crew."

They were not aware that the King was standing by the door until he cleared his throat to announce himself. He greeted James as if he hadn't heard them talking and asked him how he was feeling. James told him that he was much better and was ready to come to the King's hall.

"If you are not well," the King said, "we can make other arrangements for the future."

"No, sir—I mean, Your Majesty," James replied. "I am fit and ready." King Wisdom smiled and walked away. Princess Grace was happy for her friend, even though she felt pity for him because he was so frightened.

She told him, "Come, I will walk with you to the King's hall." As they entered the hall, the palace band started playing their instruments. Miss Elisa was there, dressed very well, and the Queen was holding her hand and supporting her. She looked at Princess Grace and nodded.

"Stand up and step forward," Lord Paul summoned James. He did as asked.

The King spoke. "Because of the good work you did to honor King Yusuf by making his memory of this country beautiful, and the volunteer work you have been doing for the palace and with Princess Grace, from this day forth, James Wilcox, you are hereby titled Sir James Wilcox the great Journalist! You will be responsible for taking pictures and writing stories of the palace family and their visitors. You will also come up with ideas about what can be done for the arrival of our visitors and bring them to the chief of staff. You will be given some offices at the King's hotel." The King congratulated James and continued, "Stand up, Sir James Wilcox. I believe you will have to give notice to your employer, Sir James."

King Wisdom then went to Miss Elisa. He honored her for the work she had been doing at the palace and the help she had given Princess Grace. She was told that she was now Lady Elisa. She was happy, but still didn't understand much of what was going on; she turned around and looked at Queen Fiona. The Queen knew she was confused and didn't understand a thing about what was happening, but she would understand when she grew up. Everybody in the kings' hall was happy for them. They celebrated, ate, and drank. What Sir James and Lady Elisa didn't know was that there was an income that went along with the title. But since the King had long ago opened a bank account for Lady Elisa, her salary would go straight to the bank. They figured they would explain to her when she was old enough to understand. They gave Sir James the documents that explained everything, plus the income. Princess Grace also gave Lady Elisa twenty percent of the money she received as a gift for the work they did together. The Queen was responsible for Lady Elisa's bank account, so everyone who had something for Lady Elisa gave it to the Queen.

7

Sir James began work at his new Offices two weeks from the day of the ceremony. On the third month, a truck parked in front of his offices and the driver told him that his furniture had arrived. Sir James told him that he had not ordered any furniture yet. The driver presented Sir James with an envelope adorned with the Royal seal. It was from King Yusuf, congratulating him on the honor and for the new business and offices. Sir James still couldn't get used to been called Sir James. Now here was a letter from one of the most powerful Kings in the world addressing him as "Sir James."

The letter read, "I hope you like the furniture I sent for you. I believe it is fit to use in your offices and studios." It went on, "P.S. Thank you for giving us a wonderful farewell, Sir James. You are a good man and you deserve the best in life. In Jesus 'name, our Lord and Savior." Sir James smiled when he finished reading the letter. The thought of King Yusuf praising Jesus was a wonderful one. The men unloaded the truck. This was the most expensive and beautiful furniture Sir James had ever seen, and nothing he thought he'd ever own in his lifetime. He could not believe what was happening in his life. He prayed and told God that if it was a dream, he did not want to wake up.

⁓❀

Over the following years, Kings and Queens came to visit and Sir James kept busy taking their pictures and interviewing them. He had a space to publish his stories at his old newspaper. People often came to buy pictures from him. Sometimes, the countries of those visiting Kings and Queens would order certain pictures from him in large quantities; and there were times when they would book in advance to have portraits taken. Sir James's business was growing and he had become very rich. The interviews he used to conduct for free, he was now being paid to conduct. He had a studio where people came to buy pictures of the Royals. The newspaper agencies also bought his pictures for their stories. The newspaper agency he used to work for was still in touch as he used them as his publisher. They were always asking for favors from him. But the head of his old newspaper was uncomfortable talking to Sir James like he used to. He still felt guilty that when Sir James thought he was being reprimanded he showed no support. He felt as though he abandoned Sir James. Sir James did not blame his former employer for the past. He still called him from time to time to check on how he was doing and to invite him for lunch or dinner. The news of Sir James's work travelled fast. Since the day he was honored, his work appeared on the front page of the newspapers in the land. Many people were amazed at how he found favor in the eyes of the King and Princess Grace.

His fiancé used to tease him and say that she could not believe he had become a celebrity over night. "What shall I be called when we get married," she asked him.

Sir James smiled, "You will be called Lady Samantha."

"It is unthinkable to know that we are now nobles," Samantha said to James. "Have you remembered to thank the tree branch that broke causing you to fall into the garden in front of the King and Princess Grace?" she asked, laughing.

"I had forgotten," Sir James laughed, "but I won't any longer. That branch played a very important part in my life."

Sir James told Samantha that he had noticed that whomever Princess Grace brought under her wing ended up been someone special. He said, "Look at Miss Elisa and her family, Minister Jacob and me; we are highly favored after meeting the young

Princess. The anointing in her is contagious. The funny thing is that it happens without her trying to make it happen." He continued, "I'm a boy from a very poor family. Even your father was unhappy when you chose to marry me. Now, I am Sir James Wilcox. My woman will be Lady Samantha Wilcox. And I will spoil you, my dear, with gifts and a beautiful home where we can entertain Queens and Kings. You will never want for anything." He laughed and said, "For our honeymoon, I will take you to Paradise and for a wedding gift, I will buy you a train which will take you straight to the moon."

Samantha laughed and said, "There is no place called 'paradise' and no train can go to the moon!" He tried to argue with her and told her that if no train to the moon exists, he would build her one. They both laughed.

Sir James wanted to open his studio officially, but he wanted to speak with Princess Grace first since he was usually volunteering at the temple every Friday afternoon and Saturday, preparing for the Saturday fellowship. The challenging thing was that there were now more people coming to the fellowship and they were never able to address everyone. They now started the fellowship at eight in the morning and finished at eight at night. But still they could not see everybody. Sir James called Princess Grace and asked her if they could meet.

"I would love to come and see your office," she said. Sir James joked and told her that maybe she should come prepared to take pictures. But the Princess took him seriously and agreed. He took many pictures of her and told her his plans for the official opening of the office. He also said that he would like to finally be married. Princess Grace told him that she thought Thursdays and Fridays would be best. She then advanced him to speak with the King about it first.

She said, "If I were you, I would include him in my plans." Sir James took her advice and did as she said.

The following day, Sir James called the King's office and requested an audience with the King. The King was happy to hear that Sir James wanted to meet with him. The two men met the following week on a Monday afternoon at the King's office. Sir James told the King his plan to open his business officially. The King was happy and they set the date together. They discussed, at length, the program of the opening, the list of guests, and transportation. The King advised Sir James to wait a few months so that the VIPs could make arrangements to be available. He reminded Sir James that he was now a noble, so he had to do things like a noble man. The King told Sir James that he would give him the Royals' ceremony organizer to help him with the organization of his ceremony.

"There is one more thing," Sir James said to the King. "I would also like to finally be married."

The King laughed. "It's about time!" he said. "When would you like to do it?"

"I would like a Christmas wedding," Sir James said.

"Excellent," the King said. "That gives us plenty of time to make arrangements." The King handed Sir James a business card and told him to call the number on the card. "She's the best wedding planner in the country," the King said. "She has planned all of the Royal weddings." The King said that after the official opening of the business, they would speak again to discuss the marriage issue. Just as Sir James was about to leave, he asked Sir James, "What are your spiritual preparation?" Sir James did not understand, he didn't know that he had to make spiritual arrangements. The King explained to him how important it was to prepare spiritually rather than simply to prepare physically. He gave him an example of how Princess Grace always prepared spiritually before doing anything. He ended by saying, "Now you know the secret to Princess Grace's success. Go and do the right thing. Always bring God first with whatever you do. You will be successful beyond measures."

Sir James was glad that Princess Grace had advised him to discuss his plans with the King. They fasted and prayed for seven days before the opening. Sir James also called the wedding planner and asked her to help with the official opening. The woman was good but she was too expensive. However, in the end, Sir James was happy that he used her; the ceremony was a huge success. Sir James invited everyone he could think of and followed the King's list and advice. Many people came to have their pictures taken. Most of the Royals who attended were also taking pictures and some invited Sir James to visit their country homes to take pictures there. Mostly they were impressed by the beauty of the studio and the exquisite furniture and decorations. King Yusuf did not come but he sent a representative. Many people commented on the beauty of the furniture. Sir James laughed and told them that a special friend had given it to him.

Sir James was fully booked throughout the following year and he knew he needed to hire more people fast. He spoke to his former boss and presented him with an offer he couldn't refuse, paying him three times what he was currently being paid. The offer came with a company car and an entertainment allowance.

King Wisdom gave a beautiful speech at the ceremony and made everybody laugh when he told them how he had first met Sir James. He concluded by saying, "God was on his side because I could have ordered a serious punishment for that." He went on to tell them, "Whoever is going through some challenges because of a mistake they've made, I pray that their mistake should turn into a stepladder for promotion for them, in Jesus' name." He prayed for his people and thanked them for the support they were showing Sir James.

When Sir James gave a closing speech he surprised everyone, including the King and Princess Grace, when he told them that all the money made from the ceremony would be used to build a church for the city. "If anyone would like to join hands now," Sir James said, "you are welcome to." There was so much joy because the people really needed a place to worship. There were so many Christians and the stadium was always full to overflowing. The church was sorely needed.

Later, when the King congratulated Sir James on his success, he told him that he could never go wrong in his life, because he first thought of building God's house before he built his own home. He told him, "God always rewards those who diligently seek him like you did." He said, "Son, the Bible says "seek first the Kingdom of God and his righteousness and all you need shall be added unto you" (Matthew 6:33, NKJV). Right there today you have shown my people the principles of success. Those who are wise caught the message. The day you build your home, God will provide for you. He will bring men and women from all the four corners of the world to bless you. Well done and keep the faith moving." Sir James thanked the King for his kind words and blessings. He then reminded the King that the ceremony would not have been a success without his help. The King said, "I still believe that you could have still done well without me." They made an appointment to meet at the end of the month to discuss more about Sir James' marriage plans. The King advised Sir James to bring the wedding planner and his future wife.

At the end of the year, Sir James had his dream wedding. It was a huge success. Lady Samantha was a beautiful bride. Queen Fiona had made a beautiful wedding gown for her that transformed her from a simple girl into a sophisticated lady. They used Prince Lawrence's castle as agreed since he was still living with the King at the palace. The west wing of the Palace was occupied by Prince Lawrence and his wife, but he had told the King that he would move out when God blessed him with children. So when Prince Lawrence heard that Sir James was getting married, he offered his castle as a wedding venue. The gardens at the castle were the best. Prince Lawrence had always wanted to show off his garden. This was the time for him to share the beauty of his garden with other people. Sir James was very grateful and touched by his offer. Sir James and Samantha went to the castle before the wedding to look at the place. They fell in love with it. The wedding planner was so happy, she even reduced her price. She said the place was beautiful enough that it didn't need much done to it. They took Samantha's parents to see the place. They too, were so happy that they didn't know how to thank the Royal family for their generosity.

On their way back, Samantha's father told Sir James that he felt badly because of the way he used to treat him. "Can you ever find it in your heart to forgive me?" he asked.

"There is nothing to forgive," Sir James said. "You were just being a good father who wanted the best for his daughter." He held his hands and told him, "A good family man will always look at the interests of his family. That's what you did."

Samantha's father was happy with Sir James' response as he had been avoiding him for some months as he was ashamed of his past behavior. He thought Sir James would hold it against him. But Sir James was now higher than him. Sir James was a noble and Samantha's father was just a court judge. Sir James was now a millionaire and the judge was not.

To their surprise, when they got home, Sir James gave his future in-laws a check for two million Euros. He told them it was their wedding present from him and Samantha.

"We are the ones who should be giving you a wedding present," Samantha's mother said. But Sir James and Samantha told them that they wanted them to be comfortable at the time of the wedding. They had done the same thing for Sir James' parents.

What no one knew was that when Sir James's wedding plans were announced, three people spoke to King Wisdom to see what they could give to Sir James that he really needed. All of them were wealthy. The King told them that Sir James did not own his own home yet; he was still renting. So King Yusuf, Lord Paul, and one of Lord Paul's friend in one of the countries in Europe built a castle to give to Sir James as a wedding gift. It was huge and very beautiful. They brought the same man who had worked on the King's brother's garden to come and design and work on Sir James' garden.

When construction had just begun on the castle, Princess Grace—who was by now very wealthy—went to her father and told him that she wanted to do something very special for Sir James. The King included her in his plan to build a home for Sir James. One of the Royals who had come to visit and who liked Sir James a lot offered to buy furniture for the castle. But the King warned him that the furniture should be of the highest quality.

Sir James was busy looking for land and he saw the castle being built but he did not know that it was being built for him. The rumor going around in the city was that one rich man was moving into their country and was building himself a home before he came. Sir James even told King Wisdom about the castle and promised to take him to see it.

King Wisdom asked "Do you think it is a beautiful building?"

"Beauty does not begin to describe it," Sir James said. "Even though it's not finished yet, you can tell it's beautiful. I'm looking to build something similar," Sir James continued. "I'm still looking for good land." King Wisdom said nothing.

That evening, when Samantha came back home to her parents, they were waiting for her. They talked for some time before going to bed. Samantha told her parents that the Queen had offered for her school to make their clothes for the wedding. "For the whole family," Samantha said.

"You mean I would be wearing clothes that the Queen made herself?" Samantha's father asked.

Samantha laughed and said, "Yes, daddy, you will be dressed like the Royals and from the Royal collection." They all laughed and sang and dance until they realized it was after 1:00 a.m. They went to bed with smiles on their faces.

At Sir James's parent's house, they were happy. Since they had given their life to Christ, they were praising Him and thanking God for their son. When he gave them the check, they prayed and blessed him and Samantha, and asked God to continue to increase them in every area of their life. Sir James had bought them a house about three months back and bought them good furniture. He gave them monthly allowance for their expenses. It was enough for them to save some money. Sir James' life was an example of the stories of rags to riches, both for him and his family. He took his siblings to boarding schools and hired private tutors for them to help them with the subjects they had difficulty with. He even went to his uncles and aunts and arranged an allowance for them every month for food and clothing. He bought the cars for each household. They loved him a lot. All along they knew he was a good boy; but they never knew how good he was until he started doing well in life. He hired some of his cousins and uncles to work at his company. He was always blessing his families. He was the kind of a person who didn't want to enjoy the good life alone. He was a giver. He also went to the local schools he had attended and donated one-hundred-thousand Euros to each school. Some people advised him to enter politics; they were sure he'd be elected.

"It's not for me," Sir James said.

He received lots of gifts for his wedding. Some Royals came from their countries to attend the wedding and most sent monetary gifts. Sir James could not believe the amount of money his accountant told him he had received for his wedding. He told his wife that the money was enough to take care of his family for the next three to four generations. Just when he thought he had more than he could ever need, the King presented him with an envelope. Inside was a house key and an address as well as a card signed by all the people who had contributed to the building of the castle. He could not believe his eyes. He fell to his knees and praised Jesus with tears of joy on his eyes. He stood up and hugged the King, which he had never done before. In the excitement and joy, he hugged him without thinking. He presented the envelope to his wife. She opened it and her mouth dropped open but no words came out. They both went and personally thanked everyone who had signed the card. They declared blessings upon their lives.

Meanwhile, Princess Grace heard what her uncle had done for Sir James. She went to him and told him that she wanted to thank him and his wife for helping her friend. They told her that it was the least they could do for him as Sir James was like family.

Princess Grace asked, "Is it true that you want children?"

"It is true," they said. "We are waiting for God to bless us."

"May I pray with you?" the Princess asked.

They prayed together. The Princess turned and put her hand on the stomach of her uncle's wife and said, "It is done. God has answered our prayers." They looked at her in doubt. She sensed that they were doubtful and she told them that it doesn't matter if they have doubt. "I know that God has answered our prayer and that you will have more than one child since you doubted." She bid them good night and left.

After six weeks, her uncle's wife fainted and a doctor was called.

"She needs more rest for a woman who is about to become a mother," the doctor said. Princess Grace's uncle jumped up and down with excitement. He was so happy that he couldn't stop kissing the wife and calling himself "Daddy."

They remembered that Princess Grace prayed for them. They went to Princess Grace's chamber to tell her the good news in person. The pregnancy went smoothly, but they were not able to attend Sir James's wedding as the wife had to be admitted to the hospital early to be monitored. Princess Grace asked what was wrong with her and she was told that nothing was wrong, but that her uncle's wife was carrying seven babies and needed to be closely monitored. Princess Grace took her Bible and walked away. After six weeks, seven healthy children were born. There was a great joy at the palace. They remembered what Princess Grace said after she prayed for them. She said they would have more than one child because of their doubt. They thought it would be twins, not septuplets! They called Sir James and asked him if he would be the godfather to their children. He was happy to be and Lady Samantha was the godmother.

After six weeks, Prince Lawrence and his wife moved with their babies into their castle with the King's blessings and help. Prince Lawrence told his brother that God has over paid them for all their past years of waiting. "Since this is your fault," Prince Lawrence said to Princess Grace, "perhaps you should move in with us to help us take care of all these children!"

The Princess laughed and told the uncle that she was not the one who put the children in his wife's womb. Everyone laughed. Princess Grace told him, "However, I love you, uncle but you should find the person who did that to help you." King Wisdom prayed for them and blessed them.

8

Princess Grace continued her work in the Kingdom of God, winning souls, performing more miracles, and preaching the Gospel to all. Many times there were people waiting at the palace gate with their sick loved ones to catch Princess Grace as she came out to pray for them. She was growing fast and her wisdom was increasing every day. There were talks that whenever Princess Grace touched someone, their life changed for the better. Some people came just to be close to her, while some came to help in the ministry of God. Some came simply to take a picture next to her. But she never changed. Her encouragement to all was to bring the Kingdom Of God first always. On every Princess Grace's birthdays, a big celebration was held for soul winning and giving to the poor. She used to say that "there are no poor men in the kingdom of God. The poorest man on earth is the one who does not know the Lord Jesus." That is why she was so concerned with the people who didn't know the Lord. Now all the Royals' family started doing the same thing. Their birthdays were celebrated by giving to the poor and soul winning, and most people in the country started celebrating their birthdays the same way, including Sir James and his wife. As much as Princess Grace was giving away her birthday gifts, she was increasing in wealth rapidly. She was the richest among the King's children. It was as if the more she gave, the more she received from all over the world.

After the Princess's thirteenth birthday, she was walking in the garden when she noticed a man standing by the palace gates looking sad. She realized that she had seen the man the previous morning. She walked towards the gate and approached the man.

Princess Grace was inside the gates and the man was outside but they were very close to each other. She noticed something strange about the man. He was wearing makeup and pink lip-gloss. He looked very pale, as though he was sick. But Princess Grace felt like as though there was more to him that she didn't understand. She took one step closer and said, "God bless you, sir." The man lifted up his face and his eyes met Princess Grace's eyes. "How are you?" the Princess asked.

The man began to cry and said "What do you see in me? Leave me alone. I am not worthy to speak to you."

"Please, come inside," the Princess said.

He asked her, "You want me to come in? You mean just like that? You are not going to do a background check?"

"It's not necessary, please come in," the Princess said. The Princess could always sense someone who needed urgent help.

The man came in and said, "Young lady, your father would not like to see you hanging out with people like me."

The Princess asked him what he meant. He told Princess Grace that he was the son of a very rich man in Germany and that his father had rejected (disowned) him because of his sexual orientation. She asked him if his father wanted a girl. She proceeded to asked him if that was the reason he was putting on makeup like a girl. The man realized that this young woman didn't know anything about being gay/transgender. He explained to her that although he is a man, he believes he is a woman trapped inside a man's body, and he is attracted to men. He said that he was sick and would be dead in a few months.

The Princess said, "No, listen to me. God never makes a mistake. If you came to earth as a man, then you are a man and that is final, Furthermore, God is the healer."

The man said that he believed that with him, God had made a mistake. He shocked her by telling her that he was married to a man but that now that man was dead and the same sickness that took his partner was taking him too. For the first time, Princess

Grace didn't know how to react. She ignored what this man was saying and asked him if she could tell him a story. She knew this man needed Jesus immediately. She also sensed the spirit of suicide in the man. She told this man how God had created a man from the beginning to worship Him and praise Him. She told him about Adam and the fall of Adam and she told him about Jesus' birth and how he died a terrible death in order to save them from sin, sickness, and all kinds of evil things. She explained to him how Jesus suffered and how he was mocked; but because of the love he had for human nature, he had to go through with it for his sake and for her sake. She told him that Jesus trusted them to do the right thing. Jesus never gave up on human kind and never would.

When she finished speaking, the man was crying uncontrollably. He has heard this massage many times but never like the way he was hearing it now. This young woman wasn't judging him either. She was not afraid of him. She was even holding his hands as though they were friends. He knew that she was a very strong Christian who doesn't know sin. He told Princess Grace the stories he heard about her and how shocked he was that she was not judging him. He said, "They say outside there in the world that you know no sin." She told him that everyone is born a sinner until you are born again. The Princess asked if she could introduce him to the Lord of Hosts, Jesus Christ. The man told her that he was not worthy to receive Him; he deserves hell. She advised him to just receive Him as he is and leave the rest to Him.

"He always takes care of all the loads of sins people come with," Princess Grace said. "Trust me on this one; Jesus always knows what to do." She led him to Christ.

Meanwhile, the Princess's brother, Prince Hope was watching and listening through the window. He could hear everything going on in the palace garden. He was trying to control his laughter because he could tell from the beginning of the conversation that his sister was ignorant about gay life. But he had to admit, she was a master soul winner. The way she shared the good news of the Lord Jesus was so impressive that the young man did not hesitate to accept Jesus Christ as his Lord and savior. What they did not know was that Princess Grace prayed every morning to commit the souls she was going to meet into the hands of the Lord Jesus and asked the Holy Ghost to speak through her.

After the salvation prayer, Princess Grace told him all things had passed and all things were new. He was now a new creation in Christ. She advised him to go to the bathroom and wash away the makeup on his face. He did as he was told like an obedient child. Princess invited him for dinner at the palace. She went to look for her brother to come and meet their visitor.

Prince Hope asked the young man how long he was visiting.

"I don't know," the young man said. "I came to this country to heal and figure out my life's journey." He then asked him his name. He told them he was called Eric Smith and that he was from Germany.

Prince Hope talked to his father the King and asked him to give the young man a room at the king's hotel on the palace's account for three months. He believed that the best way to help the young man was to give him love and to keep him close to them. The King agreed and they told the young man, Eric, the news. From that day on, Prince Hope spent time with the young man, educating him on the ways of the Kingdom of God and teaching him how to live beyond temptation. Princess Grace invited Eric Smith to come to their fellowship on Saturdays and eventually he started coming Friday afternoons to help with the preparation. During the week, he would go out by himself to evangelize. He was always asking Princess Grace what he could do to help.

On the third month, Eric Smith noticed that there were arrangements been made at the king's hotel for some new visitors. This time it was different. Although visitors had been coming, the King has never asked Eric to take part in the preparation.

The King told him that he would like him to start holding prayers every morning for the hotel visitors. He sent Eric shopping for better clothes.

The King said, "Now you should know that the way you dress and the way you conduct yourself influences many young people, especially those who believe in you."

Eric liked this because he was growing every day in God's Kingdom. He was honored that the King trusted him with his visitors.

He went shopping with Prince Hope and Sir James. He liked Sir James as he was always happy and he made everyone around him laugh. By the end of the month, the visitors arrived but Eric was not there to see them as he was out evangelizing with Prince Hope. The following day, as Eric was leading the prayers, he noticed that most of the Royal family was there including the King and the Queen. It made him nervous to be preaching to the King and Princess Grace, for he considered them more advanced in God's word; he was just a beginner. As he continued preaching, he looked towards the door and was shocked to see his father standing there. For a moment, Eric stopped. Then he remembered where he was and who he was now. He then continued preaching and the Holy Spirit poured his spirit upon him, for he preached the message like he never had before. He preached with boldness and touched the souls in attendance. At the end, he made an alter call. His father stood up with tears in his eyes and went forward with other people to give their life to Jesus. He received the Lord Jesus Christ and asked for his son to forgive him.

Eric said, "No, father, you forgive me; For I brought grief and shame to you and our lord." Eric went on, "How did you know I was here?"

"I didn't," his father said. "I had been invited by King Wisdom to come for a visit and you do not turn down the invitation of a great King."

King Wisdom and his family watched the happy reunion with praise on their lips and in their hearts; For they knew that their God was the God of Unity and the God of the lost ones. Eric's father went and knelt down in front of the King and the Queen and asked them how he could show his gratitude. The King pointed at Princess Grace and said that "She was the one who brought change to your son by giving him love and introducing him to the Lord. I just helped in the growth of the young man in Christ as any father would do. And it was only because he was willing to grow." The King said, "Mr. Smith, you have a good son. Love him and help him to grow as a man without condemning him."

"I will do that," Mr. Smith told the King. "I had given up hope of ever seeing my son again. And now here he is, a complete man."

The King invited Eric and his father to the palace for dinner, during dinner, the King told Eric that he was free now to go back home with his father, but Eric had his plans. He told them that he wanted to stay behind and help Princess Grace with the work she was doing. He explained to his father what Princess Grace was doing for the country and for the people outside the country, and how he would like to be a part of that great work. Eric's father was impressed to hear what this young woman was doing and he was relieved to know that his son has completely changed. He saw that he was willing to grow and teach other people the right way to live. He asked his son what he could do to help. Eric told him there was nothing he could do in Netherlands, but that he should do the same in Germany by winning the lost souls for the kingdom of God. Mr. Smith told his son that then he would buy him a house of his choice and provide the furniture for it.

The King told them that there was land for sale not far from the palace. "I was thinking of buying it for the church, but it is small for the church since there are many Christians in this country and they are bringing more souls to the kingdom of God every day with Eric's help." The King went on, "I would like you to consider that land so that Eric can be close to the family he is now part of."

Eric's father was pleased to hear that his son wouldn't be far from the great King and his family. They arranged to go and see the land the following day and within a week, the sale of the land was closed. The King told them that construction would begin the following month. Eric told the King that he had to go and find a plan for the house first. But the King has taken care of that. He asked Eric to leave that to him. Eric was happy for he knew that the King had good taste. The next day, King Wisdom called Eric and showed him the plans for the house.

Eric said, "Your Majesty, this is not a house, it's a castle."

The King said, "Well, you are a son of the highest God, growing to be mighty in His kingdom and you are also my son. Very soon you will be entertaining and receiving visitors followed by marriage and children. You will need to have a place fit to receive them. You must start thinking like a Prince." Eric agreed with the King and approved the building plan.

The King was happy. "You have done well, son," he said.

Eric grew in Christ Jesus and became very involved in soul winning and counseling. It was as if he was a madman in Christ; after the lost souls, he couldn't rest. During the day, he went to all public places and at night, he went to places of entertainment to bring the lost souls to the Kingdom of God. Every day after the prayers in the hotel, he went to preach in the streets and to encourage people to take God's kingdom seriously. The meeting at the hotel was growing bigger and bigger. More people were coming to attend—people even came from the city just to hear him preach. He preached love, forgiveness, and salvation. The King looked at him and saw the similar passion that he had seen in Princess Grace. He knew that the young man was completely sold to Christ and there was no turning back for him. The King told Eric's father this in one of their telephone conversations. Eric's father was so proud of him.

"Do you think one day Eric will marry a woman?" Mr. Smith asked.

"Oh yes," the King said, "Your son is a complete man, Mr. Smith."

Meanwhile, the building of the bigger house of worship that Sir James had paid for was going on. People were busy giving towards the building. There was so much money given that they began to realize that they could look for more land to build another worshiping place. Some people were giving for the wrong reasons; they wanted to be noticed by the King or the Royal family, but it was still a gift. The King knew that God would use their seed money to change their lives for the best. He remembered how Sir James first came to the palace; he wanted only to get a promotion at work. Now he was highly involved in the Kingdom of God. Eric came to forget the death of his partner and to commit suicide and now he was involved in the kingdom of God. So the King knew without doubt that they would all change; and he also knew they would need more space for worship. They were able to get a second tract of land donated by a businessman. The King thanked God for his faithfulness. They looked for another building contractor to begin building. The King had formed a committee for church building. He showed them the plans and they approved them. The second building started the following month at the same time as Eric's house construction was going on. It was a very busy period for them with all the building going on, evangelism, preparations for traveling to King Yusuf's country, and many other projects.

Contributions for the churches kept pouring in. Even King Yusuf sent his contribution. Each building could hold up to eighty thousand people, but so many people were giving their lives to Christ every day.

Meanwhile, Princess Grace was talking to the church minister about raising up men and women who would teach the word of God. They had found a ministry school and applied for ten people to start. They knew they were going to need more than that but they had to start somewhere. That evening, Princess Grace talked to her father about what should be done with the ministry. The King asked her how he could help. The Princess told him they needed to move fast as they were all new at this.

"I will give a word to the school," King Wisdom promised. "Meanwhile, I will ask the school if they can send some tutors to the palace to teach you and others."

The tutors came and were given one of the King's guesthouses about three miles from the palace. They began tutoring Princess Grace by giving her a test to evaluate what she knew. To their surprise, she answered every question correctly. They gave her the test given to students preparing to graduate with an associate's degree and then the final test for those who were completing their four-year degree. Again the Princess answered all the questions correctly. They told the King that the Princess did not need a tutor. She was far beyond their students. Instead, the school honored her with a PhD.

The tutors administered the first test to others including the Minister, Eric, Elisa, Prince Hope, Prince Lawrence, and Sir James. Most of them did well with the first test and some had only a few subjects to master before they could graduate. The King told the tutors how important it was for these people to be ready when the buildings were complete.

All the students were ready when the buildings were completed. They were ordained as the Pastors to start God's work. Ordained to be Pastors were: the minister as Senior Pastor, Prince Hope, Princess Grace, Princess Sasha, Prince Lawrence, Sir James, Lady Elisa, Lady Samantha, Eric Smith, a staff member named Aaron, two people from the Princess's fellowship, Betty and Isa. The others were ordained as ministers. Eric's father came for the ordination ceremony. He was so proud of his son. He told everyone in Germany how his son was a Pastor and was no longer gay. He was always showing them Eric's pictures and videos. In the pictures, they could see Eric preaching in a stadium. Mr. Smith would call them to come and see his son teaching. Mr. Smith had to admit that his son was truly anointed to preach. He could not stop talking about him. He gave towards the building of the church the equivalent of five million Euros and twelve buses to help with transporting people to and from church. He offered to pay for three Pastors' salaries for the rest of his life. He also gave his son one-hundred-million euros. He then called Princess Grace aside and told her that words alone could not express his gratitude towards her. He was so grateful to her for finding his lost son and for bringing repentance into his life. Princess Grace told him to give God all the glory; for God alone set that meeting. She told him the meeting was not a mistake or a coincidence. It was the work of God. Mr. Smith handed an envelope to Princess Grace.

Inside the envelope was a bank check for twenty-five-million Euros. By now, Princess Grace was getting used to these big gifts. Many people who came to her country always brought her gifts of money and minerals. She thanked Mr. Smith and gave him a hug. He went back to Pastor Eric and the King and told Pastor Eric that he hoped one day he would come back to Germany to teach the word of God there.

It was getting close to the time for the King, the Queen, and Pastor Princess Grace to visit King Yusuf as they had promised two years ago. They were arranging for the opening of the two church buildings and had begun building a third one about thirty miles from the Kings' hometown. They were to leave in three months and the first church building was to open in two weeks time. The King had to begin the selection of his crew, to accompany them to Asia. He agreed with the Princess that they would take some of the ordained Pastors to help with the work of God when they arrived. Sir James was one of the Pastors chosen to go as was Pastor Eric Smith. The Princess included Pastor Lady Elisa when she was choosing among her maids to go with her. She told the King that she couldn't leave her friend, Lady Elisa behind.

"Of course," the King said. "Even I wouldn't want to go without Lady Elisa."

Princess Grace told Lady Elisa that she would be going to Asia to visit King Yusuf. Lady Elisa told the Princess that she wanted to arrange a special gift for King Yusuf so that Princes Grace could give it to him.

"You can give it to him yourself," said Princess Grace.

Lady Elisa screamed with excitement. "Does that mean I'm going with you?" she asked. The Princess teased her and said, "Let me think about it for a minute."

Lady Elisa laughed and said, "I am going. Going one! Going two! Going three!" She jumped and hugged Princess Grace and told her that she loved her more and more every day. Pastor Lady Elisa was always Princess Grace's baby, best friend, and younger sister. She loved her a lot, yet she was firm with her. That was why most of the time, Pastor Elisa joined Pastor Eric to evangelize because she knew that Princess Grace brings God's word first and she liked people who took their responsibilities in Christ seriously. But most of the time, she was with the Queen or the King.

The plans were ongoing for the church openings and the King's journey to Asia. But the people going with him didn't know they were going until two weeks before the departure date. When they were told that they'd be accompanying the King to Asia, they were all happy except Pastor Eric. As for Pastor Sir James, he could not believe all that was happening to him. He used to tell God that he had proven beyond doubt with his life that promotion comes from God. He was growing stronger and stronger in the word of God. Many people said he was always been a blessing, to listen to him preach.

The greatest wonder was Pastor Eric. He preached to the lost souls and sometimes offered his life story as an example. He told the multitude of people that if God could change him and heal him instantly, he had no doubt that He could change anyone and heal them. One night he was preaching salvation message to a city which was known to celebrate sin. Many decent families didn't go there. Pastor Eric traveled to that city, for he thought of how when Princess Grace met him, she did not discriminate against him. As it turned out, he needed Jesus more than anyone else, but if the Princess had not talked to him that day, he would still be lost or dead; a sinner going to hell. In his salvation message, he told them the story of how he had been married to a man and how he grew up without knowing a relationship with a woman, He spoke of the sickness and how he was disowned by his father. But after giving his life to the Lord Jesus, his life changed, He was completely healed and his relationship with his father was restored. He told them that Jesus made him a complete man.

"With the true love Christians gave me, I became lost in the word of God and now I can't imagine living a life without the love of Christ," he said. He then invited all those who wanted to give their life to Christ to come forward. He told them to come as they were and promised them that God would separate them from their sins for good and they would not even remember those sins.

"When you fall, he will pick you up and when you sink, he will pull you out," Pastor Eric preached. "Because He is God of mercy, love, forgiveness, and compassion."

It was said that the whole city gave their life to Christ after that message. Everyone, from those who were playing with fire, the idol worshippers, prostitutes, and all kinds of sinners came to Christ that night. Pastor Eric continued preaching the word of God passionately and he became known in the country as Princess Graces' right-hand man.

From the moment he gave his life to Christ, he never wasted time. He started spreading the word immediately. First with the support of Prince Hope, and after a month, he went out by himself to evangelize. He told his father that he had found true friendship and family in Netherlands. He could not imagine life without them. Now he had gained some weight in a good way. He looked so handsome that the ladies were always trying to catch his attention. But his heart was for God alone at this time. That was an advantage too, because when they heard Pastor Eric was preaching somewhere, they would all come and, in return, give their lives to Christ. He was moving mountains with the word of God. Pastor Eric became one of the most powerful preachers in that country. Now he was about to go international; he didn't even know it. But Princess Grace knew he would do a good job in Asia during their visit. They were going to be there for three weeks.

Princess Grace was planning how, during their stay in Asia, she would spread her people throughout the cities in the country. They would go accompanied by King Yusuf's men, to preach salvation to the nation. She intended to cover as much as they could within two weeks. She knew King Yusuf was going to want her to be close to her and her parents, but that did not bother her. She knew that her parents were always supportive of her work. She had told her father that she wanted at least ten million Bibles to be shipped ahead of them to aid in their work. Pastor Eric has written a small booklet on salvation, which he usually gave to the people who came to his gatherings. It was designed for them to give to their loved ones who couldn't attend the gathering. Many people had given their lives to Christ because of that booklet. Now Princess Grace told him that she wanted to reproduce at least fifteen million copies of those booklets to take with her to Asia. Pastor Eric was very happy to do that. He was glad to know that his work would be of help in soul winning in another country. The booklets were produced and shipped ahead, but to Eric's surprise, he received a check from Princess Grace for thirty-million-euros as payment of the booklets.

"I cannot accept this," Pastor Eric told the Princess. "I did it for God."

Finally, after much discussion, the Princess gave up. She knew that Pastor Eric was never going to take the money. So Princess Grace invested that money into the church building account.

⤨✳

Princess Grace had many success stories before she turned fourteen. She did not believe there was anything impossible as long as one had God. She believed in God and His word with all her being. So people she spent time with ended up believing the same thing. Young Lady Elisa has long ago started praying for people to be healed. The first time she prayed and saw a man stand up from his wheelchair, she jumped with joy and told the Queen that God now trusted her because he allowed her to minister healing to someone sick and they had recovered.

The Queen smiled and said, "Yes, it means you are now an elder in the kingdom of heaven and don't forget that you are now a Pastor." She told her she was no longer a baby in Christ, and advised her to take that seriously. Pastor Lady Elisa was very happy with the Queen's response.

The Queen told the King about her discussion with Lady Elisa. She was the baby of the palace. They enjoyed her a great deal and loved her like she was their own child. That is why Pastor Eric became close to Lady Elisa as well. She was always smiling and always excited about almost everything. When they went out to evangelize, Pastor Lady Elisa was always jumping up and down like it was her first time, yet she had done it many times. She was always telling them what Pastor Eric did and didn't do, and how many souls he won, and how the ladies were trying to be close to Pastor Eric, bringing him all kinds of gifts, and asking Elisa to invite them so that Pastor Eric would notice them. She was so ignorant that she didn't see anything wrong with what she was doing. But they were happy to know that Pastor Eric was taking the ministry work seriously. Then she would burst out laughing and tell them that Pastor Eric doesn't entertain their silly behavior. He always talks about God and refuses to get engaged in their silly personal talk.

Lady Elisa looked at the Queen and said, "Mama, one girl wrote on her T-shirt 'Mrs. Eric Smith'." Princess Grace stepped in and told her that was enough. She should not go with Pastor Eric to judge people. She was not to look at their funny behavior or to judge Pastor Eric. Instead, it was her duty to see how she could help them to grow strong in Christ. The Princess told her when she saw behaviors which were out of the ordinary, her duty was to pray for them. It is the duty of the Holy Spirit to convict them. It was not her job.

Everyone fell quiet. The Princess was right. They respected Princess Grace a great deal when it comes to the things of God. At fourteen, she was well-behaved and very responsible in the work of God. She did not need any supervision in anything. She was always busy helping people or looking for lost souls, and she had a way of finding them just like the way she had found Pastor Eric. Every morning and evening when she prayed, she always prayed for those who had not received Jesus Christ as their Lord and Personal Savior. She prayed to be at the right place at the right time so that she could minister salvation to them and for the Holy Spirit to help them understand the message and be saved. Whenever she thought of the unsaved people, her heart ached. She wished everybody on earth could be saved by receiving Jesus Christ as their Lord and personal savior.

King Wisdom was busy preparing to visit his friend King Yusuf. At his mines, they were busy selecting the best diamonds for the King to choose from to take to his friend. He had one of the rarest diamonds, the Green eye, to bring. They found one big, green diamond. It was the largest they have ever found since the mines had opened. The King ordered them to take it for cleaning and cutting. He told them to be very careful not to spoil it. He was very happy. The Queen asked him if he was truly going to give it to King Yusuf. He told her that yes; he was, for King Yusuf was one of his closest friends and a true brother in Christ. He told his wife that there were no coincidences in God's kingdom. They found the diamond while they were looking for the best diamond to give to the King. He told his wife he was happy with his gift for his dear friend. Queen Fiona had also been busy at her school making outfits to take with her. The school has been so busy and, at the same time, they learned a great deal because during that time, they were working together with the Queen. Some students have volunteered to work long hours with the Queen. She arrived at the school at seven in the morning and sometimes she would not come home until after midnight. There were three groups at school. The first group came at seven, the next came at 2:00 p.m., and finally, the last group came at 6:00 p.m. The Queen was there with all of them. She started the work in the morning by cutting the patterns with the morning group and in afternoon, they would be sewing. The night group was busy with the finishing touches.

Meanwhile, King Yusuf was also busy preparing for his friend's arrival. He was even happier to know that very soon he would see Princess Grace and his friend, King Wisdom.

King Wisdom called Sir James and told him that he would be accompanying him to Asia. Sir James was overjoyed. He also started preparing his gifts for King Yusuf. He looked for some of the nice pictures of King Wisdom and his family and one of Princess Grace alone. He found one of himself and Lady Samantha as a couple to give to King Yusuf as a gift. He worked on them and enlarged them. He chose expensive and beautiful frames for each one of them. He even had the picture of King Yusuf with King Wisdom's family enlarged and framed. He was very happy with his work. He told Lady Samantha to start preparing for the journey.

She was happy but she didn't want her husband to know that she had not been feeling well. She has been light-headed for the past few days and had been feeling nauseous. She thought that if she told her husband, he would tell her to remain at home. She went to her parents and told them that she would be accompanying her husband to visit King Yusuf in Asia. They were happy for her but her mother noticed that she looked pale.

Her mother called her to her old bedroom and said, "Now tell your mama."

Samantha pretended that she didn't know what her mother was talking about.

Her mother said, "Samantha, are you pregnant?"

"I don't know," Samantha said. "I am afraid to check because if I am, Sir James might not let me travel. I really want to go." This would be her first royal trip.

"I understand," her mother said. "But you must be careful not to hurt the child."

Princess Grace called Pastor Eric and told him that he would be going with them to Asia. He was concerned that there would be not enough people remaining home. He asked Princess Grace if he could remain behind and take care of the work at home. But the Princess told him that he was needed even more in Asia than at home. They would have but a few days in the country and they needed to cover almost the whole country. She told him the Father in heaven wanted them to cover the whole world and they were running out of time. Pastor Eric took his work in the Kingdom of God very seriously. He asked Princess Grace to forgive him.

"There is nothing to forgive," she said. "I understand your passion for the work of God."

With two weeks remaining, everyone was busy, even those who were going to remain behind. Prince Hope was spending most of his time with his father since he was remaining at home as head of the Kingdom. King Wisdom was handing the reigns over to Prince Hope, showing him everything that needed to be done. Prince Hope was looking for an opportunity to talk to his father about a personal matter, for he had met a girl in his visit to the hospital, and she was neither Royal nor Noble. Instead, she was of mixed blood. Her mother was black and her father was white and Prince Hope was very taken with this girl. He was convinced that he was in love with her. He tried putting the girl out of his mind but he could not stop thinking about her, as much as he tried. As a future King, he knew a great deal was expected from him when it came to choosing a bride. However, he decided to let his father leave and he would speak with him when he returned.

Lord Paul was to help him and guide him in Kingdom matters whenever necessary. King Wisdom sensed that Prince Hope was tense but he thought that perhaps he was feeling the weight of all the responsibility he would soon have. The King encouraged his son and told him that Lord Paul would be there to help if he needed it.

The Queen left Princess Sasha in charge of the school and the virtuous women's meetings. Princess Grace also left Princess Sasha in charge of the follow-up and first-timer ministry. There was a lot for them to do while the King and his crew were gone.

9

In King Yusuf's country, he was busy preparing for his friend and his spiritual mother. He had a team of people working with Princess Grace's Team, for he knew that Princess Grace was going to be busy preaching the Gospel of the Lord Jesus Christ. He was happy about that and had called for all of his family members to come and be near to hear the good news. He left out only his uncle, whom he knew would never accept Jesus. He had led some people to Christ already, even though he wanted them to meet with Princess Grace and her team. He believed they were the best in that for leading people to the kingdom of heaven. After receiving the Bibles that Princess Grace had sent ahead, he also ordered fifteen millions Bibles and stored them in storage houses, waiting for Princess Grace's team to arrive. His wish was for his whole country to accept Jesus as their Lord and personal savior, but the Princess had told him not to force them. She told him this was a matter of the heart and that people should believe with their heart in order to receive Jesus as their Lord and Personal savior. King Yusuf had also sent his men ahead to book all the big venues in the country in nearly every city. The men and women who had gone with King Yusuf to King Wisdom's country were even busier than anyone; for the King had told them that they were responsible for spreading the good news of the Lord Jesus throughout the country. After Princess Grace and her team left, they would be responsible. He had been having meetings with them three times a week. They had been reading the Bible and praying together. His intention was to ask King Wisdom to permit him to send them to his country to learn how to become ministers of the word of God.

The day, King Wisdom was to arrive in the afternoon. There was a big crowd at the airport. Bands, dancers, and the Royal band started arriving early in the morning for they wanted to be in front to see the great King and his daughter. They wanted to see for themselves who the world was talking about. Some people even took their sick loved ones to the airport because they had heard rumors that when Princess Grace passed close to where they were standing, they could be healed.

The flight for King Wisdom was scheduled to arrive at 3:00 p.m. King Yusuf decided that he wanted to be there an hour before they arrived, to make sure everything was as planned with the Royal preparation and band. He arrived at two o'clock and he could not believe his eyes. It was even difficult for him to enter the airport. It was like the whole city was there. Some people were raising signs that said, "Welcome, great King Wisdom and his family!" Some read, "Welcome the children of the true living God!" There were so many messages but all of them were good. He was so pleased with his people particularly because he had not forced anyone to come and welcome the visitors. They had all come by their own free will. When his car arrived, his people were cheering him and sending him love messages which he never seen before. He remembered what King Wisdom had told him; when you love your people and care for them, they don't have to be afraid of you. Instead, they will respect and love you. He felt loved and respected and he could see the proud looks on his people's faces.

Many groups had formed all kinds of entertainment. King Yusuf didn't know that his people had such talents. He stopped and took the microphone in order to greet them. There was so much joy. He told them that he loved them and that he always prayed for them, for he believed it was his responsibility to pray for his people. Just as it was their responsibility to pray for him and their country. The noise of joy was louder than anyone had ever heard. The people could see that their King was truly a changed man. He saw a woman with a small baby of about six months; he got out of the car and went to her and asked her the name of the baby. She told him, and he lifted the baby and kissed him. He told the baby to grow strong and to take care of his mother. He then blessed the baby and the mother.

He told them a little about the family that would be arriving soon. He explained how he had been received in their country and the love they showed him and his crew. He even mentioned Sir James and what he did for him and how King Wisdom promoted him with the title of "Sir" after what he did to honor him (King Yusuf).

The King said, "So you see, my people, no good job goes unnoticed or unrewarded. You will never know how the good job you do for someone you don't know can change your life for the better."

King Wisdom's flight arrived at 2:55 p.m. The crowd went wild with joy, singing, and praising. When they looked down from the plane, the visitors could not believe their eyes. They were not expecting such a huge crowd. Princess Grace saw it as an opportunity for soul winning at her very first hour in the country. The soldier's band played a gospel song and they sang it beautifully towards the plane's entrance. They formed a wall and King Yusuf started to march forward to meet his visitors. To everyone's delight, he started marching and dancing.

King Wisdom saw what his friend was doing. He told his crew "Let's all dance for Jesus and meet our host." They also started dancing. Lady Elisa went ahead of them and danced like she had never danced before. Cameramen and women were busy taking pictures. The media were allowed to take videos and pictures too. All the country's television stations were showing the ceremony live. They wanted to know who the young dancing lady was. But most importantly, they were happy to see the two great

Kings dancing for their Lord. Nobody had ever seen Kings dancing before. History was made at that moment. Their children's children would hear about it. Princes Grace cried out of joy for she knew the spirit of God was present in that place. Everyone danced and danced. Some were crying tears of joy. Many people had brought gifts to the airport to give to the visitors. Meanwhile, King Yusuf's uncle was watching on television and boiling in anger. He murmured, "Idiots."

After introductions were made by King Yusuf's governor King Yusuf asked King Wisdom to greet his people. King Wisdom took the microphone and greeted the people. They received his greeting with great joy. When he handed the microphone back to King Yusuf, the crowd began calling for Princess Grace. They were beating drums and calling her name over and over until King Yusuf gave Princess Grace the microphone. He was surprised that they have not met Princess Grace and yet they loved her so much.

Princess Grace called Lady Elisa to lead them in a song. She had composed a song called "Let the Spirit of God Take Over This Country." She sang it and everyone was quiet. It was such a beautiful song and had so much anointing in it. When Pastor Lady Elisa finished singing, there was a moment of stillness. Everyone was quiet for some time. It was obvious that the song had ministered to them.

Finally, Princess Grace said, "Let's pray." She first thanked God for the safe journey and then prayed for the country, the King, the Royal family, the people of that country, and for the sick. She preached the salvation message right there at the airport and asked those who wanted to know Jesus to lift their hands up and repeat the prayer of salvation after her. Almost the whole crowd lifted their hands up. King Yusuf watched with amazement.

When she finished, she said, "Now I can pray for the sick to be healed right here, right now." The Princess asked them to touch the part of their body that was sick and she prayed for healing. She prayed and declared them healed with the peace of the Lord.

She said, "If you believe in the prayer, say amen."

The multitudes of people said "Amen!" and there were lots of screams. People were experiencing miracles. Some left their wheelchairs and cripples began to walk, those who were on oxygen support began to breathe without assistance. Many people were healed. The very first hour in that country, there were testimonies right at the airport. The King has created two websites and a telephone station with over five-hundred lines for people who received the Lord Jesus and those who received healing. For he already knew what the power of God could do. He announced that the people should log on to the websites and give testimonies of their healings and salvation. Although King Yusuf did not plan to be any preaching at the airport, he was happy that it had taken place. For there were over ten-thousand people who had given their lives to Christ right there at the airport. There was a schedule to keep. Princess Grace was to begin preaching to the people in two days.

10

As they were leaving the airport, the visitors looked outside their car windows and admired the beauty of the country. Just as Princess Grace was about to take a nap, she saw him; a young man growling on his stomach, followed by a lady who looked elderly and disappointed.

"Please stop the car," Princess Grace said.

"Miss," the soldiers said, "We cannot stop here. It is a dangerous area.

"Please. Please stop," she said.

The car stopped. Princess Grace opened the door for herself and ran back to where she had seen the young man. The soldiers ran after her. As she arrived, she felt such compassion for the young man. She knelt by him and introduced herself to him. The young man smiled for he knew who she was. The crowd rushed to the place where she was. The young man told her that he had just given his life to Christ and he knew that God was going to restore him one day. He told Princess Grace that he had never walked but he believed that one day he would be able to walk. Princess Grace congratulated him on been born again. She asked a nearby soldier where their next meeting was. When he told her, the Princess asked him to take the young man and the woman he was with to the meeting. She told him these were her very special guests. She turned to the crippled boy and told him that he was going to preach the good news of the Lord Jesus Christ to the whole world one day and he would testify to his healing and his goodness.

"Amen. Amen," said the young man. He was very pleased that God had chosen him to preach His word. She asked the officer to find a cab for the young man and he did. They parted and the young man was overjoyed. His mother was even happier. She thanked Princess Grace before their cab drove off.

As the King's convoy arrived at the palace, they were surprised to realize that the Princess's convoy was nowhere to be found. King Yusuf became very worried but King Wisdom told him to relax that he knew that wherever they were, they were safe. They arrived after half an hour and King Yusuf rushed to their convoy and asked the captain what had kept them so long. They explained to him that Princess Grace had seen a boy crawling on his stomach and had demanded the cars to be stopped so that she might talk to him. The officer told the whole story that transpired during that time. He asked the officer to take him to their place later since he had their address. He then called the workers to take his visitors to their rooms. He wanted everyone to settle in and he told them to rest for two hours before dinner.

King Yusuf then asked the officer to take him to the place where the young boy lived. They drove there and when they arrived, the King was touched by the poverty of the place. The boy and his mother had no place to live. They had a small room made of plastic and boxes to sleep in. His officers wanted to go and knock, but he told them to let him do that. He got out of the car and called the boy's name, Emmanuel, by the entrance.

"Come in," said the young man. He was surprised as he did not often receive visitors. The King entered the shack. The boy and his mother were shocked to see the King himself inside their poor and dirty house. He asked them how they were doing and they apologized for having nothing to give him. He told them that he just wanted to see them so that he could know how to help them. Immediately, he called his officers and told them to arrange transport to take them to one of his hotels close to the palace so that they could have easy access to the palace and to the place of worship. He told them also to arrange for clothes and good food for them. He asked the boy his name even though he already knew it.

"My name is Emmanuel," the boy said with a smile.

The King was surprised that the boy had a Christian name. He asked the boy's mother how she had come across the name and she told the King how she had been believing in Jesus Christ for a long time but that she had been afraid for her life and the lives of her son, so she had never dared show her faith. She told the King that she had schooled in the United States and had come back home to be married. Her husband had left her after realizing the boy would never walk.

The King smiled at her and told her that she was now free to worship almighty God anywhere and anytime without fear. The King was quiet for a moment, considering what this woman had gone through and how her husband had left her because of Emmanuel. He told her that God was going to bless her in a mighty way, and that her husband would regret ever leaving them. The King assured her that God was going to do mighty work thorough her and Emmanuel. He told the woman that whatever happened in life, she should never lose faith because God is a God of miracles.

The transport for Emmanuel and his mother arrived, and the King told them they would be staying at one of his hotels until a home was found for them. If there was anything they need in their present home, they should take it because they would not be coming back there ever again. The King also told them to leave behind their clothes as new clothes and blankets would be provided for them. He held Emmanuel's mother's hands and told her that he promised that she would never lack clothes or food again in their lifetime. Emmanuel was quiet all along before he spoke.

He said, "My King."

The King turned toward him and said, "Yes, Emmanuel?"

Emmanuel said, "Do you know I am going to be one of the greatest preachers on Earth?" For he believed, without a doubt, in the Word of God, Princess Grace had given to him.

The King laughed and said, "Anything for the Kingdom of God, my boy."

Emmanuel and his mother took few things such as books and family pictures.

Emmanuel showed a picture of his father to King Yusuf. "One day, he is going to be proud of me," he said. The King was very disturbed as he looked at the picture and noticed that this man was one of his high officers. Tears came out of the King's eyes and he told the woman that he was one of his senior officers.

The woman said, "Yes, I know."

King Yusuf asked her if he had ever given them money for food. She told the King that he never had. The King told them it was time for them to leave. He went back to his car, and Emmanuel and his mother went into the luxury transport the King had brought for them.

The officers saw that the King was very disturbed but they thought it was because of the poverty and Emmanuel's physical state. When they arrived at the hotel, the King went in with them and told the manager to give them first class treatment as well as the two best presidential suites remaining at the hotel. They told the King that the best suites were already occupied because of King Wisdom's arrival. There were many visitors coming to meet him. He told them to give them whatever their best available rooms were and to give them the Royals treatment. The King told the manager to bring in the best herbs to bathe them and to call his designers to make clothes for them. He asked the manager to make sure they were ready for the meeting with the King and his visitors tomorrow at the palace. He told the manager that he had the morning to make things happen as he wanted to meet with them for lunch at the palace. The manager told King Yusuf that it would be done.

The manager watched the news and they showed the young Princess Grace from the foreign country running towards them and talking to the boy who moved around on his belly. He thought he knew why they were there. He assumed they were there to visit the young Princess, but what he didn't know was that the King was not going to let them go back to that poor area again.

As soon as the King left, the manager called the house of design for the King. They had already gone home so the manager called their personal phone number, one he had been given and gave him the orders the King had given him. He told the hotel manager that he would send his people right away to take the measurements and to start work immediately. He then called two of his best designers to go to the hotel and take the measurements of the King's guests. Then he called the other four designers to go back to work and wait for the measurements. He said that they should select the best materials to start working as the work should be ready in the morning. He told them that the work should be first class, and that the King would be dining with the people wearing the clothes so they must be elegant. It was going to be a busy night for the workers, but working for the Royal family required occasional long days.

When they arrived at the hotel, the hotel staff had already given the guests their baths, cut Emmanuel's hair, and delivered food. Emmanuel and his mother were eating while wearing the hotel robes. They were told to wait until they finished eating. Emmanuel told his mother that if they were having a dream, he didn't want to wake up.

His mother laughed. "It's not a dream," she said. "Jesus has come through for us. Jesus is now in our country and the first thing He does is take care of His people."

Just then, there was a knock at the door and they told the person to enter. The tailor's entered and took clothing measurements including shoe sizes. As they left, the hotel manager told them that they would be dining with the King the next day at noon. They tried to control their excitement but as soon as the hotel manager left the room, they started shouting and singing in joy. The hotel manager could hear them from outside. He just laughed; he was happy for them. He had noticed that they were such humble people.

The next day at nine o'clock, the dressmakers arrived for their fitting. They fitted the clothes and went back to the factory to make some alterations. They were back by eleven o'clock and the clothes fit extremely well. They had even made a cushion for Emmanuel so that when he crawled, he would not hurt his stomach and get his clothes dirty.

The transport from the palace arrived at half past eleven. Emmanuel and his mother were so happy. As they were on their way to the palace, they were excited because it was going to be their first time at the palace. They would be among the Royals. Emmanuel was thinking of the young Princess he had met the day before. He told his mother that all these good things were happening because of the young Princess.

"It's true that whomever the young Princess comes into contact with, their life improves," he said. He went on to tell his mother that only yesterday people didn't care to look at them twice and now they were favored by the King and given the treatment of the Royals.

He looked at his mother and said, "Mother, our lives will never be the same, no matter what happens."

His mother said, "Yes, my son and it is God who favors us. That is why the King is showing us favor. Remember when I told you that. If God is with us, no one can be against us." Emmanuel told his mother that he remembered and that he also remembered the meaning of his name.

They arrived at the palace and were escorted into the dining room where the King was waiting with his visitors. There was a wheelchair waiting for Emmanuel. They showed Emmanuel the wheelchair and he laughed and said he had always wanted one of those. He sat in the wheelchair and told his mother that he could now help her with some chores or even do the shopping for her.

He made everyone laugh when he said, "Mother, I am now the man of the house. I can do the man's work in our home and you don't have to do everything by yourself anymore." His mother went and kissed him then told him that he had always been the man of the house.

When they entered the dining room, they were introduced to everyone. Princess Grace was not paying attention as she was thinking of the young man she had met the day before. The King introduced them and still Princess Grace did not react. The King asked her if she was all right. She said she was, it was just that she was thinking of a young man she met yesterday. She went on to tell the King that she wished to meet him before the service tomorrow. The King started laughing.

He then said, "Perhaps if you entertain my visitors, you will forget about the young man." Princess Grace asked the visitors to forgive her and went on to tell the King that after lunch she will like to visit the young man. Emmanuel was laughing too because he knew she was talking about him and that she did not recognize him. King Yusuf whispered something to King Wisdom and both Kings laughed. Now Princess Grace sensed that something was going on.

She looked closely at Emmanuel and said, "Are you…? No, you can't be. Yes, you look like… No, you can't be." Everyone laughed. The Princess screamed and ran towards him as Emmanuel reached out from his wheelchair to meet her.

Princess Grace hugged him and looked up at him with tears in her eyes and said, "Thank you, Jesus, thank you, Lord." It was as if they had known each other for a long time.

Pastor Eric stood up and went to them. He also hugged Emmanuel. Lady Elisa came too and told him that she did not recognize him from yesterday. She told him that he looked handsome. Emmanuel blushed. It was the first time in his whole life that someone had told him he looked handsome except his mother. People started leaving the table to join in the reunion. Emmanuel's mother looked on with tears in her eyes. She could see the love in the King's visitors and she knew everything was all right for them. She couldn't thank God enough.

King Yusuf has promoted Emmanuel's father to be one of his close bodyguards. He did not say anything to him about it. Emmanuel's father was very happy and told his wife that this meant they would be invited to the palace someday. He thought he might be promoted to a higher level in future. He was to start work the following day. The King wanted to see how he was going to react when he saw the ex-wife and the son he had abandoned.

There was so much laughter, jokes, and old memories being shared between King Yusuf and King Wisdom. King Yusuf changed the topic and said, "King Wisdom, I read something in the newspaper which I think is a lie."

King Wisdom said, "Well, there are lots of untrue stories in the newspaper. But tell me what you read, Great King."

King Yusuf told him that he had read that Sir James was discovered while he was spying on the King and his daughter from the top of a tree and that he fell at the King's feet. Sir James laughed so loudly that everyone joined in with laughter. Then Sir James told King Yusuf that the story was very true indeed. It was King Yusuf's turn to laugh loudly. He could not believe it.

King Yusuf said to King Wisdom, "Please, my dear friend, tell me the whole story about this one."

Sir James continued laughing and said, "Please, my King, I really want to hear this one myself from the Great King." They both laughed before King Wisdom could tell the story.

King Wisdom told the story and everyone laughed as he narrated for them how Sir James, the big and tall man, had fallen out of a tree while he was spying on Princess Grace. He told them how Sir James was so nervous and trembling from fear.

"Now picture Princess Grace four years ago and look at Sir James," King Wisdom said. Everyone laughed again. Even Princess Grace who always controlled herself could not help it and joined in the laughter. Emmanuel and his mother had been nervous when they'd first came to the palace, but now they were all laughing and had forgotten about being nervous. They felt at home. They didn't know the great Kings could laugh and share jokes.

The afternoon went by very fast. At three o'clock the palace staff brought in the tea. The palace staff was still afraid to look at the King and his visitors even though he had told them that they could. He told them that they were no longer servants. They were all workers with salaries and benefits. They were happy about it but still found it difficult to change.

At that time, the King remembered that he had to talk to his visitors about his plans for soul winning during their stay. He explained everything to them. And when he finished, he asked King Wisdom and Princess Grace what they thought of the whole arrangement. Princess Grace was pleased and told King Yusuf that Sir James would take the other part of the country and Pastor Eric would take the part the King suspected might be resistant to a change in belief. She told King Yusuf not to worry but to leave everything in God's hands. King Yusuf told Princess Grace that he wished she could be the one to take the part of the country that was resistant because those people were very caught up in their old ways and did not take any changes easy. Princess Grace told him to be at peace; Pastor Eric would do just fine. She told the King that Pastor Eric was highly anointed in soul winning and was qualified to deal with such people. Princess Grace knew that if there was anyone who could handle those people, it was Pastor Eric.

The next day, the first crusade began at ten in the morning. People started arriving outside the gates many hours earlier, from five o'clock in the morning. The media reported that some people had slept outside the gates. By six o'clock that morning, the whole place was full of people. Because of the crew that Princess Grace had sent ahead, large screen televisions were set up to allow people to watch the proceedings from as far away as twenty miles. Everyone in the palace had risen at six o'clock to start preparing. Emmanuel and his mother were also up at six as Emmanuel's mother began praying. The Princess had told Emmanuel to open his heart in order to receive the miracles, for surely tomorrow would be his day to receive such miracles if he focused his energy on the Maker. Emmanuel could not sleep at night. In his head, he kept hearing Princess Grace's words ringing in his ears. He was more than ready. Their transport arrived at seven o'clock to take them to the palace. Emmanuel's father was already working at the gate when they arrived. He asked the driver and officers where they were going and they told him they were going to pick up the King's special guest. He told the man that he wished that some day, he would be considered the King's special guest. The other officer laughed and said, "Only in your dreams would any of us be the King's special visitor."

Emmanuel and his mother were driven back to the palace. The car passed but Emmanuel's father could not see who was in the car and the passengers were not paying attention to the gate attendant as they were all praying. Emmanuel's mother was claiming the healing miracle for her son. She told God that she knew that he is the God of the Impossible and that she surrendered Emmanuel's case into His mighty hands.

They finally arrived at the entrance to the palace. They were escorted to the breakfast table but it was nearly empty. However, Emmanuel's mother said she would not be eating because she was praying and Emmanuel was also not allowed to eat. Princess

Grace came out and told them to eat but they told her they were not going to eat until after the ceremony because they were praying for a big miracle for Emmanuel. King Yusuf's personal assistant came and told Emmanuel and his mother that they would be riding with King Yusuf. They were shocked and happy at the same time.

They left at nine o'clock for the King wanted to have time to greet his visitors outside the city. When they arrived at the gate, the King called on Officer Soyab. The officer approached the car and was shocked and afraid to see his ex-wife and his son sitting inside with the King. The King greeted him and introduced his visitors. Officer Soyab could not look them in the eye. He was too ashamed. The King told him to keep up the good work and that he was looking forward to working with him. Then he left. Emmanuel's mother asked the King, "Your Majesty, are you aware of who that man is?"

"I am very much aware," the King replied. "But I do not intend on asking him anything. Please, do not say anything. Let him be himself in whatever way he wants to be."

Officer Soyab was very disturbed and was hoping that his wife would not say anything to the King. He thought to himself that she had no reason to be quiet considering the way he had left her and his son. He could not pay attention to his duties after that as he was distracted by thoughts of his ex wife. He realized that he still loved her. However, with Marina, he believed that he stood a chance of being someone of substance. He did not believe that he had that with his ex wife. But Officer Soyab began to doubt his logic. After all, his ex wife is riding with the King and not even Marina's father can ride with the King. Officer Soyab excused himself and went to the bathroom and cried. He asked himself what he had done. He knew he could seriously be punished for what he had done. First, he would be punished for leaving his wife for another woman, and second he would be punished for leaving her with a crippled child. In his culture, this was not allowed. Finally, he would be punished for not taking care of them. The worst offense of all was that he had not declared that he was married before, and that he still was. He was so afraid that he could not even stand up straight. He returned to his post. The other officer noticed that he looked sick. "Go home," the other officer told Soyab. "I will inform the Captain that you are not well." Officer Soyab refused to leave. The Captain came and saw him and was disturbed by his appearance. He ordered Soyab to go to the hospital at once. Officer Soyab returned home. His wife Marina was worried about him. She asked him what had happened but he could not tell her. She tried to touch him but he pulled away; he didn't want her close to him.

That night, Officer Soyab shivered all night long. Marina called his father to come see her husband. He came and asked Soyab what the matter was but Soyab could not answer. He had never been so afraid in his life. He kept asking himself what he was going to do, but he could not decide on an answer or course of action. He started thinking about suicide. He felt like that it was the only thing he could do to overcome his problems. That night, he thought of the Jesus the city was talking about. He asked himself if Jesus could help him. He felt that the answer was no, that his problem was beyond help. Soyab told himself that not even God could forgive him for what he had done. For seven years since he'd left his wife and son, he'd never checked on them or bought them food.

The crusade was a big success. Many souls gave their life to Christ, yet there was still a great deal of work to be done. Princess Grace preached to the millions of people as if she was talking to a single person. Each person received the message as if Princess Grace was addressing them alone, not a crowd of millions. When she finished preaching, nearly everyone was ready to receive the Lord, even those who had come with the intention of creating a distraction. King Yusuf has taken care of many things including places where the follow-up meetings would be held. The trucks came loaded with Bibles. They were given to most people who had accepted Jesus as their Lord and Savior. Nearly every half mile people were distributing Bibles and giving out the booklet that Pastor Eric had written. At five o'clock in the evening the Royals left. Princess Grace was about to go inside her transport when someone pulled her from behind. She turned and saw an empty wheelchair. The person who had grabbed her was hiding behind her. She turned around quickly and there was Emmanuel, standing up and smiling. His mother was standing away from him with tears in her eyes. Princess Grace screamed with joy. The Kings turned at the noise and saw Emmanuel. Everyone began crying tears of joy. King Wisdom started praising God. He told God, "How wonderful you are and how wonderful are your works!" Princess Grace told those assembled that if she had accomplished nothing more than witnessing Emmanuel walk, it was more than enough for her. King Yusuf couldn't move for some time for he could not believe what he was seeing.

King Yusuf turned and saw Emmanuel's mother shaking and crying. He went to her and told her it was okay to cry. "Crying gets out all the pains and aches of the past life." He held her tightly and let her cry. People were watching with wonder for they knew that Emmanuel was the boy who could not stand or walk. Some were asking if that was the same boy who used to crawl like a snake. All those nicknames they used to call him vanished. Nobody would call him snake boy any longer. Just then Soyab woke up and decided to turn on the television. He saw his ex wife and the King and he could tell that she was crying. He wished he could hold her. Then the camera showed Emmanuel and the broadcaster spoke about the young boy who was born crawling like a snake but who could suddenly walk. "How do you feel?" the broadcaster asked Emmanuel.

"I feel as though I am in Heaven with Jesus," Emmanuel said. Then the broadcaster turned to Emmanuel's mother and the King. Emmanuel's mother was still crying and the King held her with tears in his eyes. He told the reporter that the lady had been through a great deal and now God had answered her prayers. The reporter asked the King if it was true that he had taken them in and given them rooms in his hotel. The King told the reporter that they were his family and nothing was going to change that. He would do anything for them. "As for young Emmanuel," the King said, "I will send him to the best school in the world."

Soyab watched this and felt even guiltier, thinking of how he had run away from them. He saw that the King took them in and loved them unconditionally. His wife came into the room to join him and he moved into the guest room and locked himself in. Marina didn't know what to do. She thought that it would be better to take Soyab to the crusade, perhaps the Christians would pray for him and make him well. She thought that if they could only use their magic on her husband, she would be happy.

The King's convoy returned to the palace and when they arrived at the gate, the King realized that there was a new officer on duty. "What happened to the new man?" the King asked. He was told that the previous officer had taken ill after the King left and had gone home. They reported that Soyab was shivering and sweating and he could not even stand up. The King knew what the problem was. He told his chief staff to arrange a place for Emmanuel and his mother to sleep at the palace. He told them he would take them to the hotel the following day.

They went inside and he called King Wisdom and told him about Emmanuel's father. First, King Wisdom was upset and asked what kind of a man would leave his wife alone with a child like that. Later on, he asked King Yusuf what he was going to do. "It is a difficult situation for sure," King Yusuf said. "Especially since Soyab is now married and he never told his new wife that he was already married."

King Yusuf told King Wisdom that he was very upset about the situation. "If this had happened before I was born again, I would sentence him to death or life in prison!"

"Whenever I find myself faced with a difficult decision like this," King Wisdom said, "I always ask myself what would Jesus do?" King Yusuf told King Wisdom that he would tell him to go back to his wife and repent.

"Yes, but which wife?" King Wisdom asked.

King Yusuf replied, "The first wife is the wife. Furthermore, there are no children with the second wife."

"What about the man's heart's desire? King Wisdom asked King Yusuf. He advised King Yusuf to let Soyab choose where he preferred to be.

King Yusuf told King Wisdom, "He never divorced his first wife. He just run away."

"Unfortunately," King Wisdom said, "that is common. Most men who don't know Jesus run away when they are afraid." King Wisdom advised King Yusuf to act fast before the man did something stupid. He concluded by telling him that if Soyab never divorced his first wife, then he was still married to her.

King Yusuf called his chief of staff and told him that it was very important that Officer Soyab be brought to him straight away. He told the chief to act fast and to be careful because Soyab might be suicidal. His concern was that Soyab was married to one of his Lord's children; but he remembered that he also had a responsibility to investigate the person marrying his daughter. If that was not done, some of the fault was theirs as well. King Yusuf knew that if Soyab chose to go back to his wife, there would be problems with Lord Ishmael's family. This seemed an impossible situation. King Wisdom advised King Yusuf to call Princess Grace. King Yusuf asked King Wisdom if the Princess was not too young to be involved in matters such as this. King Wisdom told King Yusuf that Princess Grace might provide the King with the answer he was seeking.

King Yusuf called Princess Grace in and told her the whole story. Princess Grace told the King Yusuf to speak to Emmanuel's mother before he spoke to her ex husband because it is possible that she had moved on and wanted nothing to do with Soyab. Emmanuel's mother was summoned and asked if she wanted her husband back. "I have forgiven Soyab," she answered, "but I can never trust him again." She told them that she did not mind Emmanuel knowing his father, but she believed their marriage had been over since the day he left them with nothing in the house and eventually lost the house. When Soyab left, he had not thought of what she had given up to be with him. She further told the King not to punish him because she had forgiven him. King Yusuf was relived and thanked her. He then told her he had sent for him. Princess Grace and Emmanuel's mother left the two Kings alone. King Wisdom asked King Yusuf what he thought. He laughed and told him that all the time the answer was right in front of them but that they were going about it the wrong way. King Yusuf then told King Wisdom that he was right about Princess Grace. He told his friend that Princess Grace did not even hesitate for a minute. Instead, she answered right away.

The messengers returned with Soyab. He was now more afraid than ever. King Yusuf asked King Wisdom to stay and help. He asked them to show Soyab in to meet the two Kings. Soyab was a mess. He looked sick. He was shivering and sweating in the cold weather. King Yusuf looked at him as he was sweating and shivering and felt pity for him. "Do you know why you're here?" the King asked.

"I believe so, Your Majesty," Soyab replied.

"Why do you think that is?" King Yusuf asked.

Soyab answered, "I have been bad. I left my wife and son for a rich young woman."

"How do you feel about your decision?" King Yusuf asked.

"I feel bad," Soyab replied.

"What do you want to do about it?" the King asked.

"I don't know. All I am asking the great King is to give me a chance to apologize to my wife and son before I am sentenced to death," Soyab answered.

The King asked after Soyab's wishes.

"I wish I could be with my family," Soyab answered.

"Which family?" the King asked.

Soyab answered, "My one true family; Emmanuel and his mother." The King then asked him what he thought Emmanuel and his mother were feeling. Soyab told the King that he thought they probably hate him. The King asked Soyab if he thought his family would want him back. Soyab told King Yusuf, "I doubt they want anything to do with me," Soyab told the King, "But I am willing to try for the rest of my life, that is, if I am given a chance to live." King Yusuf looked to his friend for help. King Wisdom told Soyab to return home and tell his current wife the truth. "She may chase you out in the middle of the night," the King said, "Or she may forgive you. She may let you go with nothing, so you must be prepared for the outcome." The King continued, "You should also know that Emmanuel's mother might not take you back."

"I am willing to fight," Soyab said. King Yusuf told Soyab not to harass Emmanuel's mother. She had been through a lot and she needed peace. King Yusuf then told Soyab that if he tried to hurt Emmanuel's mother in any way, he would surely answer to him, and the meeting would not be a peaceful one.

The King dismissed Soyab and told the driver to take him home. Soyab was about to walk out of the living room when Princess Grace saw him. She greeted him and asked him to sit for a moment. She told him that whatever he was going through, Jesus is the answer. She talked to him about Jesus and the Kings emerged from the study and found Princess Grace ministering to him. They both smiled because they realized that they had forgotten to lead Soyab to Christ and, as usual, Princess Grace was doing it. They sat and listened to Princess Grace's message which always felt new whenever they heard it. Finally, the big question came. Princess Grace asked Soyab if he wanted to receive Jesus as his Lord and savior. Soyab said that yes, he would like that. He prayed the prayer and Princess Grace told him that all his sins were forgiven and that he was a new creation in Jesus' name and he should not allow anybody to tell him otherwise. She told Soyab to go and sin no more and to help in spreading the Word of God. He looked at Princess Grace with tears in his eyes and asked her if she could pray with him for he had a very big problem to solve that night. Princess Grace told him to go, because God had already taken care of it. She told him the problem would be solved as he entered his home. Both Kings looked at each other with confusion. Soyab went home but he felt peace within him and as the driver parked the car to let him out, he noticed that his wife was packing her things in the other truck. He asked her what was going on and she told him she was leaving him and that she did not wish to discuss it. He then noticed that her cousin from the next city was helping her. Soyab asked his wife if she had been sleeping with his cousin while they were married. Without guilt, she told him "Of course, this is the man I truly love." She explained that the man was not her cousin but was instead her boyfriend and they were leaving together to get married.

Soyab said "Whoa, things were really happening here." He went inside and asked her if she could leave him a couch to sit on and one single bed. The King's messenger watched all of this. He could not believe what was happening to this man. Marina told Soyab that he was too late, she had packed everything and left him with only his clothes. Soyab entered the house and discovered that she had taken some of his clothes. He asked her why she would take his clothes. She told him that she had done it because she bought them and now she was going to give them to her new husband. The King's messenger felt for this man. He asked Soyab if there was anything he could do to help. Soyab answered that there was nothing anybody could do. He bid the King's messenger good night and went inside the empty house and closed the door.

The King's messenger was so disturbed that he didn't know what was happening in this man's life. He felt pity for him and he was afraid that he might do something stupid. He arrived back at the palace and asked to see the King. He told the chief of staff that it was very important. He entered and found King Yusuf sitting with King Wisdom and Princess Grace. The messenger told King Yusuf that he wanted to talk to him in private about the man he had taken home. King Yusuf told him he was free to speak openly. The man described the scene he had witnessed at Soyab's house. Both Kings looked at Princess Grace in astonishment. They were about to ask her how she had known when she bid them good night and left. Both Kings laughed and King Yusuf told the messenger to call the manager of the King's storage houses. He then told him to take the furniture and blankets to Soyab immediately as well as some food. He also told the messenger to leave him with some money for expenses in case his wife had taken all of their money. The Kings were surprised by the way things turned out but they knew somehow that Soyab was relieved that his wife had left and that he did not have to explain anything to her or his father. He was very afraid of her father and the King knew that Marina's father was going to be a problem if Soyab had left his daughter.

Marina's father was watching television when he heard a knock at the door. He opened the door only to find Marina standing at the entrance. They greeted each other and he offered Marina something to eat or drink. Her father asked after Soyab and if he was feeling any better. Marina told her father that she had left Soyab. At first, he did not understand. When he finally grasped what his daughter was telling him, he demanded an explanation. Marina explained that she was now going to marry her old lover. Her father told her to go back to her husband before it was too late. She refused. Her father told her that this would create problems for him since Soyab now work for the King and the King's soldiers would hunt her down until they bring her to trial. She told her father that she didn't care and she left. He ran after her but he was too late. She jumped into the truck and told her boyfriend to drive away fast. Her father got into his car and went to see Soyab. He was surprised to see Soyab sleeping on the floor with no blankets or bed. There was nothing, not even a chair, in the house. He asked him if his daughter took everything. "She did," Soyab answered. He asked Soyab what happened.

"I do not know," Soyab said. "The King sent for me and when I returned, Marina was leaving." Marina's father became angry with Soyab and asked him why he couldn't stop her. "If you came to yell at me," Soyab said, "please leave." His father-in-law apologized and asked Soyab to come with him to his house to use one of the children's bedrooms. "No thank you," Soyab said. Just then, there was the sound of a truck outside. They thought it was Marina coming back. Soyab told him to tell her not to come in because he did not want to see her ever again. There was a knock at the door and Soyab told the person to go away. The knock came again and a voice on the other side of the door claimed to have been sent by the King. Soyab jumped and answered the door. The Chief of Staff and other palace workers stood on the doorstep. They told Soyab that they had brought him furniture with the compliments of the King. They unloaded the furniture. It was first class furniture with beautiful expensive blankets and sheets. Soyab was shocked and did not know what to say. For a long while, he could not move. Marina's father was even more afraid because he now knew that the King knew what had happened between Soyab and his daughter.

Soyab invited the Chief of Staff and palace workers in for a cup of tea. When he got to the kitchen, he saw that all of the cups and the food were gone. He came back and apologized to the men. They laughed and Marina's father turned red with embarrassment.

The Chief of Staff handed an envelope to Soyab and told him the King thought he might need it for his food and to buy other things like pots and plates. Marina's father was even upset with himself because he didn't bring any money or a checkbook to help. But he had not known that his daughter had packed everything. He was happy that the King's Chief of Staff found him there and knew that he did not approve of what his daughter had done. At least they would tell the King that they found him with Soyab and left him there with him offering support. The men told Soyab that the King gave him the rest of the week off to take care of his business. The men stayed for some time before bidding them farewell and left. After they left, Lord Ishmael told Soyab that he would come in the morning to see how he could be of help. But Soyab told him he really wanted to be alone for some time and that he would call him when he was needed. Lord Ishmael was happy that Soyab promised to call. Soyab told him when they arrived at the door that he did not blame him; Marina had a mind of her own. Lord Ishmael was so relieved to hear that. He then told Soyab to tell the same thing to the King. Lord Ishmael was so happy; he told Soyab he would always be his son. It did not matter what happened between him and Marina, he would always treat Soyab as his son. Lord Ishmael left feeling better for he was afraid of facing the King. But now he believed Soyab would make things easy for him.

When the messengers arrived at the palace, they thought the King would be asleep, but the two Kings were still up chatting and laughing. It was after one in the morning but it didn't look like these two Kings intended to go to bed. King Yusuf saw his men and called them. He asked them how Soyab was and they told him everything. They laughed because King Yusuf had just been telling King Wisdom how Lord Ishmael was going to panic since it was his child who had dropped the ball. He was happy that everything had worked out for the better. He asked King Wisdom what was going to happen since Rashidah, Emmanuel's mother, did not want her husband back. Did he think Emmanuel's parents would eventually make peace and get back together? He told him to leave it to God, that it is now not their problem. King Yusuf told King Wisdom that he wished to take care of Emmanuel and his mother, Rashidah, and to make sure they have the best in life. King Yusuf decided that tomorrow morning he was going to call his lawyer and accountant to open bank accounts for Emmanuel and his mother and give them a house to live in. King Wisdom was happy with that. He told him, "Blessed is the hand that gives."

In the morning, Emmanuel and his mother were called to the King's study. They found the King with four men. He introduced them as his accountant, lawyer, realtor and assets manager. He told them that each man would sit with them. The first thing would be with the bank accounts that the accountant would take care of. He gave them papers to sign and they were shocked to find that they were signing for accounts with millions in each account. There were three accounts; one for Emanuel, one for Rashidah, and a third one was in Rashidah's name for their daily expenses. The lawyer then came in and told them that they each had life insurance and they would be protected under the King's Law firm. If anything ever went wrong with them, the law firm would handle it.

Then came the realtor who told them he would be taking them to look at three castles and they should choose the one they like. The assets manager told them when they were through with choosing their home that he would bring the King's decorators to choose the furniture and all that is needed to make a home comfortable for them. He would then provide them with drivers and a pool of cars all to themselves. The King then told them not to worry, that his people have very good taste. If they didn't like anything, they were free to say and it would be fixed in a second. He told them that the Chief of Staff would hire staff for them and train them, and they would give them some of the staff from the palace to train those who were new. The King finished by telling them that the staff would be under the palace payroll.

He then turned to Emmanuel and said to him. "Now, young man, I want you to spend as much time as possible with me here in the palace and I will be taking you with me when I go on trips. Do you hear me?"

Emmanuel said, "Yes, sir. I mean, yes, your majesty."

King Yusuf laughed and said, "It's 'sir' now because I am now your father. It does not matter whether your father returns as you will always be my son." Emmanuel was very happy because while they were giving them everything, he was getting worried that maybe they would not see the King anymore and he really loved being around him. He went to the King and hugged him and told him that he was a good man and he was happy to call him father.

Rashidah was quiet and tears came to her eyes. The King asked to be left alone with Rashidah. He beckoned her to come close. Rashidah did as she was told and the King asked her what was the problem. She told King Yusuf that he was so good to them that she wished they could stay at the palace because for the first time in their life, they felt like they had a family. The King told her that the palace would always be their home and she was welcome to visit anytime to the palace without making an appointment. He then told her that he wanted them to be secure in case anything happened to him. That way, nobody would take anything from them. He then asked her to look at him. He told her that he was doing this for their own good, he wanted them to have something that belonged to them and their grandchildren. He would always visit them too. She was grateful and told the King so. The King then told her it would be announced that they should come to the palace as they pleased and that whenever there was a ceremony, they would be part of it. The King asked her if he understood and she told the King that she did.

King Yusuf then called on the others and the Chief of Staff. The King told the Chief of Staff that in a few months, Emmanuel and his mother would be going to their home but they were welcome at the palace any time. The King said that he actually wanted them to come more often, at least three times a week if they were not too busy. He told the Chief of Staff to put their names in the family book so that they would be allowed unlimited access to the palace. He also wanted to begin the process of setting up their chambers in the palace. The Chief of Staff told the King that it would be done immediately. The King told his Chief of Staff to arrange for good bodyguards for both Emmanuel and his mother as well as some battlers. The Chief of Staff told the King that it would be done. King Yusuf turned toward Rashidah and told her that she should arrange for time to sit with his designers to go through some catalogs so that she could choose her own clothes. She would also be able to choose clothes for Emmanuel. The King told the lawyer to arrange for tutors for Emmanuel to start after the visitors left. He then looked at Emmanuel and said, "Son, you have to start school so that you can be somebody." Emmanuel told the King that he wanted to be a preacher. The King told him that he would have his wish.

"I think this is enough for one day," King Yusuf. "I will continue to make arrangements for you but you should rest."

The next morning, guests (Emmanuel and his mother) arrived at the breakfast table at five minutes to nine. Princess Grace, Lady Elisa, Pastor Eric, Sir James, King Wisdom, and the Queens were already there worshipping. The guests joined in the worship and they prayed that for the rest of their stay they would be filled with testimonies, for divine protection, and favor. Princess Grace usually asked King Wisdom to close the prayer and to bless them. This time King Yusuf closed and blessed them and they sat and ate. During breakfast, King Yusuf noticed that Emmanuel's hands were still very rough from crawling. He told Emmanuel's mother that he was going to arrange for Emmanuel to be seen by a plastic surgeon so that he might remove the roughness from his body. Princess Grace asked, "Why would he choose to help God in what he has started?"

King Yusuf was puzzled and looked at her and said, "But the boy is not complete with the roughness in his body."

She told him that Emmanuel knows what to do. God healed him and He is able to make Emmanuel whole.

Rashidah told Princess Grace that Emmanuel was only nine years old and was therefore too young to understand many things. Princess Grace corrected her by telling her that whoever God touches, He imparts His spirit upon that person, and God's spirit is love, power, sound mind, wisdom, understanding, and His knowledge. Everybody became quiet. Emmanuel spoke and told King Yusuf and his mother that Princess Grace was right. He told them that since he had been healed, they had never thanked God. Instead, they were excited and overcome with joy. But none of them had thanked God for Emmanuel's healing or even given testimonies in the crowd like they promised God they would do if He saw fit to heal Emmanuel. Emmanuel asked if everyone could stand up and join him in thanksgiving. Everyone stood and praised Almighty God. Lady Elisa sang and they danced and forgot about breakfast. During the worship, King Wisdom noticed the way Emmanuel was dancing and saw that the roughness in his hands was gone. He touched Emmanuel's mother's hand and pointed at Emmanuel's hands. His mother saw it as well. They continued with praising and dancing for God. They finally finished at eleven-thirty. They were surprised as how time had flown. Then Emmanuel's mother asked her son to raise his hands and show them to everyone. He was not even aware that God has already made him whole. He raised his hands and saw the difference. He then went to Princess Grace, hugged her, and thanked her for her counsel.

King Yusuf took hold of Princess Grace's hands and said, "My mother in the Lord, as always you have such wisdom beyond my understanding. I will always look to you for counsel. You are truly filled with God's spirit." Princess Grace told him that she would teach him the art of listening to God. The King was happy with that. They were about to sit down and discuss those who were traveling outside of the city to conduct evangelism when Lady Samantha passed out. Queen Fiona ran to her and looked at her and asked them to call the doctor quickly. The doctor arrived within two minutes. The doctor spent a few minutes with Lady Samantha in the quiet room and when he emerged, he looked at Sir James with a smile and said, "Congratulations." Sir James did not understand. The doctor told Sir James that he was going to be a father. He jumped up and down screaming and began calling himself father of many. King Yusuf looked at Sir James with tears in his eyes. He was happy for Sir James but he had never felt that elation himself. One of the main reasons he loved Emmanuel so much was because Emmanuel has accepted him as a father. Queen Fatima broke out in a cry. Queen Fiona held her hand and told her that it was never too late for God. She was now fifty-years-old and she had never been pregnant.

Princess Grace whispered something in her mother's ear and she called her husband and told him they should all pray for King Yusuf and Lady Fatima to be blessed with a child. They prayed for them and Queen Fiona laid her hands on Lady Fatima's womb and King Wisdom laid his hands on King Yusuf groin. Princess Grace prayed a short closing prayer. "Father, we thank for always answering us when we call upon you. Thank you for the seed in this house. Amen."

11

King Yusuf announced with a smile that Lady Samantha's presence was now officially canceled from the trip. Sir James would travel without his wife. Everybody laughed and they began loading their things. The trucks were already loaded with bibles and booklets. King Yusuf told Princess Grace that he had about fifteen storage houses filled with bibles because he had ordered fifteen million bibles. Princess Grace thanked him.

At two o'clock, the Pastors and their men left. Pastor Eric was traveling a greater distance than Sir James. They each had over five hundred men and soldiers with them. Sir James arrived at six-thirty in the evening and Pastor Eric arrived after eleven at night. They met with their soldiers for almost two days and discussed what they had done in preparation and what still remained to be done. Both Pastors were happy with the work their men had done.

That night Pastor Eric had nightmares. He dreamed that at ten o'clock on the dot, the stadium in which they were preaching burst into flames. He woke up and prayed. When he fell back asleep, he had the same dream again. He woke up and prayed for an hour. He slept and had the same dream again. That is when he realized that God was warning him. He went to look for the Captain of his crew and told him to lock all the gates to the stadium and to make sure that by ten o'clock, no one was inside. He told him to warn the people that they should stand back as far as possible. At that moment, King Wisdom was also having bad dreams. He woke up and started praying for Sir James and Pastor Eric.

Princess Grace could not sleep. She spent the whole night worshipping. King Yusuf could not sleep either. He was walking the halls when he heard Princess Grace worshipping. He knocked and asked her if she could come to the family room so that they could worship together. She did and as they were praying, Emmanuel's mother came and joined them. They were soon joined by King Wisdom and Queen Fiona. They prayed until five in the morning.

No one went to bed after that. They knew something was not right but they did not know what exactly it was. Princess Grace told them that something was not right with Pastor Eric's men. King Yusuf immediately dispatched some soldiers for reinforcement. He told them that he knew the people from that town were hard-headed. They called the hotel where Pastor Eric and his men were staying and spoke to the Captain to see if everything was fine. He told them what Pastor Eric has ordered him to do that morning in regards to the stadium and he was preparing to go to the stadium with some of his men to carry out the order. King Wisdom then encouraged him to do as Pastor Eric has instructed. Princess Grace asked to speak to Pastor Eric. When he came to the phone, Princess Grace asked him to tell her what was going on. Pastor Eric told Princess Grace about the nightmares he had three times in the night. He explained what he had decided to do at that time and why. Princess Grace told him that there was wisdom in what he did. She said they would keep checking up on him. King Yusuf was concerned for their safety. He told King Wisdom and Princess Grace that it might be better for them to come back. Both King Wisdom and Princess Grace refused and told him that God s' work would prevail and that he should not worry. God would protect them just as he had already begun to do. Princess Grace told King Yusuf that Pastor Eric was the right person to deal with these types of issues. She trusted that he would always use the wisdom of God.

At ten fifteen, they were watching the news when they saw that the stadium, in which they were supposed to hold the crusade, had burst into flames at ten in the morning. The news reporter told them that no one had been injured or killed as the people who were supposed to hold the crusade said that God had warned them. The reporter finished by saying, "It looks like this God doesn't sleep, he was watching over his people the whole night." The reporter asked Pastor Eric questions. Pastor Eric told the reporter that nothing and no one can stop God's plan for that country. He told them that God's plan would prevail. They were happy. Pastor Eric then told them that the other venue was ready and they would be starting at twelve noon. The soldiers were already at the new venue inspecting it and the bomb squad were there too checking and making sure. They also checked on all the people coming in. King Yusuf instructed them to establish tight security checkpoints on all the roads leading to the crusade.

The venue was full by eleven in the morning even though they were not scheduled to begin until twelve noon. Pastor Eric prayed for that nation and the city before he began preaching and inviting the Holy Spirit to convict them during the message. He then preached salvation and repentance. When he made an alter call, many people raised up their hands. It was as if the whole stadium raised their hands up. He led them in salvation prayer and when he finished, he told them that there was someone there who did something terrible and his conscious could not rest. He then asked that person to come forward. There were several people who came forward. Among them were the people who raped women and killed other people. These transgressions seemed to be very common in that country. Pastor Eric counseled and prayed with them. Just when he thought he had finished counseling them, another man came forward and stood in front of Pastor Eric. He stood still for about five minutes without a word and with tears streaming down his face. He told Pastor Eric that he had done a very terrible thing. He informed the Pastor that he was the one who had planted a bomb in the first stadium where they were supposed to hold their meeting. He told Pastor Eric what he did and that he did not do it alone but that the others did not regret what they had done. He also told Pastor Eric that he could not find peace yet he was supposed to be happy. Pastor Eric asked him if he had received the Lord Jesus Christ as his savior. The man said that he just did. So Pastor Eric told him to go and sin no more as his sins had been forgiven. Instead, he should go and preach the good news to other people. The man asked Pastor Eric if he was not going to report him or punish him. Pastor Eric told him no. God had forgiven him and who was he to carry forward what God has forgiven and forgotten? The man thanked him and asked him what he could do to help. Pastor Eric gave him the salvation booklets and asked him to go every place in the city and give it to the people who could not come to the ceremony. He asked him to give it to those who had helped him plant the bomb. Pastor Eric told the man that God would be with him. The man took four boxes of books and went back to Pastor Eric and asked him where he could find him if he needed more books or help with some of the people. Pastor Eric gave him the name of the hotel where they were staying. They parted at five in the evening.

At eight at night when everyone was eating dinner, the hotel manager came to Pastor Eric and told him that there was a man looking for him at the reception desk. He said his name was Danny. He was one of the most powerful businessmen in the country. The Captain told him to bring the man to their table; for he wanted to be sure Pastor Eric was protected. He came in and Pastor Eric was surprised to see that he was the same man who had tried to kill all the people in the morning with a bomb. He told Pastor Eric that he had distributed the books but there were some people asking him questions he could not answer so he brought those people to Pastor Eric. They all left the dining room to go outside and see the people he was talking about. There were more than five hundred people outside. Pastor Eric and his men looked at the multitudes of people this man had brought and collected within three hours. They were shocked to see what he had done in such a short amount of time but they were happy to see that he had brought them.

Pastor Eric was quiet. He did not have any words. For one thing, he had not expected this from this man. He finally asked him if he had led them to Christ. The man told him yes and no. He explained that he had led others but left those with questions for he wanted him to do the honor of answering the questions and leading them to Christ. He then asked the hotel manager to allow him to talk to them for thirty minutes before sending them home. The hotel manager gave him the loudspeaker. Pastor Eric preached the message of salvation to the people and more people started coming when they heard his voice. Within a few minutes, the media arrived and began filming the whole meeting on every television station.

At the palace, they were having their dinner when the Chief of Staff came running and told the King to watch the news. They all went to the TV room and saw Pastor Eric with the loudspeaker at the hotel. They saw people running toward the hotel and they estimated there were over a thousand people. All the while, people kept on coming. By the time he led them to Christ there were more people. The news reporter told them that the people cannot get enough of Jesus. They prayed the salvation prayer with them and many people watching the television prayed with them. Some were not allowed by their families to go to these Christians meetings, and he called the man who brought them and prayed for him. When Pastor Eric finished praying for him, he told him his work had started in the Kingdom of God. He should go and do more and the Father in heaven would reward him. He should come early in the morning to help them with the preparations for the meeting to be held at ten in the morning.

Danny was happy to see that Pastor Eric trusted him and he wanted him to come and help. He knew if it were his people, they would never trust him after what he had done. But this man truly does what he preaches. He told Pastor Eric that he wanted to discuss another problem with him. He told Pastor Eric that he was married to seventeen women and he had met the love of his life but that she lived overseas in United Kingdom. He told Pastor Eric that he could not even touch his wives since he'd met this woman. He told Pastor Eric that he wanted to be married to one wife and that was his first wife until her father took her away because by then he was very poor and her father did not want her to be married to a poor man. What could he do because he wanted to be with his only true love and no one else? Pastor Eric told him to pray about it and God would guide him. Some people came forward and gave Pastor Eric money and told him it was their contribution to the work he was doing. They wanted him to know that they were available whenever he needed help. Some people gave him money and told him it was for his personal use.

Danny, who had brought the people gave Pastor Eric a bag full of money and told him that it was about two million Euros. Pastor Eric asked him what his name was again for he had forgotten. He told him his name was Danny. Danny told Pastor Eric that the money would help with the work he was doing and that he should buy himself something nice. Pastor Eric went inside and prayed and blessed the money he had received. He also prayed and blessed those who came and gave him money including Danny. Pastor Eric told God that he was truly the provider since he did not ask for money but he had provided for his work and not turned the missionaries into beggars. Pastor Eric called the Captain to come and help him count the money. He came and was surprised to see that kind of money. When they finished counting, they had three and half million Euros and two million dollars from the single night. They were tired after counting all that money. Pastor Eric told the Captain that he would report the money to Princess Grace, but that he suspected the Princess would use the money for church buildings or education for Pastors in that country.

That night, Pastor Eric was lying on his bed thinking of the question Danny had asked him about his wives. He asked himself what he would do in the same position. He knew the answer immediately; for he had never felt the love like this. He surprised himself because most of the things he did wrong, he changed without anybody telling him it was wrong. He knew it was the Holy Spirit guiding him all the time. Even the way he met Princess Grace he knew God had arranged that meeting. He was forever grateful to God for that day and that meeting. He wondered how merciful God was especially to him for he was lost and God found him. Now he lived a life of peace and joy. He understood that his life had a meaning here on earth. Before, he had never known what next in his miserable life. With the sickness he had, he had not believed there was a cure but Christ healed him within seconds. He spoke loudly to God in his room and he told God that he loved his life. He told God he was happy for he belongs to Him. He then started praising Him and rejoicing in the Holy Ghost. What nobody knew was that when Pastor Eric was alone, he would sing, praise, and dance for the Lord for hours. He enjoyed that moment alone with the Lord.

Danny prayed like Pastor Eric advised him to, concerning his situation. After prayer, he decided he was going to talk to his wives and give those who wanted to leave permission to do so. He provided provisions for their lives and their children for he knew most of them did not love him as he did not love them. He knew they were there because they had no choice. He went home and called them and told them how he had given his life to Christ and how he was now a changed man. He told them that he wanted to give them freedom. Those who wanted to leave should and he would help them in whatever they needed including money to take care of them and their children. He would allow them the choice of their own place to stay and he would also give them the money to build their own homes if they chose to do so. They were afraid at first that he might be tricking them so that he could kill them for they knew that he was one of the most merciless men in the city and that he was not afraid to take life. So they all kept quiet and decided not to say anything. He then told them about the love of his life and how he would no longer sleep with any of them since he wanted to be married to one wife and to be able to give most of his time to Jesus Christ and do His work. But those who did not want to leave would be provided for. He would continue to provide them with food and clothing and anything they needed. One of them spoke. She had decided she would take a chance and if he killed her, that would be it but at least she could try. She told him that she had also given her life to Christ on television. He jumped and hugged her and told her that they were now sister and brother in Christ. He told her that she had done a good thing. She then told him that she would like to leave with his blessing for she had never loved him but respected him and feared him. Danny told her he understood very well for he did not like the person he had been. He then went to his room and gave her a suitcase and told her there was five million Euros in it and she should look for a house and he would come and see if the house was good enough for her and the children because he did not want her to suffer in any way. He told her that if she needed more money to help with buying the house she should not be afraid to tell him. He told her to use the money wisely. One by one, Danny's wives told him how they wanted to leave too and start fresh. He told them all that even though he was letting them go, they were the mothers of his children and he did not want them or his children to be abused by anyone. He warned them that if anyone tried to hurt them, they should let him know.

Danny realized that he had never confessed his love to any one of them. All of them had been given to him by their parents by force. Danny remembered very well how some of them were crying because they had lovers and some were engaged to be married to their lovers. But because he was a young, rich, and arrogant boy who enjoyed seeing them suffer and their lovers crying for each other, he paid their parents a lot of money for the right to the women. They were young and beautiful and from poor families who could not even afford one meal per day. He remembered how one of them refused to sleep with him after the wedding and how he had enjoyed taking her by force. He was hurt and he wanted to hurt as many people as possible in whatever way he could. Looking back, he could not believe how evil he had been. Because of that, he hurt that poor girl so much that she could never have children. He told himself that he was going to do more for that particular girl.

Danny sent his worker to call the girl. When she arrived, he offered her a drink and told her to relax, he was not going to hurt her for he could tell that the girl was afraid of him. She used to lock herself in her room when it was her turn to spend the night with Danny. He apologized to her for raping her and forcing her to do things that she did not want to do. He told her he was truly sorry and asked if she could find it in her heart to forgive him. She agreed because all she wanted was to be out of his life at all costs. She also did not like talking; she was always quiet. Danny told her that he wanted to give her more money to buy a big house for herself and her true love. The girl just kept quiet. He wanted to ensure that she had enough money to be able to help her lover in whatever way he needed. She was surprised that Danny remembered that she had a lover. He then gave her another five million Euros. He told this girl who was the youngest of them all that if she wanted to have children, he was sure the Christians would pray for her. He said that if she wanted to go overseas to see a specialist, he would pay for it. The girl told him that he had done enough by giving her ten million Euros and that she appreciated him apologizing. She said she would try the Christian God first as she believed this God would help her to have children. But she did not know if her boyfriend was still waiting for her because the last time she heard from him, he was in a mental hospital. Danny felt badly for he knew why he was in the mental hospital. He felt there was nothing he could give or do to correct his mistake. For the first time, the girl smiled and hugged him. It was the first time Danny had seen this girl smiling and hugging him willingly. He then promised to introduce her to Pastor Eric as well as to take care of the bills of her past love and to do anything possible to help him. The young lady left and went back to her house with a smile on her face.

After they had all retired to their quarters, Danny had a moment by himself and looked back on how money and bitterness due to the loss of his wife had changed him into a selfish, rude, bitter, and arrogant, murderer, rapist, and self-centered person. He thanked God for giving him a second chance to start all over. He had asked those wives with which he had children to let him see his children and to help them with their upbringing. He also asked that the children be allowed to visit him. He was going to help the young wife find a house and furnish it for her. He felt that was the least he could do for her. He poured himself a drink and took the phone and called his wife. They talked and he asked her if she wanted to move into their home or she wanted them to find a new home. She told him he should first finish helping the Pastors and then he could call in the cleaners to remove every trace of other women. As time went by, they would decide what to do with his home. They could find land on which to build a house that suited both their tastes. She asked him how his other wives had responded. He told her they were all good, just like they had been good to him all these years. He explained to her that those women were good but that it was him who was taking out his disappointment and anger on them. He said that he wished he could turn back the clock. She told him she understood for she had a difficult life when she arrived in the UK. She had not been proud of the person she became, and she wanted to hurt her father so badly that she would make him regret what he had done. They were both not proud of the people they turned out to be. Danny had already decided that he was not going to stay in his home for long. He was going to give his home to the King so that it could be used as a guest house for the Christians. Just when Danny was mulling over his thoughts, he heard a sound behind him and he turned around. He was shocked and could not believe what he saw. He thought he was going crazy. He rubbed his eyes and opened and closed them quickly, blinking fast. He felt a hand touching him and he opened his eyes. He heard a voice that said, "Son, do not be afraid."

Danny fell to his knees and said, "Lord, it is you?" Nobody had to introduce him, he immediately knew this was the Lord Jesus. Danny offered the Lord a drink.

The Lord said, "Give me the lost souls, Danny. Go all over the world and bring the lost souls to my father's kingdom."

Danny said, "I thought you were the father.'

"I am the father whoever had seen me had seen the father. The father is in the son and the son is in the father," the Lord responded.

Danny looked at his beauty and could not understand the peace he felt in the presence of Jesus. Jesus began walking toward the door. Danny asked him, "Lord, can I come with you?"

The Lord said, "Son, you have a lot of work to do here first before you can come to me." With that, he was gone.

Danny was so excited he picked up the phone and called Pastor Eric and screamed, "I saw Him! I saw Him! He was here and He said I should go through the world and bring the lost souls to the father's kingdom. Pastor, I saw Him! He is so beautiful! Oh He is very much alive. Jesus is alive! Jesus is alive! Did you hear me, Pastor?."

Pastor Eric had never seen the Lord the way Danny has seen him, but he could imagine how he would feel if he had seen Him. He knew he would also be excited. He told Danny that he was very happy for him. Danny went on and told him how he was standing there talking to the Lord and how he touched him and how he called him "son." He told Pastor Eric how He told him that he was going to come to Him when he finished his work.

Danny said, "Pastor, I am going to heaven, He has accepted me." He told Pastor Eric that Jesus told him if he had seen him, he has seen the father. He told Pastor Eric that people said if you see God, you will die. But he is alive and he saw him, and he was going to tell the whole world that Jesus is alive and he wants all the souls to come to Him.

That very night, Danny called his men and told them to go through the city and tell the people who want to go to the Christians' meeting to come to the hotel in the morning and transport would be provided free of charge. He told them to tell as many people as possible and to go to the night clubs and the bars and any place they knew where people would be gathering. He then called all his store managers and told them to give people the following day off so that they could go to the Christian meeting. He told the managers for his bars and night clubs to make announcements that there would be transportation for the Christian meeting and that they should all be at the hotel in the morning to catch the buses to the other city. He told them to close the clubs early and not to open tomorrow until he spoke to them and told them what to do. He then ran to the houses of his wives and invited them to come to the meeting. He started telling them about the unconditional love Jesus Christ he has given him and how he had never been the same since he had given his life to Him. The wife who gave her life to Christ supported his statement and told them to come and they would leave after knowing Jesus. She said that Jesus would make life easy for them and He would guide and protect them. Danny told them how Jesus came to see him after they had left and he explained what Jesus had said to him. He said to them, "Can't you see? We now have somebody who loves us unconditionally." He told them to please come and receive Jesus first and to bring all their children. He would arrange for the drivers to take them in one bus and bring them home afterwards. He advised them to prepare food to eat and take drinks and water since they would be there the whole day. He looked and sounded like a mad man for he was not the Danny they knew. But they liked this new Danny and because of the change in him, they decided they would also go to see the Christians and hear what they had to say. They thought that if they could change somebody who was as evil as Danny had been, then they could change anybody or anything. Princess Grace was very happy with the work Pastor Eric was doing and she was excited about the number of people giving their life in that country. King Yusuf went to Princess Grace and told her that, as usual, she had been correct about Pastor Eric. He told her that the man was God's fireworks. Princess Grace laughed because of the way he said it. They finished their dinner and dessert was served in the TV room. They were waiting to see how Sir James was doing but the reporters there were not covering it live. King Wisdom has witnessed Sir James preaching salvation and knew that he was another of God's fireworks, like King Yusuf had said. He knew Princess Grace had chosen well when she had decided to bring them with them. Pastor Eric called the palace to give the report to Princess Grace and told her that they had a couple million Euros and dollars given to them by the people of the city. He told Princess Grace that the men who bombed the stadium had given them 2.5 million Euros. He would bring it with him when they returned. He also told the Princess about Danny and how he called him last night because the Lord Jesus visited him. He told Princess Grace that Danny could not control his excitement and he was the same man who had brought three buses full of people to the meeting. Now he had told Pastor Eric that every day he would do more. Princess Grace was happy to hear about Danny and she told Pastor Eric that she would like to meet him. Princess Grace told him they would discuss it in more detail when they arrived.

The following day was the grand finale for Pastor Eric in the city. He would soon move to another city, roughly fifty miles away. Danny arrived at the hotel with four buses full of people at seven in the morning. He waited for Pastor Eric and his men to have breakfast. Pastor Eric was not eating breakfast as he was busy praying in his room with the Captain. The manager went to his room and told him that Danny was outside with people in four of his buses. Pastor Eric told him to tell Danny to come and join them in prayer. Danny came and started praying with them. He was a man hungry for God. He listened to how they prayed and started praying too. When they finished, Pastor Eric told him that they would be going to another town the next day and he wanted him to join them since he would be helping with new souls in that town. It would be better for Danny to come with them and learn. Danny was happy to come and told Pastor Eric that he had relatives in that city and he had also invited as many people as he could to come to the meeting and he was giving them free transport. Pastor Eric asked how many people were coming and Danny told him he was going to bring six big buses to the hotel and they would take as many people as possible.

They all left the hotel at nine in the morning to go to the stadium. There were long lines at every entrance waiting for the doors to be opened. They knew that it was another big day for them for the multitudes of people outside were so great. The Captain asked Pastor Eric if it was always like that, with people waiting for hours and he was told that it was. The Captain then told Danny that the King was going to send him to ministry school to do God's work and he was happy about it. He told him that he thought the King would give him this city to work in. Pastor Eric told him that he better try to remember the people and take Danny's contacts for he would need people like that to help with the work. Pastor Eric was happy because he saw that the men he came with were eager to do the work and they were open to learning new things and for change.

The meeting went well but there were lots of people who wanted counseling and the lines were long. Pastor Eric and his men took the chairs and asked people to make lines to see each one of them. He asked Danny for help in controlling the lines and Danny was happy to help. Pastor Eric's men were positioned every twenty feet talking to people. By eight-thirty, they were finished and went back to the hotel to prepare for their trip the following day. They arrived at the hotel only to find more people waiting for them. People were hungry for the word of God and they could not get enough. Some told them that they would be following them to the next city and they heard the rich man called Danny would be giving everybody free transport. Some people told them that they would follow them everywhere they went and they also wanted to work for God like them. This was encouraging and Pastor Eric told Princess Grace and the Kings about it later when he spoke to them. Danny kept on telling more people that he would help with transport if they were at the hotel in the morning.

The media wanted to talk to Pastor Eric but he was avoiding them even though he appreciated that in a way, they were evangelizing for him. They would be announcing where they were going to be next, what time they would be there, and how many people had accepted Jesus as their savior. Pastor Eric also met people like the ones who were waiting for him at his hotel telling him they had accepted Jesus as their Lord and savior by watching the television. Finally, he spoke to the media. They wanted to know if he was going to stay in their country to continue with the work he had started. He told them that there were people in the country who were good enough to do the work themselves and he felt they were ready to start the work. They wanted to know who those people were. He avoided the question by telling them that they were well-trained and anointed to the do the work and they were still identifying more people who would also help in doing the work. He excused himself and went inside the hotel. Danny was happy to hear that more people were being identified. He had made up his mind that he would sell all his businesses and follow the King to perform the work for Jesus.

The Captain was very happy with his response to the media. He told him, "Good job and thank you for preparing for us. They will now respect us when we come." The Captain asked Pastor Eric if he thought he would ever be able to preach like him. Pastor Eric told him that it was quite possible, but that each one of them had a path that had been designed already by the Maker. He should open his heart for anything in the Kingdom of God and always ask for God's guidance. He told Pastor Eric that the King wanted him to be a preacher and he had been asking them to study the bible to prepare themselves for preaching.

They had their dinner with Danny and the hotel manager told them it was on the house. He gave them the best dishes from their kitchen and the best wines they had in the cellar. Danny was very happy and he liked Pastor Eric a lot. He told Pastor Eric that he was a very wealthy man. He had enough money to take care of him and his family for the next ten generations so if he decided to follow Jesus' work, he will still have more than enough money. He also told him that just yesterday, he had given his ex wives up to one hundred million Euros and he still had a great deal of money in addition to the two million Euros his businesses brings in each day. Pastor Eric asked him what kind of businesses he had. Danny told Pastor Eric that he had apartment buildings, business buildings, bars, nightclubs, schools, transportation, and farms. Pastor Eric told Danny that as a child of God, he would have to part with the bars and nightclubs as it would not be appropriate to encourage people to drink and engage in bad behavior. But he could keep the apartment buildings and most of the buildings he was renting as he would need that money to help the poor and move the Kingdom of God forward. He told Pastor Eric that he was already preparing to do that. He then asked Pastor Eric what he could do to help financially. Pastor Eric told him that first he should rebuild the stadium he had destroyed and build a place for people to worship because they will need such a space. Danny took him very seriously. He asked him whom he should give the money to for the building. Pastor Eric told him to talk with the King, but for the stadium, he should go to the city council and tell them he wanted to donate the money to rebuild the stadium. He told Pastor Eric that nobody could get in to see the King. Pastor Eric told Danny that for matters dealing with the church, the King would see him. Pastor Eric told Danny that he would make an appointment for him to see the King. Danny was becoming afraid. He told Pastor Eric that if the King knew that he wanted to kill everybody in the stadium, he would sentence him to death without appeal. Pastor Eric told him that the King would not do that and he would see to it that Danny was safe. He would tell the King about all the good work that Danny has done and that he had repented. He further told Danny that he was now a new creation in Christ, just like the King and old things had passed away and all things were new for him. Jesus had forgiven him and he gave him the spirit of love, power, and sound mind. Therefore, he should not be afraid. Fear was not his portion in Christ Jesus. Danny liked the way Pastor Eric was speaking. He promised him that they would go back with him so that he could meet Princess Grace and King Yusuf.

Pastor Eric advised them to go to bed early so that they could have some rest for there was a lot of work ahead of them. He asked them to meet in front of the hotel at eight in the morning. Danny told him he would be there at six. Pastor Eric told him to rest as he wanted him strong and alert for many hours the next day. He introduced Danny to the Captain and told the Captain that he should include Danny in his plans as he was the right person to move the ministry of the Lord Jesus ahead in that country. The Captain was happy to meet Danny and was thrilled that Pastor Eric was helping them to organize a strong team for them to move the Kingdom of God forward in their country.

In the morning, Danny arrived at the hotel at seven o'clock with seven buses. He had already spread the word that those who wanted to go to the Christian meeting in the next city should come to the hotel for a free ride. Some people began arriving at six and many people were still arriving hours later. When Pastor Eric's men came out and saw what was happening, they called the Captain. He came and greeted Danny and told him he could surely use him in this work. He needed people like him. Pastor Eric arrived at eight and found the buses were full with the people ready to go to next city. He asked what was happening and they just pointed at Danny. Pastor Eric called Danny and took a walk with him. He told him he had done a good thing. He told Pastor Eric that he would do it tomorrow again as he would be coming back to his city after the meeting to bring the people back home. Since most of them were poor, they could not afford the hotels and even if they could, there were not enough hotels for everyone. Pastor Eric told Danny to find someone responsible to control the buses because he wanted him close to them at all times. Danny could not control his excitement. He screamed out of joy. Pastor Eric just laughed.

Pastor Eric left the hotel at eight with his men and the buses. They arrived at the city at nine and were met by a soldier who informed the Captain that the Royal family was waiting for him. They escorted Pastor Eric and his men to the room they had prepared for them. The Captain went to meet the Royal family. He knew it would be the King's sister for she had a farm twenty miles from that city. The Captain found the King's sister with her son and daughter. He escorted them back to the area that had been prepared for the Pastor and his company. They found Pastor Eric on the phone with the King. The King was telling him to tell the Captain to go and look for his sister. Pastor Eric handed the phone to the King's sister. She took the phone and told the King to stop babysitting her. He laughed and told her that he will stop when she was old enough. His sister laughed. Pastor Eric turned to go and sit down when he saw the most beautiful girl he had ever seen. For a moment, his heart skipped and he quickly turned away to look for some other place to sit. The girl also noticed him. She told her brother to check to see if he was married. The brother went to him and told him in a loud voice that his sister wanted to know if he was married. Everyone heard the question including the King who was on the phone. The sister was so embarrassed that she ran away.

The mother told the King that she had to go because Marisa had ran away because her stupid brother had embarrassed her. The Captain began to look for her and told other soldiers to help him find her for there were many people and she could easily be kidnapped or get lost in the crowd. He told the mother to stay put so that she would be there for her in case she came back. The mother was upset with the son. She asked him if he could be secretive about it. Why did he always have to embarrass his sister? She then went to Pastor Eric and apologized and told him that her daughter was not always like that. In fact, it was the first time that her daughter had done something like that. Pastor Eric told her there was nothing to apologize for. He then introduced himself to the Princess and they talked for some time. She introduced herself as Princess Yeti, the sister of King Yusuf.

Pastor Eric was very embarrassed; he didn't know what to say or do. At the palace, King Yusuf told King Wisdom what had just happed with his sister's daughter. King Wisdom told him to make sure that Lady Elisa did not know about it for if she knew, she would make fun of the situation, especially if it involved Pastor Eric. King Yusuf told him he knew that by now. He asked King Wisdom if he was married or if he had someone special in his life. King Wisdom told him how Princess Grace had met him and about how his father had come to his country and how Pastor Eric refused to return with him to Germany. King Yusuf told the King that he still liked him. He told King Wisdom that he was just too beautiful a man and that is most likely the reason other men corrupted him when he was young. King Wisdom told him that everywhere he went, girls were after him. However, he was not interested in settling down yet. But he was no longer interested in men.

They found Princess Marisa and brought her back. She was so embarrassed that she could not look at Pastor Eric or anyone else in the group. Her mother called the King and told him they had found her. They spoke for some time and when they finished, she went to Pastor Eric and invited him and his men to dinner. Pastor Eric accepted the invitation and asked Princess Marisa's mother if he could be given permission to greet her daughter. She told him that might help to make her feel better. Pastor Eric went to Princess Marisa and introduced himself and she told him her name and apologized for the brother's actions. He told her there was nothing wrong with that. He told her about the invitation for dinner and asked her if she would be comfortable with him accepting it. She told him she did not mind and she began to feel better.

It was now time for Pastor Eric to preach. He began by telling everyone how blessed they were because God had written in His book that today was the day he would deliver them from the Kingdom of darkness and into the Kingdom of light. He then told them that before he continued he would like to recognize the presence of the Royal family, Princess Yeti and her two wonderful children, Princess Marisa and Prince Brian. The people were happy to know they were attending the same meeting as the Royals. He then continued with his message. By the time he finished, everyone was quiet even though the stadium was full and the overflow was huge; you could hear a pin drop. He made the alter call and from behind him, Princess Yeti and her children,

Princess Marisa and Prince Brian came and stood by Pastor Eric. They lifted up their hands. The people were happy and shouted for joy. It was as if everyone in the stadium and outside on the street had lifted their hands up to receive Jesus. At the palace, they were watching on the television and King Yusuf saw his sister and her children accepting Jesus. He started jumping up and down like a baby in his excitement at seeing his own sister accepting the Lord Jesus as her Lord and Savior. They saw a part of King Yusuf they did not know existed. He was as happy as a child at Christmas.

King Yusuf then reiterated that he really loved his sister by saying, "Lord, thank you for my work as the head of the family. If you take me now, I will go in peace." He then went to Princess Grace and thanked her for introducing him to the Lord Jesus Christ. He told them that, there was something Jesus gave to him every time someone received Jesus as his Lord and Savior. He experienced a joy he could not explain. He told them that the first time he led people to Christ at the palace had been the biggest day in his life and he even wished that Princess Grace had been there to see what a wonderful work he had done. Queen Fatima laughed and told them that on that day, it was not King Yusuf with her but rather the young Prince Yusuf. She had to hold him at night to make him sleep. He had excessive energy and had spent almost the entire night dancing for Jesus in their chamber. Princess Grace laughed and told them that about her own, similar experience. She held herself together in public but when she got to her chamber, she danced and sang for the Lord. She laughed and told them that it was funny because she never danced in public because she was not a good dancer. That was one skill God hadn't given her and one that she never asked for. King Yusuf was happy to hear that he was not alone. To his surprise, everyone at the table began confessing that they also felt the same thing. They had all experienced the joy that comes into your spirit after winning a soul for Jesus.

At the meeting, Danny was busy working hard. He never rested and the Captain's crew was also very busy. Pastor Eric was so happy with the amount of people he had. He had also added quite a few people from the city as well. He kept encouraging the Captain to know these people and get their information, so that he could keep in touch with them after they left. The Captain was happy about it too for he saw the multitude of people they had led to Christ and knew that no man could manage them by himself. They distributed the bibles and gave three to the Royal family; one for each member.

The dinner at the King's sister's house was a huge success. Everyone enjoyed themselves. Princess Yeti asked her daughter to serve Pastor Eric even though there were more than ten staff members serving dinner. She was nervous at first but she eventually relaxed. The Captain asked Pastor Eric if he was going to do something about the situation with Princess Marisa. Pastor Eric told him that he did not want to burn bridges by pursuing the King's niece. Furthermore, she was a Royal and he was not, so the Royal family most likely had someone in mind for her. But the Captain told Pastor Eric that he thought the mother of the girl liked him as well. He believed that she was encouraging her daughter. The Captain did not see any problem. Pastor Eric wanted to be a friend and see how things were going first. Towards the end of the dinner, Princess Yeti asked Princess Marisa to show Pastor Eric the property. They left the others eating and took a walk around the property. Princess Marisa told Pastor Eric that she was twenty-five-years old and she asked the Pastor how old he was. He told her that he was too old to name his age and they all laughed. Princess Marisa told him that she bet he was not yet thirty. He told Princess Marisa that he would be thirty in a month's time. Princess Marisa wanted to know if he was married or if he had someone special in his life. He was quiet for a long time remembering Prince Brian's question. Princess Marisa apologized and Pastor Eric told her there was nothing to apologize for. He then told Princess Marisa his whole life history. When he finished, Princess Marisa smiled, happy that he no longer found men attractive and she told him so.

They walked in silence for some time and Princess Marisa broke the silence by asking him if he had any intention of getting married. He told her that yes, he did, when the time was right and when he met the right woman. She asked him what qualities he looked for in the right woman. He told her that the right woman is one who would help him build the Kingdom of God, the one who would bring God's Kingdom first. She told him she understood because he was a Pastor. He told her that even if he was not a Pastor that was his passion. He would still bring the Kingdom of God first. Pastor Eric asked Princess Marisa whether she worked or was in school. She told him that she had never worked and no one could afford her even if she did. Being a Princess is her work; she made appearances and visits and she was paid for doing that in addition to drawing a salary. However, she explained that a Princess doesn't need money. She explained how her uncle wanted to send her to spend time with Princess Grace in her country. Pastor Eric asked her if she had met Princess Grace already. She told him that she had not but she had spoken to her on the phone. She was happy to do so because even though she was younger than Princess Marisa, Princess Grace sounded quiet mature and she was able to hold a sound conversation. Pastor Eric told her that Princess Grace was more mature than most adults and she was quite exceptional. He told her that she would learn a lot from Princess Grace because even he was still learning from her. Princess Marisa was surprised to hear Pastor Eric admit that he was learning from a woman and a young girl. Pastor Eric told her that the Princess is her boss and that he should call her "mother" in the ways of God. He then looked at his watch and told Princess Marisa that he had to take his men to the hotel as they had a busy day coming up. She asked him if she could keep in touch with him. He told her that he would like that and they exchanged numbers.

Princess Marisa was the first woman Pastor Eric had ever had that kind of a conversation with and it felt good and right. However, he still wanted to take his time. Princess Marisa looked at him and told him he was very good looking and that she bet girls chased after him. He just smiled and did not respond. They walked in silence to join the others.

Pastor Eric asked Princess Yeti if she minded if they introduced Jesus to her workers. The Princess told him that she would be happy with that. He asked the Captain to gather the workers and minister salvation to them. It was the first time for the Captain, but he performed very well. He was shocked at himself too for he didn't know he could be that good. Pastor Eric asked Danny to bless them and he did a good job as well. They went back to the hotel. Danny felt as though he had been asked to minister to the whole stadium. He could not believe that the Pastor asked him to help and he knew that he really meant everything he had said to him over the past few days. Pastor Eric was happy with the growth and passion that Danny had for God and he knew he was going to higher places with God.

Later on that night, Princess Marisa apologized to her mother for her behavior at the stadium. She explained that there was something about Pastor Eric which made her lose control. She told her mother that she thought she had found her husband. Her mother asked her how she knew because she had been refusing all the young men who had been asking for her hand in marriage. She always found fault with them. She told her mother that she just knew and that one day Pastor Eric would propose to her. She acknowledged that it might take time because he was more in love with Jesus than with anything or anybody else. Her mother told her that Pastors do get married. Princess Marisa told her mother that Pastor Eric was more at peace with the relationship he has with Jesus and she was afraid that he might forget about marriage. But she knew that at least now, she was his friend and he needed her. Her mother laughed and told her that she could see that she was smitten with the Pastor. Princess Marisa admitted as much to her mother and thanked her for making her serve him because she liked that a lot. She wished the night could just go on and on without ending. Her mother asked her if she was aware that Pastor Eric might not want to stay in their country. She told her mother that she knew that and she did not care where they stayed as long as she was with him. Her mother asked her if she would leave her own mother for a man. Princess Marisa told her mother that she loved her very much but for this man she would leave her and call her every day to see how she was doing. They both laughed and went to bed. Princess Marisa could not sleep that night thinking of Pastor Eric and how it would be to be his wife.

Pastor Eric was also thinking a great deal about her and praying to God to help him make the right decision. But he knew he had never felt this way for any woman or anybody before and he guessed that he might be in love. He remembered that she was of Royal blood and that he was not. He told himself to forget about her because nothing would ever happen. The Royal family would not allow a man without a noble title or Royal blood to marry their daughter. He then remembered the promise of God; He said, "But seek first the kingdom of God and his righteousness, and all these things shall be added unto you" (Matthew 6:33, NKJV), including this beautiful girl, the Royals, and more. Pastor Eric told himself that even his past would not be a problem if God approved of her. He went to bed with that beautiful thought.

12

Sir James' activities started appearing on the television. They showed him preaching in the evening. King Yusuf and his visitors were all watching and listening. Every evening, they would finish their dinner in the television room to watch the crusades. King Yusuf could not believe that this was the same man he knew who laughed and joked all the time. He was preaching the word of God as if it were his last opportunity to do so. He was encouraging people to come to the Kingdom of God as they were, for the world was running out of time. They showed the football stadium where Sir James was hosting the meeting. It was so full that people were fighting to get in. Outside, there was an overflow of over ten-thousand people. When Sir James made an alter call, everywhere hands raised in the air. He then started to sing. There was such a powerful anointing in his voice that people watching received miracles and some gave their lives to Christ over the phone. Since King Yusuf had created a call center for people to call for testimonies or prayer; many were calling. But many were calling to say they had just given their life to Christ. The manager for the call center called the King to tell him they had so many calls that the lines were continuously full. He wanted overtime payment for his workers because people were still calling and many were on hold.

The reporter covering Sir James' work reported that the meeting venues were always full every day and some people were sleeping at the meeting place to make sure that they would be able to get inside the following day. Many people had received Jesus Christ and many were still waiting to receive Him as trucks and buses from the nearby towns and cities began arriving with more people. The reporter said that in her life as a reporter, she had never seen people gathering in one place like that for a whole week. She said, "Fellow countrymen and women, this Jesus reins in our country. He has taken over. Our people have received Him like no other."

At the end of the broadcast, King Yusuf had no words. He stared at the television as though he had seen a ghost. He asked King Wisdom how he trained these men to be fireworks like that. King Wisdom pointed at Princess Grace and told him that they were always with Princess Grace as they were her children. Princess Grace told them it was because they opened their hearts to receive Jesus without reservations; then the Holy Spirit filled them. She further told them that God was always looking for willing hearts to use.

The reporter announced that they would be following Pastor Sir James to the next city. She said that they should be aware that this Pastor was a noble and a very wealthy man but he still preached and forget about his title on earth. Just then, Pastor Sir James arrived and they asked him if they could interview him. He told them that first he wanted to know if the reporter had given her life to Christ. The reporter laughed and said, "Not yet Sir." He asked her what she was waiting for. She laughed and he led her to Christ on live television. When he finished, he told her that now she could talk to her. He was so aggressive when it came to God's Kingdom but as an ordinary man, he was very soft. King Yusuf knew he had a lot of work to do after these people were gone and that he was left with big shoes to fill. He wished Princess Grace could leave these men behind, but he knew better. He knew that with Princess Grace, they were always busy winning souls for the Kingdom of God. But the King had a better idea. He thought that he would let a few of his men and his niece go and work with Princess Grace for a few months and he knew that when they returned, they would never be the same. He made up his mind that he was going to choose some men and women to go to King Wisdom's country to learn their ways and come back to teach his people. He also wanted his country to belong to Christ completely. He dreamt of the day everybody in his country would be a Christian for he knew the reward for that was peace. King Yusuf told his visitors that if there was one thing he did as a King which he was proud of; it was his visit to King Wisdom.

King Yusuf went to Princes Grace and sat next to her without saying a word. They sat there together without talking for almost thirty minutes. Finally, the King asked her how he was going to fill the shoes of the men when they left. He knew the people needed to continue to be fed with the word of God. Princess Grace told him that his men were ready. She told him to leave everything in the hands of God and that God never forsakes his children. Princess Grace had seen his men at work and had also received reports about them, especially the one with Pastor Eric. She knew they were ready. They were the ones leading the meetings in prayer and counseling the people. King Yusuf reminded her that there was still the west and north parts of the country waiting to receive the word of God and that was the areas that everyone was concerned with as all of the bad things happen in those areas. She promised him that those areas would be done by next week and that the people there would change and choose Jesus Christ as their Lord and Savior.

The last broadcast from Sir James answered King Yusuf's question. The butler told them to watch the TV and they would see something amazing. The reporter showed the meeting in the first town that Sir James was responsible for and reported that it was the last meeting in that town. When they were expecting to see Sir James, they saw one of King Yusuf's men. He took that microphone and asked the crowd who they loved. They answered, "Jesus!" He asked the question three times and each time, the crowd answered the same way. He asked them to spell that name for the Heavens, the earth, and hell to hear it loud and clear.

When he finished, he told them how the son of man was killed by the Romans. He told them step by step how He was killed, the beating, the carrying of the cross for us, the whip while he was carrying the cross, and the thirty-three lashes he was given before they made him carry the cross, the part where they nailed him to the cross, the giving of the vinegar when he asked for water, the piecing of his side with an arrow, the massive bleeding, and the water coming out on his side, and the mocking. He spoke of Jesus' request to the Father to forgive them because they did not know what they were doing in the middle of pain and mockery and how at the end, He announced that it was finished. He spoke of the earthquake, darkness, and the thunder of God. He told them he finished the oppression of the devil on us. He finished the hell path for us. He called on his fellow countrymen and women and told them that their King, King Yusuf, had seen the vision and he was good or kind enough to want to share it with them. The rest was left for them because he could not force them to believe. He could only give them the opportunity. By now, everyone was crying including those who were watching the television. The preacher himself was crying.

He concluded his message by telling them how Jesus had done that for them because of the love he had for the people of this world. "He went through all of that for you and me." He told them it was not funny, it was not nice, and it was not enjoyable. It was humiliating, disgraceful, and painful beyond the pain of death and it was all endured on our behalf. God then looked down and said, "All power is given unto my son, Jesus both in heaven and earth and whosoever believes in him shall have everlasting life. Not Buddha! Not Apollo! Not the creature in the mountains! Not the God of fire! Not the God of Alaska who sent the cold to kill all warm-blooded animals! Not one of over a million Gods men made for themselves, but the true and only living God; the Creator of Heaven and Earth. I am I am, Rock of ages, Alfa and Omega. The Almighty God who died for you for worshiping other Gods, for killing one another, for taking your brother's wife by force, for raping children, for lying, for talking badly about your neighbor, for selling your child for prostitution in the name of hunger, for talking badly about the people who He sent to bless you and for despising others; the one and only true God."

He then said, "There is life beyond this life, brothers and sisters. Do not be fooled. There is no other one than Jesus Christ. The time for repentance is now. Jesus has given us that opportunity by His death to start fresh. It's time for love. There will be a time when we wish we could have this time and it will be too late." He asked them to take each other's arm and pray the salvation prayer. The spirit of God then took over.

Princes Grace told her father with tears in her eyes that she had never seen such a moving sermon. She told her father that there was so much anointing in that man that it was affecting her just by looking at him on the television. King Yusuf was also crying. Even Lady Elisa who was always watching people and making fun of them was crying like a baby. The service was reaching the souls of the people right to their cores. When he asked if they would like to receive this mighty Jesus as their Lord and personal savior, everybody, including those who were already born again, lifted their hands up. Even in the palace, they all fell to their knees and lifted their hands up. They could not believe that this was the same man they had eaten with and joked with. He led them to Christ speaking in English when all of a sudden, he began speaking in tongues. No one knew he spoke in tongues. He sang the song Lady Elisa loved to sing, "Oh, I love Jesus," and it was like the whole nation was singing together.

The person filming the service was so moved that his hands were shaking towards the end. Then they heard the reporter saying that the cameraman was speaking a strange language and the preacher was on the floor. They knew immediately that the Holy Spirit had taken over the service. Then someone took the camera and came back and started showing the cameraman and recording him speaking in tongues.

King Wisdom said, "Oh my God, they are such powerful tongues." Just like that, the reporter started speaking in tongues right there on television. It was as though everyone at the meeting had received the Holy Spirit. The cameraperson did not know where to shoot.

Another woman they did not know took the microphone and said, "Pardon my English not good. Everywhere you are watching this. The Holy Spirit of the Jesus has possessed the people." Although her English was poor, they understood what she was trying to say. She went on to say, "Me not reporter but reporter drunk and everybody drunk with God spirit. So there is no more news. My name Mado." From there the cameraperson who had taken over went to the side where the Pastors were. All the Pastors were on the floor as well as the soldiers the King had given to escort Sir James and his men. Sir James had folded his arms and stood watching as though he could not believe what he was seeing. The cameraperson gave him the microphone.

Sir James said, "If there is anyone there still able to hear, what you are seeing here is that God Himself has taken over the service." He then sang the song, "The spirit of God is mighty in this place, mighty is my heart and mighty in this country." He then handed the microphone back to the man carrying the camera. It was as if there were only three people still standing in the whole stadium.

Princess Grace told King Wisdom that they had to call the butler to take King Yusuf and his wife to their chamber as they were also down and had been for the past hour. They went to the main door where the butler usually watched television with other members of the staff. They were all down. King Wisdom and Princess Grace looked at each other. It was as if they were the only people remaining in the whole palace. They took a walk in the palace and went to other places where they knew some palace workers would be. They were down in tongues as well. They finally went to the main gate. There was no guard on duty. They both stopped and looked at each other without saying a word. They walked back to the palace. They have seen the hand of God in the past but had never witnessed anything like this in their whole ministry life. Princess Grace finally broke the silence and asked King Wisdom what he thought of the presence of God in that country. She went on to tell her father that she suspected the whole country was the same as in the palace. King Wisdom asked her if she wanted to go out and see what was happening outside the palace.

They decided to call on Emmanuel and his mother at the hotel. They called and there was no answer. They called the hotel receptionist and finally a man with a shaky voice said, "Hello, is someone there? I don't know what is happening. People are sleeping and some are talking in a funny language." They told him not to worry and that everything was fine. Princess Grace asked him where he was when it happened. He told them he was cleaning the kitchen and they had gone to the lobby to listen to the preacher.

He said, "Haw! This is the kind of witchcraft I have never seen; Bewitching people on the TV!" Princess Grace found herself laughing and she knew the man had not accepted the Lord Jesus as his Lord for whatever reason.

Finally, the phone rang at the palace. King Wisdom answered it and it was Sir James calling. The King laughed and asked him what he had done. Sir James told the King it was not him but that it was one of King Yusuf's men. Sir James told King Wisdom that it had been two hours and people were still drunk with the spirit of God inside the stadium and outside in the overflow. He asked what he should do. The King told him to wait until God finished His work. He asked King Wisdom if he had ever seen anything like that or even heard of it. The King told him that it was the end of days. God was pouring his spirit out like never before. Things like that should be expected more these days. He told Sir James that he did a good job and he was very proud of him. Sir James then asked after Pastor Eric. The King told him that he was also moving mountains where he was and that over five million people had given their lives to Christ in his region. Sir James told him they had also led a lot of people to Christ, probably around the same number. King Wisdom told him that they had been watching him on television.

He laughed and said, "So I am now a TV preacher?" The King agreed with him. He asked the King if he could say hello to King Yusuf and King Wisdom told him that the great King was unavailable as he was at the table with the Lord drinking the Lord's cup. Sir James asked King Wisdom who was awake with him. The King said that Princess Grace was the only one still awake. Sir James could not believe that the anointing affected those people who were watching the television. King Wisdom told him how everybody in the palace and in the hotel where Emmanuel and his mother were staying were all drinking from the Lord's cup. Sir James told the King that he believed that God wanted a few people to remain to be able to tell the story to the next generation. King Wisdom told him that was true but that he wished he could be enjoying the Lords' presence like everyone else. Sir James told him they were enjoying the Lord's presence just in a different way than the others.

Sir James told the King that he tried calling his hotel to ask them to bring him some food as they had been fasting the whole day but no one answered the phone. Three times he tried calling. King Wisdom told him that it was obvious what they were doing. Together they both said, "Drinking from the Lord's cup." They laughed together. They talked for some time and King Wisdom told Sir James to start praying because that was what they were going to do until all the people woke up.

Princes Grace came in and joined her father spoke to Sir James for a while, and they began worshiping and thanking God for His spirit and for the work He had done so far in that country. They were praying when Queen Fatima finally woke up and asked them what had happened to her and everyone else. They told her the Spirit of God had happened. They helped her to stand up and they continued with the worship. As everyone awoke, they began joining in prayer. Finally King Yusuf and Lady Elisa joined them, as they were the last ones to wake up. They all praised Almighty God. One by one, the palace staff came and joined them. This time they were not afraid of the King. They finished the worship and closed the prayer and by that time, it was three in the morning when everybody went to bed. The King told the staff not to wake up too early but to start work at nine in the morning instead of five as they usually did. They all left without discussing the matter further. For the first time, Lady Elisa was quiet and very serious. Queen Fiona said, "What a blessed night." As they were about to leave, everyone said, "Amen." Without another word, they all retired to their separate rooms.

13

Pastor Sir James and Pastor Eric returned to the palace after one week of performing their job with their men. King Yusuf was very happy with them. He welcomed them all and went to the man who preached the sermon that had left everyone drunk with the spirit of God and told him that he had a lot of work to do. The King told him he was very proud of him. He turned to the Captain of Pastor Eric's crew and told him that he had heard about the good work he had done at Princess Yeti's farm and he was very proud of him too. He then told Princess Grace that she was right and that he did have some of God's fireworks in his country. Princess Grace told him that he was still going to see more of them the coming week as they were now going to be given an opportunity to preach and lead the meetings.

King Yusuf hosted a very big dinner party for them and invited most of the Royal family to come and meet them with the hope that many of the guests would give their life to Jesus Christ. God answered his prayer. Among the relatives who attended were Princess Yeti and her two children, Princess Marisa and Prince Brian. Princess Marisa was happy to finally meet Princess Grace in person. Pastor Eric did not know that Princess Yeti was coming until he heard her name announced when she arrived with her two children. He was happy yet afraid to show any interest in her daughter for he felt that it would not be proper. He had heard that there were many offenses in her country that could lead to punishment by death. He knew that sometimes even without the King's approval, the council would insist on punishment. The guests were taken to their tables for dinner and to Pastor Eric's surprise, he was seated at the same table with Princess Marisa. He later asked Princess Marisa if she had been responsible for the seating arrangement. She told him that she had not been and that she was just as surprised as he was. Pastor Eric was happy that Sir James and his wife were at the same table with him and his Captain. He looked for Lady Elisa and told them he had to admit that he missed Lady Elisa a great deal. Sir James laughed and told him that he did too. Lady Elisa was seated at the same table as the Kings and Queens. Princess Grace was at the table of nonbelievers. She was told as much before she sat down. She laughed and proceeded to her table, even though she had missed Pastor Eric and Sir James. She understood why King Yusuf had arranged the seating as he did.

The moment she sat down and introduced herself, people began asking Princess Grace why she was there. One of the guests asked her why she could not find herself a nice husband since she was beautiful and she could leave the race of Christianity to men and ugly women. She could not believe her ears. However, she told herself she was going to ignore the last part of the question. She told the guests that she did what she did because that is what she loved to do and there was nothing better than serving God. They asked her if she truly believed in the Christian God. She told them she did believe and started telling them why she believed. She was happy they had opened up this line of discussion. At first, they laughed and did not take her seriously but as she went on, the laughter died down and they began to pay attention to her.

King Yusuf was watching. He knew his people and he knew Princess Grace. He knew that she did not consider anything to be impossible. She spoke with them for about thirty minutes and four of them asked her how they could receive this Jesus. The other two guests remained quiet as if they were afraid. Princess Grace told them she could introduce them to Him right there in that moment. She then led them in the salvation prayer and welcomed them into the Kingdom of God. They all stood up and hugged each other. King Yusuf got King Wisdom's attention and indicated that he should watch what was happening. He smiled and told King Wisdom that he knew Princess Grace could do it. But there were two people remaining at the table, a husband and wife. King Yusuf told his friend that the man was the son of his great uncle and that he and his wife practiced strong witchcraft. He claimed that they sometimes dined with the Devil. King Wisdom laughed at the last statement. The man looked angry and asked Princess Grace how long she had believed in that nonsense. She told him that it had been since she was born.

Princess Grace asked the man if it was the life in the dark Kingdom that he had. He was shocked and did not know how she had the boldness to ask him that question. He asked her how she knew that. She told him she just knew. He was uncomfortable and he looked down. Princess Grace said, "Don't."

He asked her, "Don't what?" She told him not to do what he was trying to do because it would be a wrong move. He took his hand back and looked at her angrily. She looked back at him. She told him there were people he could play that game with but that she was not one of them. He told her he still did not know what she thought she saw.

She asked him, "Were you not about to open your briefcase?" He looked at her and kept quiet. She told him, "Now, we understand each other."

The man sat up straight and looked very uncomfortable. His wife told him they should leave immediately, but he told his wife that it would be rude for them to leave during dinner. Princess Grace noticed that the man's wife did not look well. She asked her if she was okay and she replied that it was none of the Princess's business. The other guests told her that she should apologize to Princess Grace because she was just being concerned. The husband went to King Yusuf and apologized to him. He explained that they had to leave before dinner was over because his wife was not feeling well. King Yusuf asked him if there was anything he could do to help. The man told him no, they would just go.

Princess Grace was quiet because she did not understand what had just happened. One of the guests at her table asked her if she had ever heard of Dragon, the ancient Chinese snake worshipped by many. Princess Grace told him that yes, there were stories that some people use to tell their children because they did not know better. She heard of these stories while counseling people. They told her that the man who had just left claimed he had been given his wife by the ancient Chinese Dragon. Princess Grace told them that was nonsense. She believed that the man just wanted people to be afraid of them. They asked her how, if that was the case, then no one knows where that woman comes from and no one has ever seen her family. Princess Grace asked them why the Chinese God would give the man a wife instead of giving that wife to the Chinese. One of the guests said, "Because his family was faithful to that Dragon and Snake God."

The guests watched as the man and his wife left the room. The woman looked as though she was feeling worse every minute. King Yusuf went to the man and asked him if he was sure his wife did not want to see the palace doctor. The man again refused. The King was concerned because the woman looked as though she was about to drop. Princess Grace wanted to go and ask them again if there was something she could do when the Holy Spirit told her to sit down and not go anywhere. She sat. King Yusuf came to her and asked her if there was something she could do. She told him that there was nothing she could to for them. The remaining guests told Princess Grace how in their country, the Snake worshippers were the most powerful and rich and the couple who had just left were the snake worshipers. They told her that no other religion was allowed in their country until two years ago when the King came back from visiting the Princess's country. They told her that many people were still angry with the King for bringing Christians into their country and some even threatened to kill the King in public. A man told Princess Grace that the King had been through a lot for receiving Jesus Christ and introducing Him to his crew. That is why there was always a heavy escort for the King. The man told Princess Grace that even the King's visitors were in danger for there were people out there who wanted to eliminate them so that the preaching of this foreign God would stop. Princess Grace thought about it. She now understood why King Yusuf sent the Pastors out with more than five hundred soldiers each. She realized it was for their protection.

At the table where Pastor Eric and Sir James were sitting, they were busy chatting as usual. Whenever they were together, they made a lot of noise. They were laughing and most tables had turned to watch them and see what was happening. Everyone at that table was laughing. Sir James was telling a story he had heard from a Pastor in the United States called Pastor Joel, on television, he told them that a woman had been married to a self-centered man who had asked his wife to bury his money with him when he died. The wife had agreed. The woman's friend was not happy that the wife had agreed to obey her husband's dying wish. She asked her how she was going to live without money. The wife told the friend that God would provide. On the burial day, the wife placed a small case inside the coffin. The friend was so upset with her and even her Pastor was not happy. The friend later asked her to explain that she didn't just bury the money with him as he requested? The Christian lady said that as a Christian, she honored her word. "I wrote him a check," she said.

The friend laughed and said, "You could have fooled me, Christian lady. I thought you were a fool. Now I know I was wrong. That was wisdom."

The whole table laughed at the jokes that Sir James shared. King Yusuf asked King Wisdom if they were always loud like that. King Wisdom told him, "Even worse. They play hard when they have that moment and they joke a lot." King Yusuf told him that he liked that they had a lot of humor.

Princess Marisa was happy that she was seating at the table for she could not stop laughing at their jokes. She had not thought that Pastor Eric could relax and joke like that. Sir James looked at her and asked her if she was the future Mrs. Eric Smith. Pastor Eric told him to be quiet and leave the lady alone. Sir James told Princess Marisa that he had never seen Pastor Eric comfortably chatting to any woman. He said that she was the first and he could tell there was something special going on. Pastor Eric asked Sir James how many times he would have to tell him to shut his mouth. Sir James laughed even lauder and told Princess Marisa that he was still waiting for his answer. Princess Marisa looked at Pastor Eric but he could not look at her. Pastor Eric asked Sir James if he wanted King Yusuf to kill him. Sir James told him no, but he believed that King Yusuf would like his niece to be married.

Sir James asked Princess Marisa if she liked Pastor Eric. Pastor Eric told him to shut up again. Sir James laughed and told Pastor Eric that he was talking to the lady, not him and why was he protecting her if he did not care for her? Princess Marisa laughed and asked Sir James if he was always forward like that. He told her that he was but he was still waiting for the answer because when they eventually get married, he would perform the ceremony. Pastor Eric laughed and looked at Princess Marisa and told her that he was telling a lie and Sir James was just a noisy person.

Princess Marisa laughed and surprised them by looking at Sir James and saying, "Sir, I don't like Pastor Eric, but I think I love him." She then told Pastor Eric that she loved him. Pastor Eric blushed and was very uncomfortable. Sir James stood up, excused himself, and asked his friend to accompany him to the bathroom.

As soon as they left the room, Sir James asked Pastor Eric, "What is wrong with you, man?" Pastor Eric told Sir James that it was his fault for encouraging the lady. Sir James asked Pastor Eric if he truly did not have any feelings for the lady. Pastor Eric told him that it was not about having feelings but about knowing where to draw the line. He said that they were surrounded by King Yusuf's guests and they should respect the King and his family.

The two men were quiet for some time and Sir James asked Pastor Eric to be honest with him if he had any feelings for Princess Marisa. Pastor Eric admitted that he did. Sir James advised Pastor Eric to talk to King Wisdom because he was running out of time and he would know if King Yusuf would kill him or not. But he should not let that beautiful lady pass him by, especially since she was clearly smitten by him. Sir James encouraged Pastor Eric not to be a coward. Pastor Eric was quiet for some time. Eventually, he told his friend that he would do something, but if he went down for it, he would blame him.

They returned to the table and Princess Marisa told Pastor Eric in a low voice that she did not mean to embarrass him. He asked her if she had ever considered living outside of her country. She told him that after meeting him, she had begun to think about it. He asked her if she thought she could manage being married to him considering he was not Royal and he was always busy doing God's work. She told him that she believed she could. He told her that he loved her too but that he was not Royal blood. She told him that it doesn't matter as he can become Royal blood by marrying her. After all, her father was not Royal and was not from their country.

Pastor Eric took a deep breath and said, "Now the big challenge is how to tell King Yusuf." He whispered something in Princess Marisa's ear and she nodded her head in agreement. They talked for some time in whispers so that the people sitting with them at the table could not hear. Eventually, Pastor Eric left to go and speak with King Wisdom. He asked permission to see King Wisdom alone. They spoke and King Wisdom smiled and left Pastor Eric standing alone as he went and returned with King Yusuf. They went inside one of the rooms together. Pastor Eric was very nervous; the Kings could see that as he was talking to them. Finally King Yusuf called Princess Yeti and they spoke and the Princess hugged Pastor Eric. Princess Marisa thought that was encouraging. Sir James was afraid for his friend even though he had encouraged him. King Yusuf took Pastor Eric by the hand and led him into the room. They spoke and the King gave Pastor Eric the most beautiful ring he had never seen. The King told him that it had belonged to the great Queen, his mother and that he should give it to Princess Marisa when he proposed for the ring should stay in the family. Pastor Eric was honored to see that the King approved of him and had given him his mother's ring. After thirty minutes, they came out of the room. Princess Marisa was very worried for Pastor Eric. Pastor Eric came out and took Princess Grace with him inside. Even Sir James began to get worried. Princess Marisa wanted to go to her mother to ask her what was happening but Sir James told her to wait because he knew that King Wisdom would never allow anything bad to happen to them even if they were wrong.

They were gone for five more minutes and when they came out, no one could read their expressions.

Pastor Eric sat down. Princess Marisa asked, "And so?" He did not answer her. She said, "Please talk to me. What happened?" Before Pastor Eric couldn't answer, King Yusuf asked for all of his guests to give him a moment to welcome his visitors. He introduced everyone except for Pastor Eric. Princess Marisa was now getting more worried until King Yusuf walked towards them and stood by Pastor Eric. He told the guests that the young man they were seeing was the most powerful preacher of Jesus Christ and the son of a billionaire in Germany in the motor industries. He was the adopted son of King Wisdom, and his castle was five minutes away from King Wisdom's palace. Everyone was paying attention now. King Yusuf told everyone that the young man had come and asked him if he could give him permission to propose marriage to Princess Marisa. The King then took Princess Yeti by the hand. He looked at his sister and said, "My sister and I have blessed the young man to go ahead and propose. If our daughter accepts him, we accept him too. Even if she does not, he will still be our son through King Wisdom and he will still be our Pastor who led millions of our people to Christ."

Lady Elisa was listening. She could not understand how she missed that. She looked at King Wisdom, Queen Fiona, and Princess Grace and realized that they looked as though they all knew something. She was not sure if she was hearing the King correctly. She decided to take a step forward to be closer so that she could ensure that she was not missing anything.

King Yusuf told Pastor Eric to stand up. He stood and the King told him that the floor was his. Pastor Eric turned and looked at Princess Marisa who was smiling widely. He said, "Princess Marisa, can you...?"

Princess Marisa did not allow him to finish the question. She screamed, "Yes, yes, yes!" Everybody laughed.

The King said, "Daughter, can you allow the gentleman to ask you the question please?" This was the part Lady Elisa loved a great deal. She laughed out loud and moved closer. Pastor Eric and Marisa began to kiss each other. Lady Elisa moved closer to see everything. King Yusuf turned to look at them. He seemed surprised that they were already kissing each other before the proposal was finished and before he blessed them. But he shook his head and called on King Wisdom and told him that they should find a way to keep them apart before they commit adultery and offend God. Everybody laughed.

Princess Yeti ran to her daughter and hugged and kissed her at the same time while congratulating her. She turned to Pastor Eric and gave him a big hug and told him that she couldn't have wished for a better son-in-law than him. She welcomed him to the family. Lady Elisa was already at Pastor Eric's side smiling and jumping up and down and hugging him. Pastor Eric lifted her up and asked her if she was going to behave. She asked Pastor

Eric what he would give her if she behaved. He didn't answer but instead turned to Princes Marisa and introduced Lady Elisa as his daughter. Lady Elisa told Princess Marisa that she was beautiful. Princess Marisa thanked her and told her that she was as well. She touched Princess Marisa's hair which was pitch black and shining and asked her if she dyed it. Princess Marisa told her that it was natural. They smiled at each other.

Princess Grace hugged Princess Marisa and told her that now they were sisters. Queen Fatima and Queen Fiona came and joked with them by telling them that they were both in trouble because they did not ask for their permission and spoke only to the men and Princess Grace. Queen Fatima looked at Princess Marisa and Pastor Eric and asked them who was going to cook for them since none of the men nor Princess Grace could cook. Queen Fiona asked them who was now going to make their wedding clothes. Pastor Eric told them that no one else except them. If they could not help, they would not eat or dress. They laughed and congratulated them and wished them the best.

Princess Marisa told Pastor Eric that she loved him the moment she saw him and he told her the same thing. King Yusuf gave Pastor Eric the microphone and told him to say something to the people. He took the microphone and said, "Let's pray." He committed his future wife into the hands of God and asked God to bless both of them to continue with His work. He asked God to bless their marriage and protect it jealously. When he finished the prayer, he thanked Princess Yeti, King Yusuf, and the people of the country for raising up Princess Marisa. He then thanked Princess Grace, King Wisdom, and Queen Fiona for taking him in as their son and bringing him to that country to meet the most beautiful woman in the world. He turned around and spoke to Sir James, thanking him for been noisy because something good came from it. Everybody laughed because they knew Sir James. Sir James laughed and clapped hands at the same time. He then gave the microphone to Princess Marisa. She said she wished her father was alive to see that day and she thanked her parents, King Yusuf, and the Queen. She told them that she was too excited to talk and she cried. Pastor Eric hugged her and they sat down.

Lady Elisa had changed her seating arrangement as she was now sitting at Pastor Eric's table. She asked the workers to bring her chair to her because nothing was happening at the King's table. They brought her chair and set her dinner plates. She wanted to be where something was going on. As soon as her chair arrived, she asked Princess Marisa and Pastor Eric how they met. Both of them answered her at once and said that they had met right where they were sitting. The funny part was that she believed it and she began looking around. When she saw another man and woman setting next to each other, she warned Pastor Eric and Princess Marisa that there might be another wedding announcement. They laughed. She was such a joy and so innocent at the age of thirteen.

After the excitement of the engagement, King Yusuf told his wife that he had to now invite his great uncle to tell him the news. Queen Fatima did not like the great uncle as she was still afraid of him. She wished they could go ahead without him because when she had gotten married to King Yusuf, the great uncle had not approved of her. He wanted to choose a wife for King Yusuf and he had someone else in mind. But King Yusuf had stood up to his uncle and said that if his father approved of his wife, that was all that he wanted. The Uncle told King Yusuf that he would regret the marriage. So Queen Fatima believed that the King's uncle had bewitched her and that was why she had never become pregnant.

Princess Yeti did not want the great uncle around her family either for she blamed him for the death of her husband. When Prince Brian was three-years-old, there had been a ceremony and the great uncle had taken the small Prince Brian to introduce him to his people with whom he performed black magic. Prince Brian's father was very upset with the uncle and told him not to ever come close to his children. The uncle told Prince Brian's father that nobody spoke to him like that and got away with it. He told him that he would not see the rise of the sun tomorrow. The next morning, Prince Brian's father did not wake up. He was a vegetable for three years and finally died. But King Yusuf knew that if they did not tell the uncle about the engagement, there would be trouble. He told Princess Yeti what he was going to do and why. Princess Yeti still did not want to see her uncle, but she finally agreed with the King that it was the right thing to do.

Princess Yeti told her daughter what the King had decided to do and why. She was not happy that her great uncle was coming for she feared him too and was angry with him for killing her father. She still remembered how angry he was with her father that day. She also remembered her mother telling her husband that maybe they should apologize and her father arguing that he would not be a man who could not protect his children. She told Pastor Eric about it and he told her not to worry. Later on, Pastor Eric told Princess Grace and they decided to go on fasting until the day he arrived. They were fasting from twelve midnight until six in the evening every day without fail. They prayed together before going to bed.

King Yusuf called the uncle the following day and invited him to come to the palace. He said that he had family matters he wished to discuss with him. The uncle was happy that the King wished to discuss family matter with him even though he was not happy that he had brought Christians into the country. King Wisdom also called Pastor Eric and asked him if he had called his father and told him the good news. Pastor Eric told the King that he intended to do so. King Wisdom told him that perhaps they should call him together. King Wisdom made the call and spoke to Pastor Eric's father and told him that Pastor Eric had something very important to tell him. He gave the phone to Pastor Eric and they spoke for a few moments before Pastor Eric broke the news to his father. He finally told him that he had met someone he wanted to marry and he wished that his father would give him all of his blessings. He said that if his father did not approve, he would respect his wish and not marry the young lady.

His father asked, "Did you say young lady?"

"Yes," Pastor Eric said.

"Does the King approve of this girl?" his father asked. "Is she from a good family?" Pastor Eric handed the phone back to King Wisdom. The King told Pastor Eric's father that he approved of the girl and that she was the daughter of his best friend, King Yusuf. Pastor Eric's father was impressed and asked if they approved of his son. King Wisdom knew what he was thinking. He told him that they did approve of the new Pastor Eric and they know he was the vessel of God who would love their daughter and take care of her. He knew that the two young people loved each other and they both loved the Kingdom of God and that was all that mattered. He then told him that true Christians do not judge people by their past history. Pastor Eric's father understood the King very well and the matter of his son's past was now closed. He thanked the King for being a good father to his son when he could not and said that he was looking forward to learning a lot from him in the future. The King gave the phone back to Pastor Eric and his father told him that he was very proud of him.

Mr. Smith was very happy because Pastor Eric was the only son he had. He had one son and two daughters. Now he knew that he would have someone to inherit his business.

Pastor Eric waited for Princess Marisa to wake up so that they could talk. Since they were fasting as soon as the Morning Prayer ended, he excused himself and his future wife and took a walk with her in the garden. He was impressed with the garden as he had not known that it was so beautiful. He told Princess Marisa about his whole life. He explained about where he came from. He spoke about his father disinheriting him and about how he had met Princess Grace and had learned about what his priorities were. Princess Marisa stopped and kissed him and told him she was happy they had met and she would make him forget everything. She told him that she would have never guessed that he was from a wealthy family. She told him about how her father was a Swedish man and how that was the beginning of the problems for her family because her mother had been the only daughter of King Yusuf Senior and she was to marry into the Royal family. She laughed and told him that it meant marrying your cousin. She heard that her father had the Royal blood in him too. She told him that her father was wealthy too but that he was not a billionaire like his father. She explained how her mother had two children before her, Amanda and Samuel, and both had died at the age of two. When she was born, they were praying for their God to let them have her. She told him that her father believed in Jesus but never led them to Him because he was not a strong Christian. When he heard that they could not worship other Gods in their country, he never fought for His God. He simply accepted the law. They talked and shared for hours. Finally, they decided on a date for their wedding. Pastor Eric suggested a year from that day and she told him that a year was too far. They decided to discuss it with the two Kings, their wives, and Princess Yeti.

Pastor Eric requested an audience with the two Kings and their wives. Princess Marisa requested that her mother join them. They asked them if they have come up with a date for the wedding and Pastor Eric told them that he wanted it to be a year from today and Princess Marisa felt it was too far. King Wisdom asked him why he wanted it to be a year. He told him that it was because Princess Marisa had to spend time with Princess Grace and that would help her a lot to understand their way of life. She needed time to learn the kind of life he lives in his country. He told the Kings that he wanted her to be sure of what she was getting into; because most of his time was dedicated to God's work. Princess Marisa told them that she met him while he was doing God's work and she did not see that as a problem. Then Pastor

Eric asked her when she wanted the wedding to be. She laughed and said, "Now." Everybody laughed. She suggested six months so that Pastor Eric's family could make arrangement to come to the wedding as they lived far away.

King Wisdom said, "Young Lady, hold on. We are Pastor Eric's family and there is no other family. Pastor Eric is my second son. Tell her, my son."

Pastor Eric laughed and everybody laughed and King Wisdom said, "That was very true since they lived in three different worlds, they need time." They asked Pastor Eric where he wanted the wedding to be. He told them that first, he wanted a celebration for taking Princess Marisa from her country. That would be in King Yusuf's country and then the main celebration would be in King Wisdom's country. Princess Marisa was happy with that. Then King Yusuf asked him where they would be staying. They agreed that they would stay in King Wisdom's country as that was home for Pastor Eric.

King Wisdom and King Yusuf were happy. King Wisdom turned to his friend and told him they were now related. They both laughed. King Yusuf told everyone that this marriage was a blessing for it had now connected the two countries and families forever. He stopped and said, "Correction: three countries together."

King Wisdom agreed with him and told him that they would now have to visit each other from time to time. They left Pastor Eric and Princess Marisa to come up with an actual date for the wedding.

Princess Grace and Princess Marisa spent most of their time together at the palace while Pastor Eric and Sir James left for the other parts of the country to perform evangelism. The two Princesses continued watching Pastor Eric and Pastor Sir James on television to see the great works they were doing. This time, both men were covered live. Princess Grace was teaching Princess Marisa the way of Christian life. They studied the bible together and prayed together. Princess Grace told Princess Marisa to spend more time reading the books of Proverbs and Hebrews, for they would help her in her marriage and daily life. Princess Marisa did as Princess Grace suggested and to her surprise, she enjoyed them a great deal. Some days Lady Elisa joined them and the three ladies would study the bible and pray together. Princess Marisa was surprised by the maturity of Lady Elisa when it came to God's word. She was not playful when dealing with the things of God. Princess Marisa kept telling Princess Grace that she wanted them to read the Psalms but Princess Grace told her she was not ready yet. Toward the end of the week, Princess Grace told her it was time for her to read the Psalms. Finally, Princess Grace told Princess Marisa that she should now lead them in prayer. She was uncomfortable at first but as she kept praying, she got more comfortable. Princess Grace reminded Princess Marisa that the time would come when she would go out with Pastor Eric to evangelize and he would ask her to pray for the people and she should be able to do that.

Whenever she talked to Pastor Eric on the phone, Princess Marisa told him what she had read and what they had done with Princess Grace. He was very happy about it because he could tell from her voice that she was enjoying herself. He teased her and told her that he now wished to marry her immediately. She laughed and told him that he was the one who did not want to rush the wedding so he had to wait.

Queen Fiona called Princess Marisa and told her she was going to design her wedding gown. She had heard of Queen Fiona's work and had seen the clothes Queen Fatima had brought with her from Queen Fiona. They were so beautiful that the whole country was now talking about how Queen Fatima's dresses. Princess Marisa considered herself fortunate for her wedding gown was to be designed by Queen Fiona. Queen Fiona told her she was a pretty girl with a beautiful figure and she would enjoy making more than a wedding gown for her and her family.

Princess Marisa's mother was very happy that Queen Fiona was going to design the gown for her daughter. She knew it would cost a lot but she did not mind paying. What she did not know was that Queen Fiona was secretly taking her measurements as well to surprise her with few outfits for she was a very beautiful girl too. She looked like she was in her late twenties yet she was in her late forties. During dinner, she asked Queen Fiona to give her an estimate cost of the gown and King Yusuf told her that was for him to pay for. Then King Wisdom told them it was his responsibility as the father of the groom. As they were fighting over who would pay, Queen Fiona told them that none of them was going to pay. Her wedding gift to Princess Marisa and Pastor Eric was the wedding gown.

As they were talking, King Wisdom's phone rang. It was Pastor Eric's father, Mr. Smith. He joked with him and told him to tell the people that King Wisdom was the father of the groom so it was his responsibility to pay for the bride's gown. Pastor Eric's father laughed and said, "Your majesty, that is the reason I am calling." He told him there was a very good and well-known designer for wedding gowns and he wondered if they could permit Princess Marisa to come to his country for a fitting. King Wisdom laughed and told him that if he tried to take the work of Princess Marisa's gown away from Queen Fiona, he was not going to help deal with the Queen's anger. Pastor Eric's father laughed and apologized and told the King that he hadn't known the Queen was going to make the gown. He asked King Yusuf how his daughter in-law was doing.

The King gave the phone to Princess Marisa. She said, "Hello, daddy," and left the room to speak to her future father in-law in private. She was very happy that he had asked for her. She told Mr. Smith that she loved his son and that she was going to make him the happiest man on earth. Mr. Smith liked that a lot and told her that he was lucky to have her as a daughter-in-law who loved his son as much as she did. They talked for over an hour.

No one knew what they were talking about. But Princess Marisa was laughing and everyone could tell she was enjoying whatever her future father-in-law was telling her. She promised him that she would come to Germany before the wedding. Mr. Smith was very happy and he welcomed her to the family. He asked her if he could ask her a personal question. She told him she didn't mind. He asked her where they would be staying after they got married. She told him that King Wisdom would kill them if they tried to relocate from his country. They both laughed. He told her that they would be opening another motor industry in King Wisdom's country to expand the business. Princess Marisa told him it was a good idea and that she liked that and maybe later he could consider his uncles' country too as they could do with some developments. He told her he liked that too. They agreed to discuss it after the wedding. The Princess asked him if he knew any bible distributors or wholesalers because she was considering suggesting that to her uncle. He told her he could work on that and call her before the end of the week. She laughed and asked him if she could call him "Daddy." He was very happy and he agreed. He promised to call her every week without fail. They bonded so well and from that day on, he called his daughter-in-law every day without fail.

Princess Marisa went back to join the others, and King Yusuf told her that he was very happy to see her happy but that he was jealous because there was another man in her life. She smiled and hugged her uncle and told him that he would always be the only man in her life. King Wisdom told her he was going to tell Pastor Eric. They laughed and she looked at the King and told him that Pastor Eric knows that King Yusuf was the love of her life. King Yusuf told them that it was like a mother leaving a crying child and telling the child that she would be back in a minute when she knew that she was going away for days. King Yusuf told her that Pastor Eric was a very lucky man to have her. She told her uncle that she was also very lucky to have him and she could not wait to be his wife. Queen Fiona told her that she had felt the same when King Wisdom proposed to her and she even asked him to speed it up. They had gotten married three months later but then they had been in the same country and were almost neighbors. Princess Marisa asked Queen Fiona if she was in love with him or whether she was the parents' choice. She told them that she had fallen in love with him two weeks before his ball dance where he was to choose a wife, but that she thought that she was too young. She had not dreamt of him looking at her twice. She was surprised when he proposed to her. She told Princess Marisa that she was shaking so much that she couldn't even say yes for she was so in love with him. They laughed and Princess Marisa asked her how old she had been. She told them that she was eighteen and he was twenty-nine at the time.

They looked at King Yusuf and waited for him to tell them how he had met Queen Fatima. He knew what they wanted to hear. He said, "Well, they forced me to marry her!"

Queen Fatima threw a pillow at him and said, "Old cow!"

Everybody laughed. Lady Elisa was on the floor rolling with laughter. King Yusuf looked at Lady Elisa and asked someone to bring a belt to whip her behind. She laughed even louder and ran to King Wisdom to help her. She told him that the old cow was about to hurt her. King Wisdom picked her up and cuddled her and asked King Yusuf not to hurt his baby. Lady Elisa looked at King Yusuf and said, "Don't worry, old cow, we won't tell any-body." King Yusuf pretended to grab her legs and she screamed, hiding herself in King Wisdom's jacket.

Queen Fatima told them that they should leave Lady Elisa behind for few weeks because the people really liked her. Before she could say anything, King Yusuf told King Wisdom that they would like to adopt Lady Elisa. She screamed and said, "No!" She was not leaving her family for anybody, not even Pastor Eric. They asked her why and she told them because back at home all the girls liked Pastor Eric and they wanted to be his wife, but she was the only one who didn't want to be his wife, she just wanted to be with her Daddy and Mama. They laughed and told her that the time would come when she would want to leave her parents for a man. She shook her head and said she was going to stay with them forever. Princess Marisa told her she couldn't wait to be Pastor Eric's wife, because she couldn't wait to kiss him again and again. Lady Elisa and Princess Grace made faces and stuck out their tongues out and pretended to vomit. They all knew they were children talking. Princess Yeti reminded her daughter that although Princess Grace was tall and looked mature, she was only fourteen and not mature in matters of the heart. Princess Grace corrected her and said that she was fourteen and a half. Princess Marisa was shocked as she thought that Princess Grace was nineteen or twenty.

Princess Marisa looked at her mother with confusion because most of the time Princess Grace sounded more mature. She even sounded more mature than her and even the Kings looked to her for advice. Later on that night, Princess Yeti explained to her daughter the nature of the birth of Princess Grace and how she was responsible for the Christian movement in their country. She explained how Pastor Eric and Sir James all reported to her and took their orders from Princess Grace. She told her daughter how those two men would lay down their lives for Princess Grace because of how much they respect her. She explained how Princess Grace planned everything without help and how she trained Pastor Eric and Sir James. Princess Marisa was very impressed and told her mother that she was going to ask Pastor Eric to raise their children the same way Princess Grace's parents had raised her.

14

That evening, they were watching the crusade and King Yusuf's men were preaching. He could not believe his eyes and ears for they were really good and the crowd was huge. They were leading many people to Christ. There were some times when Sir James and Pastor Eric would preach because they were holding two and sometimes three meetings a day. They often traded off when it came to preaching. But there was something about Pastor Eric. When he was on the pulpit, he became a different person altogether. He was on fire for Jesus without doubt. When he was not on the pulpit, he was shy and less talkative but when he was on the pulpit, he was bold and could talk. Every evening from seven to ten the news showed the crusades. They showed them again between ten and twelve and then from two until six. They were always calling Princess Grace to talk to her and she was always busy on the phone giving instructions. Sometimes she would tell them who to put on the pulpit and who to use for opening prayer and closing prayer. There was a time when she called Sir James and asked him why Emmanuel hadn't been on the pulpit. She told them that he was not a child when it came to the Kingdom of God. She asked them to take him with them this time. She told Sir James that there were many young people who would be more encouraged to hear from someone their age and many people who were born crippled who would also be encouraged to hear from someone who had been in their position. She said that a preacher was made when God poured His spirit into a person. They promised her that Emmanuel would preach that night.

King Yusuf called Emmanuel's mother, Rashidah to the palace that night so that they could watch Emmanuel preach together. The King was happy that Princes Grace believed in Emmanuel and had instructed her men to let him preach. That evening, they were all waiting to see how a nine-year-old boy was going to do. King Yusuf was nervous and Emmanuel's mother was nervous too. Sir James began singing. When he finished, he told the people that he was now calling on the most anointed young man of God who would be giving them the testimony of his life and how Jesus had changed his life. He told them that this young man had been born crawling like a snake and had never walked until he met with Jesus. After coming in contact with Jesus, he started to walk. Many people who knew him from the King's city could testify to that. The crowd began screaming with joy.

When Emmanuel took the stage, it was as if the people would never stop cheering. He started to sing the song Lady Elisa had sung when they arrived at the airport, "Let the spirit of God take over this country." He sang it so well and asked everybody to raise their hands up to receive the blessings from God. He reminded them that the same spirit that had healed him was there that very night. He invited those who were watching on television to raise their hands as well. He then said that if you are a woman in need of a child, put your hands on your belly for tonight is your night. He encouraged the woman's husbands to also put their hands on their wife's stomach. King Yusuf moved to his wife and put his hands on her stomach. They sang the song and when he finished, he told them how God had healed him and explained what he had done to prepare himself to receive the healing. He spoke of how Princess Grace had encouraged him to be ready to receive his healing and how he, in turn, encouraged them. He talked about the power, healing, and salvation found in Christ Jesus. He told them that he could not start the prayer without giving people a chance to receive Jesus so that they too could partake in these miracles. He told them, "Look at me. Who would have thought that one day I would be standing up, singing and dancing like this?" He told them there was no miracle too big for Jesus and no problem too big for Him either. He led them to Christ. When he finished, he prayed for all kinds of diseases to leave those people for they were now the children of the most high God. He told the sickness that darkness can never mix with light and whenever darkness sees light, it disappears so sickness should disappear because they were now the children of light. When he finished the prayer, Queen Fatima was on the floor. The spirit of God had taken her over.

Rashidah was crying tears of joy. She had never thought her son could preach like that. She took Princess Grace's hands and kneeled in front of her and thanked her for all that she had done for them. Princess Grace told her to thank the Lord Jesus for He was the one who ordained their meeting and He is the one who heeled the young man. She told the woman that she was just a vessel of God.

When King Yusuf regained consciousness, he began boasting that his son was preaching the word of God. He told Emmanuel's mother that there were going to be bible distributors for the whole country for he was going to open a business for them to sell the bibles at low prices so that people would be able to afford them. Princess Marisa told him that she had already asked Mr. Smith to look for Bible suppliers and he was going to call her back to give her the information and she would pass it along to the King. He was happy with that. He told her that, as for, Emmanuel, he would be the preacher at the church for the Royal family and workers near the palace. He could not control his excitement. He went to Princess Grace and hugged her and kissed her. Queen Fatima woke up and told them that she had seen herself walking in the garden with a twin boy and girl. Everyone screamed with joy. King Wisdom told them that it was done and they should start preparing. King Yusuf called the butler and told him that tomorrow they should start preparing a nursery because his wife was pregnant. The butler was very happy. He said, "Yes, your Majesty. If you like, I can start tonight."

The King told him tomorrow would be fine. Right there King Yusuf began planning for his coming children and Emmanuel. Lady Samantha said, "Whoa! That's a strong faith the King has here," for she could see that the King believed without doubt.

Sir Pastor James was also very shocked by Emmanuel. He did not think he would be that good in the short time since he had given his life to Christ. When he finished preaching, Sir James approached Emmanuel backstage and lifted him up, kissed him, and told him how proud of him he was. Emmanuel told him that he wished his mother and King Yusuf had seen his dream come true. Sir Pastor James told him that the King must have told his mother to watch. He asked him if he wanted to call his mother. Emmanuel said yes. He called the hotel and the manager told him that they had seen him preaching and they too were incredibly proud of him. After they congratulated Emmanuel, he asked if he could speak to his mother. They told him that she was at the palace. Sir James told Emmanuel that it was time for counseling and he would be counseling the sick and the young people. He told him that if he felt that he should pray for them while he was counseling them, he should feel free to do so. But for now, he would only see the sick people and the young people. Emmanuel was happy with that.

The evening went well and they returned to the hotel. Sir James called the palace and asked them if they had seen Emma. King Yusuf asked to speak to him. He told him how proud he was of him and how he couldn't wait to lift him up and kiss him silly. Emmanuel laughed for it was his first time hearing the King so excited. He told the King that he had dreamt of himself preaching in that very stadium and he had told his mother. He said that happened before Princess Grace told him he was going with Sir James. The King told everybody what Emmanuel has told him and his mother confirmed it. King Yusuf told them that

Emmanuel was not only a great preacher but also a prophet. They all laughed. Queen Fatima said that her husband was so happy, she knew they would not sleep that night.

King Wisdom looked at his friend for he was thrilled to see him happy. He could tell he loved the boy a lot and wanted the best for him. He told Emmanuel's mother that when he came back, he would be moving to the palace. He wanted to see Emmanuel every day. Emmanuel's mother was very fond of the King and was happy that he felt that way about her son. She felt she couldn't thank God enough for she believed Emmanuel was in good hands with the King.

Because of Emmanuel's tiny body, many people thought he was only five or six years old. So many people were shocked at the powerful voice, message, and prayers that came out of him. That night, the reporter showed many people who had been healed and some were calling the call center telling them that they had been healed while listening to the young boy. "Who was he?" many of them asked. Some cities were calling to invite Emmanuel to come to them and preach. The manager of the call center called the King that very night and told him about the kind of testimonies they were getting and how they had five different cities inviting the boy to come and preach. The call center manager asked the King if he knew the boy. The King told him that Emmanuel was his son and that the man should tell the callers that Emmanuel was the King's son. The manager didn't know the King had a son and from the sound of his voice, he could tell the King was a proud father. He told his visitors what the call center manager had just told him. He told them that the young boy was going places. Even Lady Elisa who always had something to say was speechless. The great man was too happy to care what anybody said. Princess Grace was also very happy. She told King Yusuf that he had seen more than twelve powerful preachers from his country already. Did he still think that his country would fall apart when they left? He told her that he believed they would now be all right, and he thanked her again.

Meanwhile, Soyab was watching television and could not believe he was seeing his son. It was now becoming very difficult for him to pursue his wife since it looked as though they were now prospering and Emmanuel was healed. But he knew that even if Emmanuel was not healed, he would still want to go back to his wife. For when he saw her, he remembered how he loved her and all the old feelings came back. He lay awake at night thinking of his wife. He sent flowers to her from time to time telling her how sorry he was and how he wished he could cancel everything and start over. In the last message he send to her, he told her that he would never marry again or even give himself to another woman even if she wouldn't take him back. He wrote that he knew he had done a very foolish thing to leave his wife and son like that. Emmanuel's mother thought of him quite a bit for she had never been with another man in her life besides him. She knew she would never stop loving him. But she believed in love and trust and she did not trust him. She did not even believe that he had changed. She sometimes thought of giving him an opportunity to come and hear what he had to say and she did not trust herself around him. That is why she had not met with him yet. But on her way to the palace, she saw him and he greeted her and she acknowledged the greetings. But she had to admit that it was difficult seeing him. Soyab knew that his wife and son were in favor with the King and that presented another challenge for the King had warned him not harass her. He went home that night thinking of them. He could see Emmanuel's happy voice preaching the word of God.

Emmanuel's mother did not go back to the hotel. Queen Fatima told her that she had her own chamber at the palace and they have made clothes for her so that whenever she comes to the palace, she didn't have to bring anything with her. She was led to her chamber. She loved it. It was so big and beautiful and there were shoes, clothes of all kinds, nightdresses, dinner gowns, nightgowns, suits, running shoes, dressing shoes, and so on. She couldn't believe her eyes. She never thought she would own so many clothes in her life. She asked Queen Fatima when did they do all that. Queen Fatima told her that for the past two weeks, they had been working on it as well as a wardrobe for Emmanuel. They took her to see Emmanuel's chamber. It was also big and she could not even count the numbers of suits, toys, and bicycles in Emmanuel's room. She knew Emmanuel was going to be very happy when he saw all that. She was so touched that she hugged the Queen and cried thinking of all of the years of suffering they had endured and how God had taken them out of their suffering. That night, when she was sleeping, she had a dream an angel had come to her and told her that the greatest gift a human could ever have is forgiveness, especially when the burden was as heavy as the one she was carrying. She looked at where the angel was pointing and saw that she was carrying her husband. She woke up and went back to bed. She had the same dream again. King Yusuf also dreamed of a man coming to him and telling him that he had given him Emmanuel and it was his responsibility to encourage Emmanuel's mother to forgive so that she could receive her blessings. He told him never to be afraid of anybody taking Emmanuel from him for he had sealed the deal. In the morning, she told the wife that a man told him he had given him Emmanuel and he should encourage his mother to forgive. He then told her the rest of the dream. The Queen told him to tell Emmanuel's mother to forgive her husband. King Yusuf told her he did not want Soyab to hurt her again and he didn't want to force her to forgive him but he would do something.

He decided before telling Emmanuel's mother that he would talk to King Wisdom first. He told King Wisdom and King Wisdom told him that it was an angel of God and he should unite Soyab and his wife. As a King, he had the power to do that without losing Emmanuel or his mother. After breakfast, Emmanuel's mother told the King that she'd had a strange dream she wanted to tell him about. He let her tell hers first. When she finished, the King told them about his dream and how he had told his wife and King Wisdom about it. She told the King that even if she could get back together with her husband, she still preferred to leave Emmanuel with him. She felt that the King loved Emmanuel more than anybody and that he had earned the right to raise Emmanuel. The King was happy to hear that. Princess Grace told her that was the best decision she could make. King Yusuf told her he would send for her husband to speak with him, but she should understand that their plans would remain the same. If Soyab wanted her, he would have to move to her house and if he joined her in the business, he should know that she was the boss. She would still keep her chamber at the palace and come and go as she liked. For every family gathering, she would be invited as she was now a member of the Royal family.

The meeting between Soyab and his wife was short. The King was surprised at the outcome; for Soyab told the King that even though he was Emmanuel's father, the King had shown unconditional love towards him when his father could not. Therefore, he would love it if the King would continue fathering Emmanuel and guiding him. Soyab told the King that he was Emmanuel's father but he did not deserve to take credit for what Emmanuel had turned into. He further told them how he had watched him on television and was proud of him but at the same time, he felt overwhelmed with guilt thinking of how he left his mother because of him. He concluded by telling the King that he believed that handing over Emmanuel was the right thing to do. Soyab knew there was a very strong bond between Emmanuel and the King and he also knew that the King had a very good heart. He had proven it to him when his second wife left him with nothing. The wife told him that she was also going to give Emmanuel to the King and since was God who had brought them back together, he would bless them with other children. Rashidah then told the King that although she had forgiven him, she did not want to stay with him yet. The King told her that God wanted them to reunite and therefore she should try. He suggested to Soyab that he start dating her. The King said he should take her out for dinner and drinks until they both became comfortable. He told Soyab that it was easy to break trust but difficult to build it back up, but they were fortunate that Jesus had come into their country and brought with Him forgiveness and trust. He encouraged them to talk every day and also warned Soyab not to push her. He then prayed with them.

He asked Emmanuel's mother to excuse them and to call King Wisdom for him. Queen Fiona asked for an audience with Queen Fatima and Emmanuel's mother. She told Queen Fatima that she believed that they had to counsel Emmanuel's mother. For she had been through a very rough period in her life and should not let that period cloud her judgment. They spoke to her for an hour and made arrangements with her to meet again over the next three days. Without knowing what the Queens were up to, the Kings made similar plans to counsel Soyab for the next three days.

The two Queens were busy with Princess Yeti planning the wedding. It was now clear that Queen Fiona was responsible for the gown and they had to divide the remaining duties among themselves. Queen Fatima told them it was simple; they would be responsible for the celebration in their country. And Queen Fiona would be responsible for the celebration in her country. Of course Mr. Smith was fighting with them to take over most of the planning but they would deal with him when the time came. They discussed a lot of things and they finally agreed on the plans. Queen Fatima advised Queen Fiona that when it came to the celebration in her country, she might have to hold two celebrations. The wedding had to be at the palace and the Queen's family would be responsible for everything at the palace since the palace would be Princess Marisa's home in that country. Another celebration would be taking place at Pastor Eric's castle when Pastor Eric takes Princess Marisa to her home. That one, Mr. Smith and his people would be responsible for. Queen Fiona asked Queen Fatima if anyone had ever told her that she was the smartest woman on earth. She was so happy with the suggestion Queen Fatima had given her. She stood up and gave her a big hug and they both laughed. She told them that they loved Pastor Eric a lot. To them, he was their biological son. There was no difference between him and Prince Hope. She told them how God had been increasing their family with wonderful children; first Lady Elisa, then Sir James, and now Pastor Eric. And she told them how all of them were so perfect that they could not ask for more from them. They asked her how old Lady Elisa was when they had adopted her. She told them she had been about to turn five. She laughed and told them that Lady Elisa was a bunch of joy every day in the palace. She told them that she hated to admit it, but sometimes she felt like King Wisdom adored Lady Elisa more than all the other children. He told them how the King still cuddled Lady Elisa like she was a baby and how even when she spent the whole day without seeing Lady Elisa, she was not herself. She laughed and told them about how when Lady Elisa want to sleep in her chamber, she would pretend to be fast asleep so that they could leave her to sleep and how sometimes when she saw that the King wanted to sleep in her bed, Lady Elisa would run and jump into the bed and tell the King that she was the first one to be on the bed, therefore she was the one sleeping with her that night. They laughed and told her that some gifts are always more special than others.

Just then, Lady Elisa knocked and asked the Queens if she could offer them some tea. They laughed and asked her if she knew how to make tea. She told them she did not but she could quickly find someone who knew how to make it. Princess Yeti looked at Queen Fiona and told her she thought she understood everything she had just told them. Princess Yeti called her and asked her when was she going to visit her. She looked at Queen Fiona and told Princess Yeti that she is never away from her parents. She explained that wherever they went, she went with them. They all laughed and she hugged Queen Fiona and kissed her and told her she loved her. The Queen told her she loved her more she was gone as fast as she came in.

15

Back home in Netherlands, Prince Hope was doing a good job and Lord Paul was very proud of him. He told King Wisdom when they were talking on the phone that the young man was a natural at his job. He was still meeting with the lady he had met and was still thinking of how he was going to break the news to the King. She had just graduated as a medical doctor and was practicing in the private hospital where the Royal went. She was a very beautiful girl with a pile of black curly hair. She looked like a doll. Everywhere she went people would turn around and look. Her friends used to tell her that she was responsible for accidents happening because her beauty made men lose their minds and caused women to daydream. At the hospital, her patients loved her and they were always creating excuses to see her one more time. Prince Hope told his sister that he was going to the hospital to see a doctor. His sister told him she was coming with him. He didn't want her to come but she insisted. Finally, they left and upon arriving, they were escorted into a private waiting room. They stayed there for five minutes before anyone came to see them. Finally, Liberty came. Princess Sasha turned and saw her. She said to the brother that she thought she had just seen an angel walking into the hospital. He looked and saw Liberty walking into the waiting room. Princess Sasha stood up before Liberty even entered the room. She believed she had never seen anyone as beautiful as her. She opened the door with a smile and greeted Princess Sasha and then turned to Prince Hope and asked him what she could do for her favorite patient. Prince Hope told her that the problem was his heart, it was skipping too much at the thought of her that he couldn't sleep or concentrate on his duties. She pretended to examine his heart and told him she understood his problem. She believed she had the cure for it. They became so lost in themselves that they forgot that Princess Sasha was there. She kissed him and asked him how he felt. He said that he felt a little better but not fully healed. He grabbed her and kissed her passionately. He took a deep breath and told her that it felt like it. They both laughed and Princess Sasha pretended to cough so that she could remind them she was there. They both laughed and apologized. Prince Hope introduced his sister and Liberty to each other and told his sister that she was the love of his life.

Princess Sasha was impressed that she could not make out what ethnicity Liberty was for she was too light-skinned to be black and yet a little dark-skinned to be white. Regardless, she was the most beautiful girl she had ever seen and she understood why her brother had fallen for her. Princess Sasha asked them how they met. Prince Hope told her he had met Liberty at the hospital and he could not take his eyes off her. She told them something shocking; they had actually met the day the prince was conceived. She told them how her mother had gone to the palace for their parents' wedding and Queen Fiona came to the gate to throw her bouquet to the people standing outside. Instead of the ladies who were fighting to catch it, it fell into her prima. She was only three-months-old by then and after nine months, Prince Hope had been born. She told them that her mother had kept that bouquet for her and it had stayed sealed in a box. They were all surprised and at the same time happy. They couldn't wait for the day their parents would hear the story. The ladies connected so well and Princess Sasha told Liberty that she was beautiful and she would like to have her as her sister-in-law. She laughed and told the Princess that she was not Royal and there was another problem her brother would discuss with her. Prince Hope was concerned that she was not Royal blood and that she was instead of mixed blood. He told his sister about his concern.

Both her parents were medical doctors. Her mother was a nurse from an African country called Botswana and her father was a doctor there as well. They fell in love and at the end of her father's contract, they moved to their country together. Liberty's father sent his wife to medical school since that was her heart's desire. He told his sister that both of his parents were very beautiful, especially her mother. They were also major shareholders of the private hospital.

Prince Hope had ordered flowers to be dropped off for Liberty. The flowers had just arrived when he got there. He pretended to be jealous and asked her who the flowers were from. She told him they had come from a certain Prince and that he was the most handsome and romantic man she had ever met. He told her to tell the Prince that she was taken and he had better back off. She stepped forward, kissed him, and told him she was taken and he better back off. She thanked him for the flowers and told him she loved flowers and his flowers always brought a smile to her face. He told her then she would have flowers every morning until he died. Princess Sasha asked her why her parents had given her the name Liberty. She told them that her mother had many abortions or children dying at an early age, so her grandmother in Botswana had told her to give the baby an unattractive name and she would live. They all laughed at the explanation. They kissed and had lunch together with Liberty and left. Prince Hope told her sister that he loved her more than anything in the world except for Jesus. His sister told him that she did not blame him and she would help in whatever way she could so that their parents would approve of Liberty. She said that she would love to have a sister-in-law as pretty and smart as her. Prince Hope continued his private visits to see Liberty and enjoyed every moment of them. He told Liberty that the way he loved her made it impossible to think of spending his life with anyone else.

King Wisdom had met Liberty in the past at the hospital and he had been shocked at her beauty. He had told her that she was a real beauty but he did not know that his son was seeing her in that way. Liberty told her parents for she was very close to them both. They told her to pray hard because she might end up with a broken heart, but since they were strong Christians, they did not believe that they would cheat on their wives, so she better be ready for a heartbreak. But Liberty's mother told her that there was a beginning for everything. She might be the first to be married to a Royal without having Royal blood of her own.

16

Sir James told his men to go to bed early since they had to proceed to another town in the morning. They were not sure if anybody had prepared for them in that city. He was thinking of leaving in the night but the captain told him that those were the most dangerous cities in the country. He advised him to sleep and they would leave at four in the morning. They agreed. They had their dinner early and packed everything to make sure that no time would be wasted in the morning. Sir James woke up at three in the morning and started praying before he met his men for prayer. He finished praying and took his shower and went the hotel lobby where they would all meet. There was no one there. He waited for five minutes and went up to the captain's room and knocked. The captain told him he could not open his door and his room phone was not working. He knocked on the other brother's door and heard the same story. He started running around to all the rooms where his men were staying. They were all experiencing the same thing. He saw other guests coming out of their rooms. He went to the lobby to look for the manager but he wasn't there. He went to the manager's room and found him fast asleep. He woke up the manager and told him what was happening to his men. The manager took the keys and tried to open the doors but nothing happened. Sir James called the palace and asked to speak to Princess Grace. He told her what was going on and she told him to knock at all their rooms and tell them to start to worship. He told his men to worship right inside their rooms. They worshipped for an hour and Princess Grace woke up her father and mother and told them what was going on with Sir James' men.

They started worshipping too. Other guests woke up because of the worship of Sir James' men and at the palace, everyone woke up when they heard Princess Grace and her parents worshipping in the family room. They knew that something was not right for it was very early in the morning.

After an hour of worship, the Captain tried his door and found that it opened. He told the others to try their doors; they opened as well. Sir James went to Emmanuel's room and found him still sleeping. He was unaware of what was going on. Sir James woke Emmanuel up and helped him to get ready. Sir James called Princess Grace and told her they were fine and that they were preparing to leave. Princess Grace called Pastor Eric but got no answer. He called the hotel where they were and they told them that they had left the night before. King Yusuf was not happy. He told them that Pastor Eric had to pass through a dangerous village on the way to the new city. In that village, all the Kings were strengthened. Before entering the village, the mountains only allowed one to pass if the Gods approved of them. He told them his men knew better not to try to go at night and that they were supposed to call him first. He told them that he had to dispatch the army. King Wisdom told him he did not think that was a good idea.

Pastor Eric left at nine o'clock at night and the Captain told him that he had heard many bad and fearful stories about the village they had to pass through. But Pastor Eric's concern was that nobody went ahead to help prepare for the meeting. Even though Danny promised to go, there was nothing much he could do by himself. So they had to be there at night. They could work through the night to make the place ready. Danny had called them and told them that he would meet them at the city but that he was coming from a different direction. They drove well until they arrived near the top of the mountain and saw people dressed in black robes ahead of them blocking the road. They slowed down and all of a sudden, there was a very heavy mist.

The soldiers took out their guns and got ready to fire. Pastor Eric told them not to fire and instructed them to put their guns away, for the bible says that whoever lives by the sword will die by the sword. He told them to start worshipping. They began worshiping at eleven at night but the mist grew stronger and stronger as if the worship was doing nothing. Pastor Eric told them not to stop. They worshipped until midnight when Pastor Eric began singing the worship song they had sung upon arrival at the airport. "Let the spirit of God take over this country.' All the men sang the song together. It was as if their voices were opening the gates of heaven. As they sang, the mist began to clear. They could see the people clearly though they could not see their faces.

They continued with their praise and forgot about the people in the mist. They were enjoying themselves in the presence of the Lord. Pastor Eric's men were now in the spirit. Finally, they heard a voice asking them who they were and what they wanted. Pastor Eric told the voice that they were the worriers of Almighty God and they were on their way to the next city. The voice told them they were not welcome to pass through the village and they were not wanted in the city. Pastor Eric told the voice that the world is God's and they did not need permission from man to pass. They came to pass through that village and nothing or anyone could stop them. The voice told them that if they forced matters, they would not be responsible for what would happen to them. Pastor Eric told his men to continue singing. They did and Pastor Eric instructed his men to accompany each vehicle slowly through the mountains and into the village. Together there were eight hundred men.

They sang the song and started to march their way through the village. It was a distance of about twenty-three miles but they did not fatigued as they were enjoying themselves in the presence of the Lord. They sang the same song and continued marching until they saw the sunrise and realized that they were off the mountain. The Captain told Pastor Eric that the village was about five miles away. They continued marching and singing and they saw five men standing in the middle of the road ahead of them. They arrived at the men and Pastor Eric told them not to stop. They continued marching and the five men started running away. They sang their way through the village and when they were about five miles past the village, they stopped and praised the Lord for his goodness and mercy. They continued on to the next city.

King Yusuf received a phone call around eight in the morning to tell him that the chief of that village was dead. He was not told what had killed the man but he suspected that it had to do with Pastor Eric and his men. He asked the caller if he had seen his men and visitors. The man told him they were marching the whole night through their village and they had created many problems for them. The King asked him what kind of problems. The man told him that he believed the King knew what he was talking about. He told the King that if he was the one who sent those men he did not think that it was a wise idea. He would hear from the elders of his village and the guardians of the mountains soon.

After thirty minutes, he received another call from his uncle informing him that the wife of his son had gone missing. Her name was Yika. He told Princess Grace and King Wisdom that the woman who had left the dinner party sick was missing. She had been sleeping in bed with her husband when he woke up to discover that she was gone. She also lived in the village where Pastor Eric's men had marched. He told them that the person who had told him about the death of their chief had also told him that Pastor Eric's men were marching through their village and singing the whole night. Princess Grace realized that that explained why they could not get hold of them.

Pastor Eric knew that they must be worried at the palace. As soon as they arrived in the city at nine in the morning, he called Princess Grace and told her what had happened and that they had just arrived in the city. He thanked God that Danny had already begun preparing for the meeting and had invited many people. He told Princess Grace that there was a rumor going around that someone very important was dead and that something serious was going on. Princess Grace told him about the death of the chief of the village and the disappearance of the King's sister in-law.

What Pastor Eric did not know was that they had caused a great deal of damage to that village simply by worshipping. The villagers normally went outside the village and kidnapped children to come and feed to their God. But the previous night, their God had been disturbed in the mountains by Pastor Eric's men and since they were highly protected by some unknown power, this strange God could not hurt them. However, it had become very angry. The God went into the village and punished them for bringing these people into his home. Their God had never been disturbed by any power stronger than his own until that day. While Pastor Eric's men were singing and worshipping their God, there was a powerful wind blowing through the village. Many people were killed. Some disappeared and the villagers believed they had been taken by the angry God in the mountain. When they heard Yika was also gone, they began telling the story that their God had taken the people it favored so that when he destroyed them, his favorite people would not be hurt; for even though Yika was a woman, she was the chief Priest. She was the one who took the sacrifices to the God of the mountain.

They started the meeting and to their surprise, many people came and gave their lives to Christ. Before they had been told that no one was going to come and they were wasting their time. They heard that there were groups of people spreading the word that people should refuse to attend the meeting of Christians and that if they did attend, their God would seriously punish them. Since they were all afraid of their God, they decided not to go and sent messages for Pastor Eric's men not to come. They knew that if they disobeyed, they would be used as sacrifice to the God of the mountain. But now that they heard that Pastor Eric's men had a serious fight with the God of the great mountain and that none of Pastor Eric's men was dead, but rather most people in the village and in the city had died, they were convinced of the power of Pastor Eric's God. That was why they came to the meeting and did not mourn their chief or the others who had died in the village.

Everyone in the village and the city was talking about the power of the Christian God and how they would rather be under that God than the God who kills his people and ate them every year. They heard that the Christian God did not want any human sacrifices but rather that he just wanted to protect his people. They had also heard that their King had accepted this God and that he was very happy and at peace. There was also a story going on that his great uncle could not control him any longer. Stories were going around that the great uncle had tried to kill the King using the power of the mountain God and had failed. They were preaching the message of Christ but were unaware that they were doing so. They were evening knocking at other people's doors and telling them that if they don't come and seek the protection of the Christian God, they were going to die at night because the mountain God was coming back to kill more people. Villagers were running to the city to be under the protection of the Christian God. Many people came with their blankets and sleeping bags to sleep because they were afraid to go back to the village and they asked to see the King of the Christians. They told them there was no King or Chief but there was a Pastor. They came to Pastor Eric and asked him to please plead with his God to protect them from the anger of the God of the mountain.

Pastor Eric told them to listen to the message carefully and that they would have to dedicate their lives to Christ at the end of the service. He told them that they should not accept Jesus Christ out of fear or because they were afraid of the God of the mountain. He told them that in Jesus was everything including love, riches, eternal life, forgiveness, long life, divine favor, divine protection, wisdom, and much more. He explained that they should accept Jesus because they believed in Him and that He died for them and rose again for their salvation. They told Pastor Eric they understood. There were so many people that the palace was called to provide reinforcement. They said they believed that more than ten million people were there and the soldiers and police for that town and the villages surrounding that town could not control the people alone. They needed help and they needed it fast. The King ordered the nearby cities to provide help. Pastor Eric told the King that those people needed the bibles more than anybody. He said they should look for any bible they could find. King Yusuf ordered the production of Pastor Eric's booklet and the printers were told to produce twenty millions of them. They were instructed to take them to the city where the crusade was happening. He then sent his asset manager to bring all the bibles that remained in storage to the crusade. The asset manager told him they had received more bibles the previous day and they were still counting them so that they could give the report to the King. The King told him to count the bibles while loading them onto the trucks and that the trucks should start moving right away. Princess Grace wanted to go and help; she told the two Kings that she had to be there. At first they refused but Queen Fiona convinced her husband to let Princess Grace go. Then King Yusuf asked the soldiers to fly her there immediately.

They finished the first service and asked people to make room for the next service. Many people did not want to leave. They stayed and waited for the next service. Danny's ex-wives told him they wanted to go and help with church and they would leave after the Christians meeting. He advised them to cook and sell food to the people there because he had discovered that many people did not like leaving, instead they preferred to spend the whole day and evening there. He advised them to carry supplies to cook more food there. He then gave them two trucks loaded full of food supplies and told them to look for help for he knew they would need to serve many people. They made a lot of money and their supply was exhausted in two days. They were happy that the supply was empty for they were very tired from cooking day and night. They told Danny that they needed more supplies but he was busy. They knew if they went out to buy food supply, they would not be able to come back in. So they decided that they would prepare the remaining food for the Pastors and their visitors and that they'd close for the day and leave the little bit for tomorrow for the Pastors and visitors to have something to eat. For two days, none of them slept.

The second service began and Pastor Eric was very busy counseling. He did not know how the people were going to release him to go and preach. Everyone was busy. He told one of the young men to start the service by singing worship songs. The people learned the songs quickly and they began singing along with them. They heard a powerful woman's voice behind them and although none of them were expecting her, they knew Princess Grace had arrived. Pastor Eric heard her voice and smiled. He was so happy she had come. Pastor Eric excused himself and told them that his leader had arrived. He then told them they were going to have a service to remember for a very long time. He ran to greet Princess Grace and asked her if she could take over the service. She stepped forward and encouraged everyone to join in the worship. She told them that when you worship, you make power available. She said that everyone, no matter where they were, should lift their hands and join them in worship. She said there was no distance too great for the Holy Spirit. The Princess told them that the Holy Spirit, or the spirit of God would find them wherever they were. Everyone began to come forward and concentrate on worshipping. The reporter said that it was as if the heavens had opened up. They could not explain what was happening but they knew without a doubt that the power of God was available in that place. The reporter showed the faces of the people and how they were worshiping. Some were on their knees with tears streaming down their faces, some were standing up, and some were on the ground. Some who couldn't make it inside were on top of their cars. Everywhere they looked, people were worshipping. Even in the roads, they had stopped their cars and were listening on the radios and worshipping. Truly Jesus has taken over with so much power.

Pastor Eric told the reporter that the young princess who was the leader of this Christian movement had arrived and was causing havoc in the God of the Mountains. He said, "Fellow citizens, we are witnessing the era of the fall of the God of the mountain. Power to Jesus Christ!"

At the palace, they were watching it all happen. Princess Marisa came into the family room; she did not know that Princess Grace was gone. It was her first time witnessing Princess Grace in action. She could not believe that was the same girl she had been joking with yesterday. She did not seem like the same girl who had been sticking her tongue out at her for kissing a boy. Now she was mature and in power. She now understood why her husband-to-be and the Kings respect her so much. Princess Yeti watched with tears in her eyes. She couldn't believe that same young girl was as dangerous and powerful as that. They watched the service in tears. Emmanuel's mother was glued to the television and she did not hear anything or see anything going on around her. She wanted to get every bit of anointing and blessings from the service. All she wanted was to get as much as possible from this young Princess, The powerful girl of Jesus.

The whole palace was watching including the workers who were so proud to know Princess Grace. She started to preach the message. She began by referring them to Psalm 18:2 (NKJV), "The Lord is my rock and my fortress and my deliverer. My God, my strength in whom I will trust; My shield and the horn of my salvation, my stronghold." She encouraged them to live as that scripture taught. She then quoted Psalm 20:7–8 (NKJV). "Some trust in chariots and some in horses, but we trust in the name of the Lord our God. They are brought to their knees and fall, but we rise up and stand firm." She went on, "But we trust in the one who created Heaven and earth, the giver of life, Alfa and Omega, Rock of Ages, the founder of salvation, the God of forgiveness; The granter of Wisdom, Peace, and the father of Love and the owner of all riches in the Universe. I AM, I AM, Lion of Judah, Rose of Sharon. That, ladies and gentlemen, is my God whom I am proud of and have confidence in." The crowd went crazy for Jesus. They said she introduced Jesus in a way they had never heard before. You could fall in love with Jesus the way she introduced him.

When she finished the message, she led them to Christ and announced that they were going to be there the whole night. The crowd was very happy. They were cheering, clapping their hands, and jumping up and down. They were so happy and ready to worship the whole night. She then told them that they had to pray for the people who were missing that they would be released back to their families. The reporter told them that nobody could count the number of people who gave their life to Jesus Christ and the God of the mountain had lost the battle. The reporter told them that even he had given his life to the true God and he was happy about it.

They prayed for the missing people and she encouraged them to command in the name of Jesus the release of those people, wherever they were. The part they liked the most was when she told them to release the power and the fire of the Holy Spirit to destroy that creature that had taken the people away in the name of Jesus and to eliminate all the work of the dark kingdom in their country. She reminded them that the bible said that at the mention of the name Jesus Christ, every knee shall bow and every tongue shall confess that Jesus is Lord. So they had power in the mention of the name Jesus. They started commanding in the name of Jesus Christ. They looked up at the mountain where the God of that area lived and directed the power and fire of God to that area. People of King Yusuf's country witnessed the warfare prayer they have never seen before. They worshipped the whole night, singing and dancing to the Lord and praying. From time to time, they would lead people in Christ for the benefit of those who had just arrived. During the night prayer, many people were healed and the lame began to walk. With Pastor Eric's assistance, Princess Grace led the service the whole night. Around two in the morning, they saw a light on the top of the mountain. People began paying more attention to light, but Princess Grace told them to continue to pray and not to allow themselves to be distracted. Around three o'clock, the soldiers came to the pastor's entrance with five people; two women and three men. They claimed they were taken by the God of the mountain and they were able to escape because of a major earthquake that had been followed by fire and they saw the road leading to the village and began running. That was how they had met the soldiers who had brought them to the meeting. Princess Grace asked Pastor Eric to lead them to Christ and pray for them together with the soldiers who had brought them. They were surprised that she didn't pay much attention to their stories. She told the multitudes of people to continue to pray until sunrise.

Pastor Eric asked her why she did not care to listen to those people. She told the Pastor that they had to be aware of the tricks of the enemy. When they were praying they should not let anything cause them to lose focus. Whenever your prayers had been answered, the enemy has a way of causing distraction and sometimes the distraction came with the answer. But you should always remember that when you make a commitment, that you are going to pray until this time. You have made an appointment with God and you have to keep it. Don't stop because you found the answer. Stop at the time you told God you would stop. Because when you say you are going to pray the whole night, the angels of God are dispatched to be at that prayer meeting.

Because of the appointment you made, you must keep it and not let anything make you break your promise. Only then you will you get your answer followed by miracles and more blessings.

In the morning, they were surprised to realize that there were still as many people as the day before. Pastor Eric held the morning session to give Princess Grace time to rest. They divided the men into three groups. Some took their rest with Princess Grace and at two o'clock, some took their rest with Pastor Eric. Finally, some left at eight o'clock but did not want to sleep so they came back around ten that night; others came back at twelve. They spent the second night praising and worshipping again. People were still coming and most people did not leave. The next day which was also the last day, Princess Grace shared with them some scriptures to always refer to which would encourage them to stay strong in the Lord for He would guide and protect them at all times. She further told them that their King would send a minister for that region soon and they would be able to have a leader near them every day. They were very happy to hear that. She prayed for them and introduced all the men who had come to minister to them. She had a gift for them from their King, King Yusuf. They made joyous noise to hear that their King had sent them gifts. She then instructed his men to distribute the bibles among them. There were people distributing the bibles at every entrance as well as in every row inside. King Yusuf was very happy to see how happy his people were to receive the bibles

Pastor Eric introduced Danny to Princess Grace and told her that he was the one who had brought the women who had been cooking for them. She asked Danny to call those women. They came and she prayed for them and blessed them. She told them she was grateful for the work they had done and she told them that their work in the ministry had started. She told them to take the bibles and help with the distribution and they should see the Captain so they could register their names to be workers of the Kingdom of God. They were very happy that she had prayed for them and allowed them to be the workers in the kingdom of Heaven. Danny asked her if she could pray for the young wife who could not have children because of the injuries she had sustained at his hands. She asked him to bring her in. She came and Princess Grace called Pastor Eric and together they prayed for her. She told the young woman that she had a big heart since she was able to forgive the person who had hurt her so badly. The Princess told her that God would bless her and she would be caring for a child of her own at the same time the following year. She believed it and she was very happy. She asked Princes Grace if she could pray for the man who was supposed to marry her, since he was admitted in a mental hospital due to heartbreak. Princess prayed for him and used her as a contact point. She told her the young man was healed as they speak. Princess Grace invited Danny to come with them to the palace since she had heard of his good works. Princess Grace told all the people to study their bibles seriously since the word of God was their weapon against evil. She told them that they needed to know the word of God and to know what God said about them and they would never be afraid of anything or anybody. She encouraged them to keep coming to the stadium to worship as one and share the word of God together by studying the bible together. The leader would arrive shortly and they should support him and those who could give time to help should do that. She told them they had a lot of work to do in that country and they needed people to help to move the Kingdom of God forward. People were already asking where they could register to help with the work.

The day they were leaving, they spent most of their time counseling and taking the names and contacts of the people who wanted to help with the church and prayer. They held the service that morning. After the service, people did not want to go back. They wished they could stay there. Danny was happy to see the Captain holding meetings with his ex-wives and to know that they will be doing God's work. He told himself he couldn't have asked for a better ending than that. They distributed the books that Pastor Eric had written to give to their loved ones who couldn't make it to Christ. They should go out into the world to share the good news of the Lord Jesus with everyone they met.

They packed their things and bid farewell to the multitude of people they had met. Many people drove along beside them for a long time, singing gospel songs. The people had enjoyed the visit very much and they did not want them to go. Princess Grace called King Yusuf on their way to tell him they were coming back. She told him that people in that city needed a minister quickly. He told her that the same man who had preached with so much wisdom was being sent there. He was with Sir James at the moment but the King would tell him as soon as he arrived. King Yusuf heard the noise and asked her when they would start coming. She told him they had left an hour ago. He wondered what the noise could be. She told him that many villagers and city people were traveling with them and that they were singing loudly. She laughed and said, "Guess what?"

"What?" the King asked.

The Princess told him they were passing the same mountain and the people had come to escort them through the mountain which meant they were no longer afraid of the mountain. They were singing and marching. The King laughed because he knew that they had completely won the battle. Princess Grace laughed and told King Yusuf that fear had been defeated and the Devil had lost. King Yusuf was very happy to hear what Princess Grace had just said and to know that they loved them so much that they'd escort them without fear. They had clearly received Jesus as their Lord completely.

17

The King's uncle was very upset with what had been going on and he was preparing to go and meet with King Yusuf himself. He told his people that it was time to finish up the King or silence him for good as punishment for what he had done in their country. He reminded the people that since the beginning of time, no other Gods had been allowed in their country. But since the King had traveled to a foreign country and brought back his belief in a foreign God, he had brought that God of the dead man into his country. Now people were being harassed by a Ghost God. He told them that he had been telling people that it was a Holy Ghost. The King's uncle told the people that he was sick and tired of all of it and he would end all the rubbish that was going on in his country. It was time to show King Yusuf who is and has been ruling the country all along. He told them that when he arrives, they would know he had arrived because they would hear it on the news and they would be back to controlling everything again. They could celebrate by returning to their God all those people who had been rebellious. He wanted to arrive before his visitors returned so that he could humiliate the King in front of those visitors. He warned his people that if those visitors were not careful they would go down with him.

The people knew trouble was coming because of how upset he was. They knew what happens when he got upset. He told them that no one belittles his country, his people, and his Gods and gets away with it. They should watch and see. He told them that from that day on, the people of that country would know never to cross him. He told the people that he thought it was about time they started thinking of inviting the Queen mother to handle the situation. They pleaded with him not to call the Queen mother because the rumor was that when the Queen mother fought, she killed everyone, even those who were on her side. The old stories were that she moved with a heavy wind to make sure that she was not seen and the wind destroyed everything in its path. Houses were destroyed and many people were blown out to sea. He finally told them that he would not invite her just yet, but if King Yusuf did not stop the madness of Christianity in their country, he may have no choice but to invite the Queen mother. He told them that one thing was for certain; King Yusuf could not rule their country anymore. He had done enough damage and it was time for him to go. The people agreed and told the King's uncle that he would make a better King than King Yusuf. They told him they were all behind him and that they would support him in whatever he wanted them to do. He laughed and asked them how they felt about staying in the palace. They were so happy, they told him they would like that very much and they would forever be at his service.

One of the men told the King's uncle that he thought he should cool down and not make a hasty decision as more than half of the nation had accepted the new God of the Christians. He became so angry with the man that he asked him who he thought he was. The man told him that if he did anything wrong, they would all have to pay for it. The King's uncle was upset and asked the rest of the people if anyone else thought that way. They were all quiet. The King's uncle asked them if they were just going to sit there and listen to their leader being insulted. They became angry and sentenced the dissenter to death. They killed him right there and left his body to be fed to their God of the mountain.

After they finished, the King's uncle called the King to tell him he would be on his way first thing in the morning. He told the King that there was a lot at stake because of what he had done. He told the King that he could not protect him anymore.

The King told him he did not need his protection as he had Jesus. His uncle told him that he would regret his words and he would know that he was just a small boy once they were finished with him. King Yusuf told him he had better watch his mouth because the last time he checked, he was still the King. The King's uncle became very angry with the King and reminded him that even his father, the great King Yusuf, could not talk to him like that. He told King Yusuf that he was too weak to be a King and he was going to prove it when he arrived. He asked King Yusuf what made him so bold when he knew very well that he could destroy him quickly. King Yusuf told him he wished he could destroy him, but he could only do that in his wildest dreams. The truth of the matter was that he could never destroy him. The King's uncle was boiling with anger. He wished he was close to King Yusuf so that he could choke him. He said as much to King Yusuf. King Yusuf was also getting angry with his uncle because he was treating him like a small boy. His uncle told him he had behaved like a small boy by forgetting the foundation of his country.

While all this was happening, King Yusuf was with his wife. She left and called King Wisdom for help. She asked King Wisdom to tell King Yusuf to stop and apologize to his uncle for she feared that the King's uncle would kill them all. King Wisdom arrived in time to hear the furious exchange and he could tell that King Yusuf was not giving in. Queen Fatima begged him to be quiet but he would not. As he hung up, Queen Fatima asked him if he knew that his uncle would not forgive him and he was going to kill them all. King Yusuf told her he would not kill them because Jesus would not let him. He told his wife that gone were the days when his uncle ruled them with fear and it was time for his uncle to give him the respect a King deserved.

King Yusuf explained to King Wisdom how his uncle had been controlling his country with dark powers and now he was angry because of the Christian crusades. He was upset that the people had given their lives to Christ. King Yusuf explained how in the past, he had gone along with his uncle's wishes because he was afraid of him. King Wisdom told King Yusuf that they should only fear the Lord and no other human being. He asked King Yusuf if he remembered what he had told him about the palace staff in his country. King Yusuf said he remembered. He told him that was the correct way to live so that people had mutual respect for each other and not fear. Fear is of the devil. Queen Fatima told him he did not understand the King's uncle. They told her that she should trust in the Lord and fear no man. King Yusuf told his friend that his uncle had made the people of his country fearful of him, as if he was God, but that it was time for that fear to come to an end.

The King's uncle went to bed very angry that night. He called some of his members and told them how a small boy who calls himself King had insulted him and even threatened to kill him for telling him to stop the Christian madness. They listened to him carefully and asked him what should be done. They all told him that the King had to die and it had to be a disgraceful death. He was happy with them. He told them he was going to sneak into the King's chamber at night with the black mamba snake. He would instruct the mamba to kill both the King and his wife, since he has tried using magic from a distance and did not work. After that he would assume the King's powers and sentence any dissenters to death. His followers were happy with the arrangement and they asked him if he needed any help. He told them he did not, that he would take care of the King and Queen by himself. He would teach the whole world that nobody opposes him and gets away with it.

Princess Grace and Pastor Eric's group arrived at the palace first. Princess Marisa was taking a walk in the garden, picking flowers when she saw them. She dropped her flowers and run as fast as she could to meet them. Pastor Eric was talking to some soldiers but when he saw her coming, he met her and they hugged. She told him she missed him as though he had been gone for a whole year. He laughed and gave her a gift he had brought. He had told Danny that he was engaged to the most beautiful girl in the world and he wanted Danny to find him something from that city to take with him to give to her. Danny knew who the girl was for he had been there when they first met. Danny laughed and told him he did not know that Christians could be romantic, especially Pastors. They were such a beautiful couple. Princess Marisa was beautiful with her shining long black hair. She was tall and slim as well. Pastor Eric was tall with blond hair. When it came to beauty, this couple was perfect.

Princess Grace was in the truck behind them and she looked at them and smiled for they were adorable together. She knew Princess Marisa was going to make Pastor Eric a very happy man. She came from a land where wives are obedient to their husbands, and she knew that Pastor Eric would not abuse her. Princess Grace started walking towards them and Princess Marisa saw her and ran to greet her and told her she had seen her on television and she had been fearsome and beautiful at the same time. Princess Grace laughed and asked Marisa if she was talking about her or somebody else because she could not imagine herself being fearsome. The two ladies laughed and Princess Grace asked her if she had seen Pastor Eric even though she knew she had. Princess Marisa told her that she had but she knew that whenever Princess Grace was around, Pastor Eric became serious. Princess Marisa told Princess Grace that these men respected her a great deal. She told her that she respected them as well. Princess Marisa laughed and told her she did not understand the power she had on people. Even the Kings respect her. Both ladies laughed and Princess Grace changed the subject.

Just when they were about to enter the palace, Sir James' group arrived and they went back to welcome them. That evening, the King asked his cooks to cook something special for the soldiers of God. At the dinner, King Yusuf told them he had never been as proud of anybody as he was of them. He proposed a toast to the great God's Warriors. The whole time, he held Emmanuel's hand and kept looking at him. He finally picked him up and kissed him and told him he had made him the happiest father in the whole world. He told him he was going to start preaching in the church near the palace. But while the church construction was underway, he was going to send him to King Wisdom's country for three months to learn more and he would come and start ministering in the Royal Church when he returned. He told Emmanuel that he would spend most of his time with Pastor Eric. He looked at King Wisdom and smiled. He then told him he would be calling him every day to hear how he was doing. Princess Grace laughed and told Emmanuel that the King should just tell him the truth, that he would be babysitting him by phone. Everybody laughed. The King said, "You can't blame an old man for trying." He also told them that in four months, there would be some tutors coming to his country to teach ministry school and all of them were going to attend. They were very happy. They stood up and cheered and thanked the King. One of the Captains proposed a toast to King Yusuf.

King Yusuf told them that the Lord Jesus had been accepted in the country. After they sat down, the King told the man from Sir James' group who had preached with the heavy anointing that he would be sending him to the city from which Pastor Eric had just come in two days' time. He should take the contacts of the people who were going to help him from the Captain of Pastor Eric's group. The minister's name was Rocky so the King joked and told him he might have to change his name to something more suitable for a Pastor. Rocky told the King that it was suitable and that he should think of him as Pastor Rocky! King Yusuf told him he was right and that it sounded dangerous and fearful. Everybody laughed.

Since Danny had taken Pastor Eric's advice and had come with them, he was happy to hear King Yusuf mention his name. Pastor Eric told the King that they had come with Danny. King

Yusuf asked him to introduce him. He was sitting at the other table. They called him and the King told him he had heard of his work and the great contribution he had made and he was very happy. He wanted Danny to be one of the ministers so he should attend the ministry school in four months. Danny was so happy to know that the King was happy with him and that he knew him by name. He also told him he heard of the work of the women he brought. He wanted those women full-time in the ministry. He felt like jumping and screaming with joy. The evening was a huge celebration.

Sir James and his wife were sitting at the same table with Pastor Eric and Princess Marisa, Princess Grace, Prince Brian, Lady Elisa, the two Captains of both groups, and the two other men from Sir James' group. Lady Elisa and Prince Brian were busy playing and giggling at nothing. Princess Grace and Princess Marisa had tried to silence them on several occasions but finally gave up. Princess Yeti was at the same table with the Kings and Queens together with Emmanuel and his mother. Unfortunately for Soyab, his captain had chosen him as one of the people to guard the dinner celebration. He was standing at the far end of the room but he could see that his wife and son were at the same table with the Kings and they looked happy and very comfortable. As for Emmanuel, no one had to ask how King Yusuf felt about him; it was obvious. Princess Yeti was embarrassed by Prince Brian's behavior when she saw him and Lady Elisa making funny faces at some of the food. She told them that it was her fault as she had never given Prince Brian an opportunity to grow up. Since his father had died, she had been treating him like a baby. That was why at fifteen, he still behaved like he was eight. King Wisdom told her that children will always be children and it was useless to try to change them into elders. What they didn't know was that Prince Brian used to sleep in his mother's chamber until two months ago. When King Yusuf heard that, he told Princess Yeti to stop that madness immediately. He told her that he was now grown up and he had to learn to sleep in his own chamber. He slept with the light on and Princess Yeti put the baby monitor in his room.

Prince Brian was the next in line for the throne if King Yusuf did not have any children. The King was concerned with how his sister was raising his nephew. She had been afraid of the great uncle stealing her child.

On the other side, Lady Elisa still ran to the Queen's chamber and pretended to be asleep so that they did not send her to her chamber. It looked like Prince Brian and Lady Elisa were now friends because Lady Elisa did not run back to the King's table as much as she used to. She was enjoying herself. Prince Brian did not run back to his mother either, which was a relief. They seemed to be enjoying their silly behavior and jokes together.

One of Sir James' men told Sir James that since the beginning of the kingdom, they had never seen the King laughing, joking and eating like he had been that evening. Now the soldiers were able to sit and eat in the same room with the King. Before, the soldiers had only been allowed to guard the Royals; talking to them was forbidden. The man told Sir James that Jesus really was God as He had brought the change to their country. The man said, "Look at us now, we are Royals." He also told Sir James that he would remember this evening for the rest of his life. Sir James laughed and told him that Jesus always brought peace, unity, and love. That was why they had to let the whole world know about Him. They needed to bring peace to other places where people were still oppressed. Sir James looked at the room and decided he was going to write a story about his journey. He told King Wisdom and the King told him that he should write a book about the whole country. Sir James decided he was going to write a book about the two great Kings; one from the east and one from the south. King Wisdom laughed and told him he would buy that book.

Sir James began writing his book that night and made sure he remembered the names of the cities they had travelled to and the names of the people he had worked with. He wrote down the miracles Princess Grace had performed in the name of Jesus. He titled the book, "The Great Evangelism of the Two Kings and a Princess," but Lady Samantha told him it should be called, "The Power of the Innocent Mind." He agreed.

The Captain of the group told Sir James that he could have named the book, "The Rise of Jesus and the Fall of the Wicked God." Sir James laughed and told him that when he finished writing the book, he would understand why he gave it the title he did, but for now, he was just going to start writing something to make sure he did not forget most of the things he had experienced. He asked Sir James when they would be coming back. He was told that the work in their country was done, but they would come for a visit to see how everyone was getting along. He reassured them that he would definitely be coming back to attend Pastor Eric and Princess Marisa's wedding. Sir James told him that his wife was expecting and he was not sure if they would be able to travel, but if she was not doing well, he might come by himself and leave her with her parents. His wife laughed and told him he was not going to leave her alone, she was coming to witness the wedding of the Royals.

King Yusuf looked at the young girl sitting in front of him and tried to imagine how a young girl could produce results like the ones he had seen and how she could organize people like she had when she did not have a business background or education in any way. He also noticed that all the people working with her respected her a great deal; including her parents. He had to admit that even he had started respecting her for everything she told him had came to pass. She knew what she was doing. There were many thoughts going through his mind and many questions he wanted to ask but he did not want to offend his visitors. He was wondering how God had poured His power and blessings into a young girl. Then he remembered the story Sir James had written for the newspaper few years ago called, "The Power of an Innocent Mind." He spoke out loud, unaware that he was doing so, "So God wanted to work with innocent minds." They asked him what he said and he was startled. Princess Grace had heard him so she told them that he was summarizing the article Sir James had written when he'd first met her. King Yusuf was surprised that she knew what was in his mind. Before they could discuss the topic further, the butler came in to announce the arrival of his uncle. King Yusuf warned them about his uncle who practiced the dark powers openly. The mood in the room changed immediately. King Wisdom asked him if he wanted them to excuse them. He told them no, he wanted them around. He told the butler to escort his uncle to their table.

18

King Yusuf's uncle entered the palace. He greeted his nephew and ignored his visitors. He looked at Princess Marisa and told her she had grown. She just sat there and looked at him without saying a word. He became angry and asked Princess Yeti if these were the manners she taught her children. Were they not taught to respect elders? Princess Yeti told him not to start criticizing her. He got even angrier and asked her what business she had talking to him with such disrespect. Did she know who he was?

"I know who you are," Princess Yeti answered. "What are you going to do? Kill me like you killed my husband and children?"

"Calm down," King Yusuf told Princess Yeti. The uncle turned at King Yusuf and asked him if he thought telling his sister to be quiet would make him forget about the conversation they'd had the day before. He told the King that Princess Yeti learned to disrespect him from him, her brother. The King was getting upset and trying to control himself because of his visitors even his bodyguards were ready to take down his uncle. The King's uncle saw the bodyguards standing and ready and asked the King what he thought they could possibly do to him.

"I will silence you along with your guards," the uncle said to the King in front of everyone.

King Yusuf said, "Get out of this palace if you came to threaten us in front of our visitors."

The uncle told his nephew that he was not going anywhere and he had come to take over the throne since the King had lost his mind and was not fit to be a King. King Yusuf stood up and asked his uncle if he was aware that he could be sentenced to death for what he had just said. He told King Yusuf that he was the God of that country and nobody in their right mind would try to carry out orders against him. One of the captains marched forward and asked the King to give him orders to remove the King's uncle and he would obey. Other soldiers stepped forward and formed a circle around their King.

"We will obey your orders," they said to the King. King Wisdom's soldiers stood by their King and his family and told him they were waiting for his orders. The uncle turned and looked at them and asked them what had gotten into them. He asked his nephew if these were his visitors who were teaching his people to believe in a dead man.

"What nonsense is this?" the King's uncle asked.

Princess Grace was not used to people insulting her Father in heaven. But instead of being angry with him, she felt pity for him for she knew that he was lost. She moved to where he was standing and asked him what he believed in. He told her that he could have built himself a God of Gold but then he realized that he already had all the gold he needed on earth. Princess Grace cut him short and asked him what he believed in. He looked at his nephew and said with pride that he chose the mighty snake. He opened his silver briefcase and there inside was a black mamba snake. Princess Grace felt even sorrier for him. She asked him if he was aware that he had chosen something which he has been given power over to believe in. Before Princess Grace could finish, he cut her short and told her that he worshiped snakes because they were the most powerful creatures on earth. They were his Gods. This particular snake originated from far away countries and it was known as the deadliest of them all. Princess Grace told him to stop speaking because that was blasphemy. She told him that he should never allow words like that to come out of his mouth.

He looked at King Yusuf and asked him if anyone had taught this young girl that women were not allowed to speak in the presence of men, especially when they had not been given permission to do so. King Yusuf told him that she was not just a woman and he had insulted the only faith she knew. The uncle told him that had been his point. King Yusuf told him that the young lady was the most powerful minister of the word of God and that they were all there to support her. The uncle laughed and told his nephew that he pitied him and that he now knew that he was not fit to be a King. He had lost his mind to defend such behavior and to tell him he was following a child. Princess Yeti told him to leave their visitors alone and get out of their palace. The soldiers tried to step closer, ready to take him out but the King told them to wait. The King's uncle was more annoyed that his nephew was not defending him and that he had chosen the side of a young girl. He decided he would deal with his nephew later. He felt anger building inside him and tried to control himself. He told them he felt like opening his case and letting the black mamba deal with all of them. He laughed to himself and told them he was imagining how they would all be screaming and begging for their lives as the great creature dealt with them. Princess Grace was boiling with anger towards him. She stepped forward.

The uncle ignored Princess Grace even though he knew who she was because he had seen her on television several times talking to his people and telling them to believe in her God. He always turned off his television when he saw her speaking. His nephew, the King had not invited him when they were arriving. Instead, he watched the ceremony on television like everyone else. Why should he show them any respect? In addition to all that, his God had warned him not to listen to them and not to get close to them. But he had come here today because he was upset with what had been done in his village and he had to bring everything to an end. While all these thoughts were going through his mind, he remembered to go back to the topic. He continued and told them that everyone was afraid of the black mamba for it is the most dangerous and poisonous snake on earth.

"Not to the children of God," Princess Grace said. She told him, "Behold, I give you authority to trample on serpents and scorpions, and over all the power of the enemy, and nothing shall by any means hurt you" (Luke 10:19, NKJV); she told him that is what our God says about us. The old man told her that talk was cheap and she was only a child. He said that she had been brain-washed but it was not her fault, it was the foolish people who had brainwashed her.

By now, King Wisdom was controlling his emotions towards him and praying for the Holy Ghost to please help him. King Yusuf couldn't take it when he insulted his friend King Wisdom and he told the soldiers to deal with his uncle. Princess Grace asked King Yusuf to give them a moment first. This was the first time he had addressed her since he arrived. He told her that if he could take his snake out, they would all scatter and run in differ-ent directions. Even her father, the King and his nephew would run in fear. Everybody was quiet during the discussion between the King's uncle and Princess Grace.

Princess Grace went to him and told him to tell his snake to come to her. He became angry and asked her how she dared challenge the power of his snake when she knew very well that her God had died on the cross many years ago. Did she know the Queen mother of all the snakes had been living for over thou-sands of years and had never died? She was lucky she was his nephew's visitor and it was his responsibility to keep them alive, otherwise she was going to regret her actions. He would probably kill them like their God had been killed. She stepped forward and, with anger in her voice, told him to open the case and to tell the snake to rise and come to her. Out of anger, he stood up and looked at everybody and told them he had warned her but she would not listen. He said what was about to happen was not his fault. He looked at her with spite and opened the case. The black snake lifted its head up. Princess Grace stepped closer to the snake and looked directly into its eyes. The moment their eyes met, the snake burst into flames. It started to burn right in front of everyone. The old man jumped and moved away from the case. He asked her what kind of witchcraft she was practicing. She kept on looking at the snake until it was completely reduced to ash. Then she looked at the old man and walked back to where she had been and asked him where his God was now. He didn't answer. Princess Grace was so angry, she took a step towards him and he began to urinate on himself. She looked at him, shook her head, and walked away.

The old man thought to himself, *The snake had burned to ashes.* She did not touch it; she just looked at it. The old man was now afraid of her. He asked her what kind of a person was she. She told him that she was the kind of person who was filled with the Holy Ghost, the one who had given her life to Almighty God, the true living God and the only God. The creator of heaven and earth and that God was Alfa and Omega, the beginning and the end of everything. She was so bold and the old man became even more afraid of her. He was now shivering and he didn't realize that he had wet himself in the process. Everyone present had seen a side of Princess Grace they had never seen before. They had seen the fall of the aggressive and rude man. Princess Marisa was so happy that somebody had finally put him in his place. They never thought a young girl would be the one to put him in his place. What they didn't know was that had been the Holy Spirit working through the young lady. They thought God would have to come down himself to deal with him. Princes Marisa was also more afraid of her dear friend Princess Grace for she felt she did not know her at all. As young as she was, she was the one defending the Kings and everyone in the palace. She was the one bold enough to answer him and to challenge him in public. She realized that she did not know Princess Grace and she told herself that she had to be careful what she said in her presence for she was like a tiger among them. Princess Grace started to leave the dining area and looked at Lady Elisa and told her to lead the old man to Christ. She left the room.

After she left, they all stepped forward and looked at the ashes inside the silver case and the powerful man who had arrived in the room with the air of arrogance and rude behavior. He had been humbled and humiliated in front of everyone. There were so many thoughts in everyone's mind but the strange thing was that even Lady Elisa who always had something to say was silent. The old man was still standing by the wall as if he was about to run away in his wet pants when Lady Elisa broke the silence by singing a worship song. Everyone but the King's uncle joined in. They praised the Lord with their hands lifted up. They glorified Him and told Him how wonderful and powerful He was. When the song ended, Lady Elisa called the King's uncle to come and stand in the middle of the circle they had formed to receive Jesus as his Lord and Savior. Like an obedient child, he stepped forward and received the Lord Jesus as his Lord and personal savior. When they finished, Lady Elisa went to King Wisdom and said, "Daddy, can you do the honor of laying hands on him so that he will be filled with the Holy Spirit?" The King stepped forward to lay hands on him. The King's uncle immediately started speaking in unknown tongues. He could not stop. He was speaking loudly and rolling on the floor. Danny was watching all this for he knew the uncle very well and knew how powerful he was. Now a young girl had dropped him from the high place and even the youngest among them was the one telling him what to do and leading him to Christ? He smiled to himself and thought that at least he was led by a man and he did not boast publicly like him. He told himself that he should never cross these young people because they were the most dangerous and powerful with their God, Jesus Christ. For now, he understand why Pastor Eric respected this Princess so much. He became afraid of her. She was really something else. She did not talk too much but when she did, she produced unexplainable power. He told himself that he had a lot to learn in this new faith. He said to himself that he wished he was a child, then Jesus would pour this kind of power into him. He looked back at his journey in life and knew that if he was given that power, he could have abused it. However, he was still grateful that he had Jesus and he had gotten him in a respectable way without being arrogant about his evil life in public.

At one thirty in the morning, they left him to go to bed. King Yusuf told his men to take him to the family room since it was the closest, for he did not trust his men as they were upset with his uncle. He knew soldiers because he had been a solider himself. The other reason was that his uncle never allowed anybody to enter his chamber, but after seeing the snake, he understood and he did not want his men to meet with the evil in his chamber. He told them to bring a blanket and throw it on top of him. The once arrogant and pompous man was crawling on the floor weeping. King Yusuf felt pity for him, for he had never seen his uncle out of control. However, he was happy that he had finally gotten the help he needed even though he didn't know he needed help.

The soldiers were still very upset with him for attacking their King in front of them and his visitors. They wished the King would just give them permission to deal with him, just for a few minutes. But the King told them they should let the Holy Spirit deal with him and strip him of his arrogance and evil powers. The Captain told the King that he would bring more soldiers to guard the King and his visitors for he did not trust the old man at all. It was done and some soldiers were placed outside to guard the family room. They had seen the soft men who were preaching the word of God like humble children turning into lions when a man threatened their King. These men were ready to kill for their King without mercy. They knew that if the King didn't stop them, something bad could have happened in front of them. That night, the King was also very proud of his soldiers. He saw the love and respect he had never known they had for him. He told his wife that he had never been as proud of them as he was at that moment. He said that he would miss them when they retired. His wife advised him to leave somebody behind to take care of him. He already knew that he would and Soyab would also be his bodyguard with the others. He was going to tell him on the last day as King Wisdom was leaving to his country.

Princess Yeti was very happy that a young girl had put his uncle in his place. She told her daughter that she wished that the whole country and world had been there to witness that. But then God does not work like that. She felt as though she could have invited him to a public place and dealt with him in front of the media and everyone for the benefit of those he had hurt while he was under that artificial power. The King's family went to bed with smiles on their faces that night. Princess Marisa and Prince Brian were also very happy and celebrating the fall of their great uncle. As for King Wisdom and Queen Fiona, they were still in shock over what they had seen their daughter do. They did not even know who she was anymore or how she knew she would be able to kill that snake. They were afraid to ask her. But then this girl was raised in a way that she knew no fear. She believed every word in the bible without question or doubt. They felt like they did not know her at all for every day they saw a different person in her.

That night. Princess Yeti had a dream of herself flying and she was shouting to her brother so that he would see how free she was. In the morning, she told them her dream. She told them that if they knew how many lives they had saved by ministering deliverance to her uncle, they would be shouting for joy nonstop, for evil was in control of their country in a big way through their uncle. Many people were scarified to this evil God. People were disappearing and small children were taken from their parents. They were told never to talk for if they told anyone, they would be given to the Gods and the Gods would deal with them. She told them people were living in fear and that most people who had money had left the country to live freely. She concluded by saying thanks to Jesus, those people were now free as well as their children and their generations to come would be free as well.

In the morning when they came for the Morning Prayer, they heard him while they were walking down the hallway, they could not believe he was still going on. They went to the family room where they usually held their morning prayer and found him lying on the floor. He had vomited all kinds of things. They looked like small snakes but they all look dead. There was also some grass and all kinds of disgusting, ugly things they couldn't stand to look at any longer. King Wisdom told King Yusuf to close the door and not to let his people inside until later after God told them what to do.

They started the Morning Prayer. Princess Grace came in a bit later and joined in the worship. They thanked God for His deliverance and salvation of the King's uncle and prayed for the nations, for the Kings, the presidents, and salvation for all souls. King Yusuf gave the closing prayer. He told his visitors that if the only thing that came from this mission was leading his uncle to the kingdom of God, he would still be the happiest man in the continent for many people's lives have been saved. He welcomed them again to his country and his palace, and told them they were his family and they would always be viewed as family. He then invited them to breakfast and called on his butler to not allow anybody into the big family room until further notice. But many people had lost their appetites after seeing what the uncle had vomited.

They had started eating their breakfast when Lady Elisa asked King Yusuf in her childish voice if he had known all along that his great uncle was eating his God's babies. Everybody laughed. Even Princess Grace could not control herself. Lady Elisa was sitting next to King Wisdom and he looked at her and asked her to come to him. She did and the great King cuddled her while laughing. When he finished laughing, he told them that the room was full of all kinds of innocent minds. He looked at Princess Grace and told her that he was thankful to her for bringing Lady Elisa to be part of his family. King Yusuf asked Lady Elisa if she wanted to go and check on the great uncle. She laughed and told him she believed that was the work for the great Kings. There was so much laughter in the breakfast room that they did not hear that great uncle had stopped until Queen Fatima said, "Good morning, uncle."

He said, "Good morning, daughter," and looked at Princess Grace and said, "Your God is fearsome yet forgiving." He told them not to enter the family room. He said, "You don't want to see what is in there"

Lady Elisa said, "Oh, we already know what is in there, great uncle." King Wisdom put his hand over her mouth to stop her from speaking but he was too late. The words were already out.

The uncle laughed and said, "So, Christians have a sense of humor too." He excused himself to go and clean up. He looked like a mess and smelled terrible. He asked the King which chamber he should use. The King called the butler to take him to his chamber he told him he had never given his chamber away. Only God knew what went on in that chamber. He did not reply to the King. He just walked to his chamber quietly. For the first time in his life, he had no words and he felt very light, as though a weight had been lifted from him. He stopped and looked back at Princess Grace and thanked her for sparing his life and saving his soul. With that, he followed the butler to his chamber.

They were still eating their breakfast when they heard a loud scream and the sound of someone running. The King's uncle ran past the soldiers and the butler and burst through the door to the breakfast room. He ran straight to Princess Grace and grabbed her like a baby holding onto its mother. He asked her to please help him. They could not believe that this rude man who had enjoyed killing people was afraid of anything. The way he ran past them and went straight to Princess Grace was shocking as she was the same person he had wanted to kill with the snake the night before. She asked him what the matter was. He could not talk. He kept on pointing at his chamber and finally he said, "There! There! Please help!" He was shaking so much it seemed as though he was about to collapse. His eyes were wide with fear and he said, "Please help. Somebody help. We are all going to die. Help please." Nothing he was saying made any sense. Princess Grace told him to come with her but he refused and told her that the largest among them should go into the chamber. He looked at King Yusuf and told him he would never again enter that chamber. They all went outside towards his chamber to see what he was talking about. They all stood behind Princess Grace, as if they were hiding behind her. Princess Grace was about to enter the chamber when the spirit of God stopped her.

She stopped and went silent for two minutes before she called everybody to come and worship outside the chamber. While they were worshipping, they heard loud banging noises inside and it sounded as if two huge bulls were fighting inside. They became afraid and wanted to run away because the noise was so loud and it sounded as if the chamber was falling apart. The palace workers heard the noise and came running to see what was going on. The noise could be heard as far as the gate. Most of them joined the worship without having to ask. They could see the walls of the chamber shaking. Princess Grace told them not to stop worshipping, no matter what happened. They worshipped as if their life depended on it. Finally, the noise stopped after an hour or two; they had lost track of time. The great uncle was standing next to the gate, ready to run at the first sign of anything wrong. He could not concentrate on the worship. They continued worshipping for about two more hours until Princess Grace told them it was time for prayer. They prayed and prayed. First, they prayed warfare prayers and it was as if the heavens were shaking due to their voices and cries unto Almighty God. They followed with praises and thanksgiving. Princess Grace gave a closing prayer of thanksgiving. Finally, she asked King Yusuf and King Wisdom to enter the chamber with her.

As they entered the living room, they saw first that many things had been broken. They began to wonder where the noise had been coming from, as the damage did not seem that extensive. King Yusuf went to the bedroom door and opened it, he was about to put his head inside when he turned and ran, leaving King Wisdom and his daughter inside the chamber. All the people outside were very surprised to see the great King running away like that. He passed the people and collected himself, remembering who he was and what he had just done. King Wisdom turned to see what he had been running away from. He looked inside for less than a second and snatched Princess Grace by the hand and began running. Princess Grace stopped them and went back inside. Both Kings, who had been commanders of great armies, ran for their lives. King Wisdom was afraid for her; he begged her not to go inside. Princess Grace invited the Holy Spirit to go inside of the chamber with her. She was there for about five minutes and came outside to tell them that all was well and that it was dead. The two Kings could not tell what they had seen, but they knew that it had been huge. They understood why the King's uncle had run away. They were sweating out of fear. Lady Elisa looked at them with her eyes wide open. She could not believe that she had just seen the two great Kings running for their lives. She said to herself loud, "Wow! another story to tell for a very long, long, long time." She looked King Wisdom in the eye but she knew better than to say anything to him at that moment. She knew her time would come. Queen Fiona took her hand and pulled her away from the King without saying a word.

Everyone began to suspect that there must be a snake or a great creature of some sort inside. What they did not anticipate was the size of the creature. It was so big that they had never seen anything like it. It had rolled on and along the bed as well as on the floor with its mouth wide open by the door as if it was gasping for air. It was as if it was ready to swallow something big. The wide open mouth was big enough to swallow a whole man with ease and its body was big enough to accommodate up to hundred human bodies or more. It filled the whole room from the floor to the ceiling and from the door to the far wall. Nothing made sense at this moment. King Yusuf called the commander of the army to come and to bring the soldiers who specialized in snakes. He asked for them to bring a big truck to carry the snake out so that they could burn or destroy it. He figured the soldiers would find a way to do that but he warned them that it was the largest snake he had ever seen.

After a while, the army arrived but the truck was too small. King Yusuf told the commander that he better get a much bigger truck. He sent his men to go and get the biggest truck they could find. The King told them to go inside his uncle's chamber and to be careful. The commander went inside with two men, looked around the living room, and went straight to the bedroom. They came back running and fighting for the door. The Kings were outside and they started laughing when they saw the great soldiers fighting for the door. It was as if, all of a sudden, the door had become too small for one person to pass through. This time everybody laughed. King Yusuf and King Wisdom were roaring with laughter because they now realized how they had looked like when they had run out of the room. The commander stopped and collected himself. He called his men and reminded them that they were supposed to guard their King to their last breath.

Princess Grace went to them and told them that the snake was dead and that they should not be afraid. They looked at her in shock and asked her how she knew that. She told them she had been inside and she had touched the snake and that it was stone cold. It had not moved when she had touched it. The commander could not believe his ears. Princess Grace had just told him that she had touched the creature to see if it was still alive and he looked at her as though she was crazy. He finally closed his open mouth. Princess Grace sensed that he thought she was crazy and she asked him if he wanted to go inside with her. He told her no, that they would find a way to deal with the snake. He looked at the Kings to read the expression on their faces. He could tell they heard what this young lady had said and it was as if they were not surprised and had no doubt about what she had just told them. He believed it was true. The commander went to the King and asked him how that snake had entered the chamber. Without a word, the King pointed at his uncle. The commander knew who the King's uncle was and what he was capable of doing. He turned and took a few steps towards the uncle without saying a word. The uncle was now afraid of the commander for he could tell he meant business. He was not going to play games with him. He remembered that he was there last year when he had threatened the King and even then he had wanted to strike and the King stopped him. Without a word, he pointed at Princess Grace.

Princess Grace could not believe her eyes. In shock, she stepped forward and asked the great uncle if he had just pointed at her. He told her that he had, that it was because of her that the snake had appeared. She had killed the baby snake and pro-voked the Queen mother to strike. Princess Grace told him that it may seem that way, but the creature had been sleeping with him all along. She was inside already because she was always with him wherever he went. She had just been invisible because of the magic he used. Because of the anointing, she had been exposed. The uncle began scratching his body and jumping from one place to another when he thought of sleeping with such a huge, disgust-ing beast. He thought about how, even with the smaller snake, he had never slept in the same room with it. At his house, it had its own room and when he went out he opened the briefcase and put it inside. At the palace, he would put it in the bathroom and even sealed the door to make sure that it would never come to him.

Lady Elisa interrupted his thoughts and said, "Oh, great uncle! That is why you were vomiting her children because Your

God was laying her eggs inside your stomach all along." She ran as she spoke the last part as the great uncle was charging after her. Everyone, including the soldiers, were laughing and telling her to run faster. King Wisdom called on the great uncle and told him not to kill his baby. King Yusuf was laughing so hard because he remembered that ever since they were young, his uncle had been the most feared by everyone.

Princess Yeti was still boiling with anger towards the King's uncle. She did not see anything funny and she did not feel pity for him. She wished that Princess Grace could have left him to be eaten by his own evil. She finally told them that in order for her to move forward, she had to tell her uncle what was on her mind. She needed to ask him three questions and she needed straight answers, no matter how painful they might be. The great uncle went to her and told her to ask him anything and that he would answer truthfully. She asked him if he was the one who had killed her husband. He took a deep breath and told her that yes, he was the one. She asked him about the two children she had lost when they were both two-years-old. He told her that it had been his duty to sacrifice the Royal blood even though with her husband had just been his pride that had been hurt. With the children, he figured that they were less painful to lose than an adult so instead of sacrificing her, he had taken Amanda and instead of sacrificing King Yusuf, he took her son, Samuel. He told her that even if he had not done that, each of them would still have been killed. He stepped forward and told her that he loved her even if he did not know how to show it. He explained that she should understand that it was their way of life. Even her father the King had sacrificed himself to save the kingdom for his children; for if he had not done that, they would have lost the kingdom to another family. Everyone was quiet, even Princess Yeti. She cried softly and told him that it had been the right thing to do because that had been his way of life. He had believed in the God of sacrifice.

He continued to tell them that they would do anything for Jesus even if it meant going to a place where most people disappeared.

King Yusuf went to his sister and held her and told her it was okay to cry. He held her for a long time. Princess Marisa went to them as well, crying. Prince Brian joined them. The Prince was the only one not crying but he looked very angrily at the uncle. King Wisdom stepped in and told them that it was all in the past and they should remember that the uncle had been born again. He was a new creation in Christ Jesus and that was why they were all standing outside because all the evil that the uncle had used was gone. That was why they had the dead creature in the palace. Forgiveness was the greatest gift of them all. For the Father to be able to forgive them, they should first be able to forgive those who had hurt and despised them with or without cause. He then asked everybody to join hands and pray for peace in King Yusuf's family. They did. The great uncle took the hand of Princess Yeti and the King came and hugged the uncle and told him that he forgave him. Princess Yeti was still crying hugged him and told him she forgave him. Prince Brian was still upset and walked away from the great uncle when he tried to hug him. This concerned the great uncle a great deal for Prince Brian was next in line for the throne if the King did not have any children or if his children were too young to rule. They heard the noise of the truck arriving just as they finished praying.

The soldiers arrived with another truck and it was huge. Now they faced the dilemma of getting the snake outside and loading it into the truck. The soldiers banded together to try to think of the best way to bring the snake out of the chamber. They could not come up with a solution. They went to the Kings and asked them to help them come up with ideas for how to get the snake outside. Both Kings told them there was only one way, for them to carry it if they could but they were not going inside with them. They called the snake experts from the zoo. They came and entered the chamber but they all ran away and told them they could not help.

Meanwhile, Queen Fiona told Lady Samantha to go inside and to stay far away from the chamber with the snake. She came back and said she was afraid to go by herself. She wanted to be around people. Queen Fiona did not want her to see the snake when they brought it out, knowing that she was expecting a child and did not know how she would react when she saw it.

The chief animal control officer came and told the King not to worry, that he was there to give him the best service. King Yusuf told him that all of his men had come running from the chamber when they'd seen the snake. He was very angry with his men and asked them what kind of soldiers and animal control officers they were. He turned to the Kings on his knees and apologized for the behavior of his men. He told the King that he would punish them for their behavior and that he was going to give the King the best service he deserved. The two Kings exchanged looks and folded their arms, waiting and watching the brave soldier angrily going inside the chamber by himself. He soon came running, passing everyone. He ran straight to the gate without looking back. By then, everyone was laughing hard. Even Princess Yeti and Princess Marisa were crying from laughing so hard. The Chief Officer never returned to service his King. He left his car and everything at the palace. King Yusuf told the soldiers that it looked as though there was no one to punish them, so it was better to think about what they could do to solve the problem at hand.

Finally King Yusuf decided it was better for them to burn the snake inside the chamber. The two Queens asked if they could see it first. Sir James, Pastor Eric, Danny, Princess Yeti, Lady Elisa, and Princess Marisa joined them and King Yusuf told them they were welcome to go in by themselves. They looked at King Wisdom to escort them but he turned around and looked in the opposite direction. They asked Princess Grace to go in with them.

She told them she had already seen it so she did not need to go in again. Finally, she told everyone that she would go and open both doors and block them so that they remained open for everyone to see what they were talking about. The palace staff came running to see as well. Princess Grace opened the doors and people could see from a distance. She switched the light in the living room on and asked King Yusuf where the switch for the bedroom was. He told her by the head of the creature. She squeezed her hand in and switched the bedroom light on. Everybody was surprised and shocked at how brave this girl was. Even the two Kings came and took a good look. They could not believe their eyes. Everybody was still afraid. It was as though the snake could catch them where they were standing. Nobody knew something as big as that snake even existed. How this one had entered their home and gotten into the bedroom was a mystery. Princess Grace went and closed the doors after they had seen. The soldiers were shocked that this young lady was not afraid at all and she would go in and touch the creature and turn her back on it without fear. Some of them remembered seeing her on television preaching. They went to her and asked her if she could introduce them to her God when they finished for they wanted that kind of boldness. She agreed with a smile and the two Kings smiled at that kind of evangelism. King Yusuf told them to burn the snake together with the chamber. That was the only possible way to get rid of it. He told the soldiers to call the fire department to come and control the fire and to make sure that nothing except for the chamber burned. Danny told Pastor Eric that he was afraid of these young Christians and he will never cross them as long as he was alive. He told Pastor Eric that as for the Princess, he was even afraid to look at her. She was dangerous. Pastor Eric told him she was the sweetest of them all once you knew her. Danny just shook his head and told him that he couldn't explain all the things she has done since he arrived; if he tells anybody what he had seen, no one would believe him. Pastor Eric told him that was the power of the Holy Spirit working in her and through her.

The butler asked if they should remove the things in the living room and the study room but King Yusuf told them he thought it was better to burn everything. He asked his uncle if there was anything that was important and needed to be saved. He told them there was a black briefcase full of Euros inside the chamber in the living room. Lady Elisa asked him if there were any snakes inside the brief case. He looked at the soldiers and told them that there was only money inside. The commander opened the door and looked inside and saw the briefcase. He went inside and brought the case and handed it over to the uncle. Lady Elisa and King Wisdom were standing by him and moved away from him. He pretended not to see what had happened but he could not blame them for their actions, since he too was afraid of everything in that room. He put the case down and opened it. To his relief, there was only money inside, nothing else. He told the King he did not have anything to wear since all of his clothes were inside and he was afraid of wearing anything from that room. The King told him that the King's designers would take care of him. The firemen arrived and the media people were standing outside the gates, wanting to know what was going on. The commander of the army briefed the firemen. After the briefing, the commander and the firemen's supervisor went inside slowly. The commander opened the door to the bedroom and the firemen could not believe what he saw. He began shaking and vomited from fear. He asked the commander how they were going to burn the snake.

They discussed how to put gas on the snake. They thought of opening the rooftop. The fireman asked him if he was sure it was dead for if it was not, it would charge at them once it felt the heat. They were now getting more afraid. If they could find a way, they could put the gasoline inside the fire truck and use the fire hose to pour the gasoline on top of the snake. That way, they would be sure to cover its entire body. They did as the fireman suggested. Princess Grace asked Pastor Eric to bring the briefcase that the uncle had his snake in to be burned with the big snake. Pastor Eric did as he was told. The Commander of the army asked Princess Grace to open the doors for them and to prop the doors open. It was done. They were now faced with the question of how to light the fire. The commander escorted the King and his visitors outside to the far end of the palace. Princess Grace remained with the firemen and soldiers. The fireman told them that if they were so sure that the snake was dead, they could break the window and put the hose through it. Princess Grace told them not to worry, the snake was completely dead. The other fireman told them he was very good at aiming. He could light his cigarette lighter and aim it to fall right by the bedroom door. They wanted the fire to start inside the bedroom first. It was agreed. The fire started to burn and when the huge snake started to burn, it was as if bombs or fireworks had been placed inside its body. There were also big blasting noises coming from the room, many of which they could not understand. They heard the sounds of children crying and a young girl singing a sorrowful song. They heard animal sounds as well.

Queen Fatima asked what the noises were and where they were coming from. The great uncle told them that the souls of all the sacrifices given over many years were coming from the burning snake. They were the sounds of animals, virgins, children, innocent blood for rain, riches and so on. Everyone looked at him and listened to what he was saying. He told them that now their souls had been released. Princess Yeti started crying again, thinking of her father, her two children, and her husband. Everyone was quiet. Then Lady Elisa said, "King Yusuf, surely your country needed deliverance. I am happy we came." He told her that he was happy they had come as well. They stayed there in silence until the commander came and told them that they could come out. They went straight to see the damage. It was not as bad as they had expected but they could still see some remains of the snake. The firemen had been able to control the fire. The whole chamber had burned. But because it had been built out of hard red bricks, the wall was still standing. The commander told the King that they would clean everything out and make sure it was ready for construction as soon as it cooled off. The King thanked them and told the butler to take them to be fed. He told the Commander that what they had seen and heard there ended in the palace. He did not want to hear anything outside. They signed the declaration of secrecy agreement. The butler then escorted them into the dining room.

The King and his visitors went inside to eat their lunch as well. For lunch, the palace served the King's favorite traditional dishes. Earlier, he had warned them that they would be eating something original from their country. When they went to the dining area, he reminded them that the meal was traditional food again. Lady Elisa asked him if they would be eating snakes. King Yusuf teased her and told her that they had roasted a snake just for her. She screamed and ran to King Wisdom. The uncle excused himself as he was still dirty from the day before and his clothes smelled bad. King Yusuf asked the butler to find him a room to use and something for him to wear. He also commanded the King's design house to start working on his clothes immediately. Everyone enjoyed the dishes and told the King as much. The butler escorted them to the great room and they all stopped when they saw where he was taking them. He told them that the room was as good as new. They would not see or smell anything. The butler told them that the soldiers and firemen had helped to clean it up. King Yusuf told the butler to call them, so that he could reward them since they had done more than what they were called to do. He did. The King told the butler to bring one of his briefcases. When the butler returned with the briefcase, Lady Elisa jumped up and said, "Not again, please!" Everybody laughed.

King Yusuf just looked at her and said, "Lady Elisa, don't worry." He opened the briefcase and removed bundles of Euros. The soldiers entered the palace room where the King was and the King gave each one of them a bundle of money. He gave the Commander two bundles and asked him to call the firefighters. He gave the same to them and gave their supervisor two bundles. They were very happy and they thanked him. He told them it was for cleaning his family room. The fireman told him that it had been easy as they had used the fire hose to suck the whole thing out. The King was still grateful for their help. The uncle told them that he was the richest man in the country and next time he comes to visit, he would call for them. He gave his briefcase to the commander and told him to share it with everyone who had helped. They thanked everyone, especially the King and the uncle, and left.

After they left, the great uncle saw that Lady Elisa was uncomfortable so he asked her if she hadn't known that he was the richest man in the country. He told her that he could buy her if he wanted to. Lady Elisa laughed and said, "Correction, great uncle, you used to be rich before both your money makers died and were burned." He laughed and told her he sometimes wished that he could cut out her tongue. King Yusuf told them that the following morning they would use the original family room for prayer. He said that perhaps after prayer in the room, everyone would be comfortable. It was agreed. The evening went well until Princess Grace asked the great uncle if he was going to introduce the people from his secret society to Jesus. He was silent for some time and told her that she was asking him to commit suicide. She told him that no one could kill him. She explained to him that if the great snake hadn't killed him last night while he was alone in the great room, then there was no one who could kill him. She asked him who the head of that society was. He told her that he was the leader. She told him that she thought as much and now they would not have much power. She told him that she would like to go with him and minister to the society. The old man told her that she might not be aware of what she was asking of him; but that it was as if she was asking him to go to hell to minister there. She told him she was very much aware but that she wanted to go to their meeting and share the good news of Jesus with them.

The great uncle was getting very afraid. He told Princess Grace that he would not do that for he knew what had happened in the past to the people who tried to oppose the society after they became members. He knew that it did not matter who she was, they would eat her alive and feed her to the snakes. He told her that she could not follow them there for it would be the most foolish thing she could ever do. It would be like following a snake into its hole in the dark. She told him that with or without his help, she would go and find the society and bring all those souls to the Kingdom of God. That was stubborn faith and she was not moved by anything. King Wisdom was listening carefully and he wished he could hold his daughter and tell her to relax and stop the madness because he was afraid of his daughter getting hurt. But he knew that he could not help her. He knew that it was her path and that nothing would stop her.

That night, when they went to bed, King Wisdom asked his wife, "What have I done?" The Queen remained quiet and finally she told him not to be regretful because God would not let anything happen to their daughter. She told him that she now had a mind of her own and that only God understood her. She told the King that although she had given birth to her, she was God's vessel and there was nothing anyone could do about it. She went on to tell the King that she was thinking that if all the Christians on earth could raise their children the way they had raised Princess Grace, imagine how the world would be. She asked the King if he could imagine having hundreds of children like Princess Grace. They went to bed with those thoughts. The King had to admit that Princess Grace was a special vessel of Almighty God

But during the night, the King was disturbed by nightmares. He knew it was not a nightmare but it was because God was angry with him for regretting the gift he had given to him. He told his wife that he needed to ask God to forgive him and most of all to repent.

During the Morning Prayer, Princess Grace shared with them that they should use the gifts of God without regret and they should never regret the life God had given them for it was a life with the greatest purpose and the rewards of that life were more than any of them could ever imagine. King Wisdom fell to his knees and asked God to forgive him. He repented for all the thoughts and words he had said the night before. He knew it was the devil putting those thoughts into him. He asked God for His will to be done in Princess Grace's life and with his family. He felt peace after that.

After the prayer, the great uncle saw that he had missed many calls from his people. He did not want to talk to them for he knew what he had done was totally unacceptable in their society. He listened to the messages they had left with fear creeping up on him. They were all urgent and some had left messages that their babies had died. He knew what they meant. He called Princess Grace and told her what had happened. She told him to invite them to the palace and to tell them to bring their briefcases. She then talked to King Yusuf. He was afraid that perhaps they would be coming with something as big as the snake they had seen the day before. But Princess Grace told him that his uncle was the head of the society and that he was their leader. King Yusuf agreed but he did not want them to sleep at the palace. That was agreed as well. The great uncle invited them to come and see him at the palace the following day at ten in the morning. They made their travel arrangements and told him that they would be there the next day at ten in the morning as discussed.

Meanwhile, Princess Grace asked everyone to continue fasting. They fasted and prayed. The day of the meeting, they were all ready and excited about meeting their visitors. Pastor Eric remarked that if Mohammed could not go to the mountain, then the mountain would come to Mohammed. They all understood his reference.

They woke up at the usual time and went to the family room and started worshipping. Some of the palace staff was worshipping in their quarters. Princess Grace asked King Yusuf why he did not invite the members of his staff who were free to come and join them. The King sent his butler to call those who were free. They were very happy and they came and worshipped and prayed. To everyone's surprise, most of them had good voices and could sing very well. When it came to prayer, there were fireworks. King Yusuf was very happy and told them that most of them were going to work for the kingdom of God. He said that he would have to hire more people to replace them. They were very happy to hear that from their King. King Wisdom asked them if they had all accepted Jesus Christ as their Lord and Personal Savior. Most of them had but a few of them had not. They led those who had not yet accepted Jesus as their Lord and Savior to receive Him. Just as they finished, the uncle's visitors arrived.

As the great uncle's visitors arrived, the butler came and announced their arrival. A few minutes later, he escorted them to the great family room as instructed. They were very happy to be in the palace. In their minds, they were thinking that perhaps the day had finally arrived for them to take over the palace as their prophecy had told them many years ago that the kingdom of darkness would take over under the leadership of the great uncle. They saw their leader and exchanged greetings. They expected him to talk to them in private but he didn't. Instead, he called them inside and offered them seats to sit. They were confused because they were expecting him to talk to them in private so that they could discuss the problems they had been experiencing. But he told them he knew about their problems and that they should feel free to talk in front of these people including King

Yusuf, King Wisdom, Princess Grace, Pastor Eric, and Pastor Sir James. It did not make sense to them but as he was their leader, they knew how arrogant he could be at times. They did as he told them. They thought that, as usual, he had some secret powers to show these people. After all, they know their leader. He was capable of many things and he liked to show off his powers. They continued with their stories and when they finished telling them everything. He told them what had happened to him two days ago. He explained how the young lady they saw sitting close to him had burned his toy with her eyes just by looking at it and how he had slept in the family room without knowing where he was. He told them that it happened because of the mighty powers this young lady had used on him. They wanted to run away, but he told them not to run.

He told them how arrogant and boastful he had been with his powers when he entered the palace and how he no longer knew anything anymore about those dark kingdom powers. He continued to tell them about how he had found the Queen mother in his bedroom chamber and how he had run to Princess Grace for help. He had not left anything behind including the two Kings running for their lives at the sight of the Queen mother. They were now smiling that the Kings had been afraid of their God. He continued and told them that only the young lady in front of them had been able to go inside by herself and inspect the Queen mother. When they heard this, their eyes grew big. They remembered how their leader would be the one directing them in darkest places especially when they had been new recruits. He also told them how the Queen mother had been seen by everybody and they all gasped. They could not believe that there was anybody on earth who could see the Queen mother and this young lady had the nerve to look at her when the great Kings and their leader were afraid of her. They knew there was something about this young lady and they wanted to have it as well. If it meant paying with all that they had, they would pay so that they too could have those powers.

They remembered the old legend that they'd been told about the King from China. In the old days, he had been given the opportunity by the Gods to see the Queen mother and he had become the most powerful, richest, and feared man on earth. They asked him if he was telling them that he had also seen the Queen mother. They called the Queen mother, "the rock of ages, and the master of the earth, the giver of all riches and wisdom." He told them that she was in his bedroom and he had run away because it was so frightening. He continued to tell them that he called the young lady for help and she came but she could not enter the chamber because she told them that her God had stopped her. They laughed at first because they did not know what comes next. As he continued to tell them what had happened, the laughter died down. He told them how they had sung their songs after two hours of singing the Christian songs that praised and spoke of life and love, the Queen mother died. He reminded them that they should remember that the Queen mother did not want to hear anything about love and peace. They were astonished. He told them that the Queen mother had died and the King called the soldiers to come and remove her but even the soldiers were afraid of the Queen mother, even though she was dead. Their eyes became huge. He continued to tell them how the fire engines were called to come and help and finally they put gasoline on her and burned her together with the chamber. He did not have the chance to tell them about the strange sounds they heard while the snake burned for they were all crying hysterically. All of them told their leader that they were left with nothing. They asked him what they were going to do. He pointed to Princess Grace and told them that she would guide them. He told them that she had guided him and helped him during a difficult time and therefore, they should do as she said and she would guide them. He told them to listen carefully. They were still crying and they grasped at their leader. He told them to collect themselves and give the young lady a chance to help them. They all asked Princess Grace to be their leader.

Meanwhile, outside, Danny and the soldiers were talking. Danny was telling them that he thought it was a bad idea to have brought all those wizards together. They could have met them one at a time. He then started laughing and told them he was so grateful; he did not boast in public about the powers he had and also he was grateful he received the Lord in a respectful manner. The soldiers laughed and one of them said that the Holy Spirit really dealt with the Great Uncle. He asked them if they saw how afraid he was of their leader after telling her she was a stupid young girl who knew nothing and was raised by fools. They all laughed, and some started to imitate how afraid he was when he saw his snake burning from the eyes of Princess Grace, and another told them they were not showing it properly, that he saw the whole thing. He then performed how the great uncle reacted. They laughed at how he did it. Princess Yeti and Princess Marisa were looking at them and listening through the window. Danny told them he was very happy he belonged to the most powerful God. He told them that in his lifetime, he will never play games with this young Christian; he has discovered that they were the most powerful. He asked them if they don't think Princess Grace is something—very quiet, polite yet firm, and fearsome when you crossed her path in the Lord. They all agreed with him that she is surely the vessel of God without doubt. He then went down on his knees and thanked God for choosing him as his child and asked forgiveness for all he had done wrong in the sight of him. All the soldiers saw and heard what Danny was doing, and they all got on their knees and prayed too.

After the visitors dried their eyes, Princess Grace told them about the power beyond all powers. She explained about the same power that had killed the Queen mother and the same power that had burned their leader's toy. She told them about the beginning of the world and the first Adam, then the prophecy about Messiah, the birth of Jesus, his horrible death, and the reasons he died. Finally, she told them about Jesus rising from the dead. She finished by explaining about going to hell. She went on to tell them that when they received Jesus as their Lord and personal savior, all their sins will be forgiven and they became new. They liked that part for they were asking themselves how they were going to face the people they had been tormenting by killing their loved ones for scarifies. When she finished, they were all crying again but listening carefully. She told them how Jesus had performed miracles and told them when he left how those who believed in him would perform even greater miracles than he had performed. She finished by telling them that they were looking for power the wrong way and that the kind of power they were looking for was temporal because it was not eternal like the power of the Lord Jesus. She told them that whoever believed in the Lord Jesus shall have everlasting life and shall not go to hell. By now, they were all paying attention and ready to make Jesus their Lord as well. She told them that the life in Jesus was not only the life of power, but it was the life of love, peace, compassion, forgiveness, and giving, just as they had been given a chance to repent of their evil doings and to have a chance to give life.

She asked them if they would like to make Jesus Christ their Lord and personal savior. They all agreed and they were eager to receive Him. She led them into the Kingdom of the most High God. After they received Him, Princess Grace sent for the rest of the team to come in and worship. They sang worships unto the Father and praised Him, thanking the King of Kings for His mercy and wonderful love for them. She took a few steps towards King Yusuf and asked him to lay hands on them to receive the Holy Spirit. He was happy to do so. He did not even touch them, he began praying and lifted his hands towards them and they all received the Holy Spirit and started speaking in unknown tongues. The King's uncle was now becoming afraid of his nephew for he did not know that he already had that kind of power as well. He now understand why he was not afraid of him. After that, they celebrated and she told them that the heavens were celebrating every time a person accepted Jesus Christ as their Lord because one more person was saved from the lake of fire. She encouraged them to go and share the same news with whomever they met. King Yusuf thanked King Wisdom, Queen Fiona, Princess Grace, and her Pastors and told them he had gotten more than he'd hoped for during their visit. He could now rule his county in peace and in one spirit. His country now belonged to Jesus Christ and it was a very good feeling. They said Amen to that. The King asked the butler to bring the best food and drinks for a celebration. He then announced that he would be sending his uncle to King Wisdom's country to go and learn how to be a minister of the word of God. The uncle was very happy about it; he could not control his excitement. The other former members of the society asked the King if they could also go if they promised to pay for everything themselves. They said that they also would like to do great works for the right cause. King Yusuf told them that he would have to call the school first and see how many people the school could take and determine when they could begin their classes. He warned them that this was a very important job and they should take it seriously as they would be the leaders of the country and many people would be looking to them for growth and spiritual feeding. He further told them that when it comes to the work of The Lord Jesus, he did not play games and anyone who abused the ministry would answer to him and he would deal with such matters seriously. They told the King that they would not fail him or the kingdom of heaven. The food and drinks arrived and everybody ate and talked, laughing about all they had to look forward to with their life in the Lord Jesus. The King told the former members of secret society that they may attend the classes in his country because some tutors would be coming, but for now they should go and help the ministers and he would get the report of how they were doing. He divided them among the ministers he was sending out. They were very happy. King Yusuf didn't want them to remain idle because they might backslide; he also wanted to separate them and not to send them to their homes.

King Wisdom was quiet watching his daughter and thanking God for the work he was doing through his daughter. After she finished, she called her and asked her if she could take a walk with her old man while everybody was eating and celebrating. They walked together. King Yusuf's garden was beautiful, but they did not have the time to enjoy it. He told his daughter that he had something to confess and asked for her forgiveness. He told her how the previous night, he had been so afraid for her life when she wanted to follow that group to their secret meeting place and he ended up questioning himself, whether he had done the right thing in bringing her up the way he did. Princess Grace stopped and asked him why he would allow the devil to put such ugly thoughts in his mind and why he would entertain them. She told him that in the future he should refuse to give voice to thoughts like that. When thoughts like that come into his heart, he should refuse to say them out loud. He should pretend he did not hear the devil and instead he should start worshipping or thinking of something good God had done for him or the people he knew and the devil would flee. She asked him if he had asked the Father to forgive him. He told her he had. She told him that she loved him very much but the Father's Kingdom comes first and her life was not as important as doing the work of the Father. She told the King that God had given her this life to use for His glory on earth and she never feared anything because she knew the one who created everything both in heaven and on earth was always with her and was always guiding her steps. She asked King Wisdom if he had not noticed that God always directed her and told her what to do if there was danger. He told her that he understood and knew that very well. After this discussion, they continued with their walk to see King Yusuf's garden. It was beautiful indeed; some of the flowers they had not seen before.

King Wisdom asked Princess Grace what was next after this journey to King Yusuf's country ended. He had a feeling that her plans may have changed. She told him that it was true that her plan had changed and she was not sure if they would go straight home. She told him that the Father in heaven was in control now. He asked her if they were going to die. She laughed and told him no, there was a lot for them to do on earth before they joined the Father in heaven. The King stopped and took a very deep breath. Princess Grace laughed and told him he did not think the great King would be afraid of death. King Wisdom laughed and asked her if she had forgotten how both he and King Yusuf had run for their life two days ago. Princess Grace laughed and asked him if he knew he was in trouble with Lady Elisa for that. King Wisdom laughed and told her that he knew and he wished he could make her forget, but he could not. Princess Grace laughed and told him that he and King Yusuf would always be reminded of that day by their favorite daughter, Lady Elisa. They both agreed. They picked flowers and went back inside.

The following day was the day that King Wisdom and his people were scheduled to leave King Yusuf's country. Princess Marisa was going to stay at the palace as Princess Grace's visitor. Emmanuel was also going to stay at the palace under Princess Grace and Pastor Eric's supervision for three months. The great uncle wanted to go, but he did not have enough clothes. The King's designers were still making clothes for him. He told the King that he did not care, he would buy clothes for himself as he was so anxious to start the work of Jesus Christ as quickly as possible. He also told the King that he can call his home and ask them to start bringing him clothes and money. It was agreed. He wanted to begin learning from Princess Grace and the Pastors who had come to his country. The truth was that he was afraid to face the people of his country who he had been terrorizing by killing their loved ones. He was hoping when he returned that Jesus would have worked on them and made them forgive him. Finally, the two Kings agreed that he could go. He would be staying at the King's hotel, and he would be under Sir James. The uncle sent for more of his clothes and money from his home. An hour before they left, his messengers were back. Princess Yeti came to him and told him in a firm voice that when he arrived in King Wisdom's country, he was to behave. She wanted to hear only good reports about him. He laughed and said, "Yes, mother. I promise I will behave."

Everybody laughed, especially King Yusuf, for he had never heard his uncle joking before and now he was catching on the sense of humor they had. It was a good sign.

The morning of their departure, everyone woke up earlier than usual and went to the family room to start praying. To their surprise, most of the palace staff was already there to join them. Even those staff members who had the day off had come to worship. When King Yusuf saw this, he was very happy with them and he told them that from that day onward they should come to join him in worship and praise every morning. They sang praise songs and danced for the Lord Jesus. Lady Elisa discovered that she was not the only good dancer; there were many talented dancers and good singers in King Yusuf's country. Emmanuel danced like he had been practicing which surprised everyone. As for King Yusuf, he also realized that he did not know anything about his staff. All of a sudden, he had a whole church choir in his palace. He told them how proud and happy he was with them.

At the end of the morning service, Princess Grace prayed for them and declared blessings upon them. King Yusuf sent his butler to bring Soyab in. In front of his Captains, he told Soyab that his good men would be leaving him in a few days to go and preach the good news of the Lord Jesus Christ in different cities and he needed new men to provide him with service. He wanted to know if Soyab was willing to take on the position of Captain of the palace together with the other Captain. Soyab fell to his knees and thanked the King for the opportunity. He promised that he would not let him down and that he would guard the King with his life. The two Kings laughed for they thought of the Chief Officer who had run away after promising to give the King his best. They all laughed and King Yusuf reminded them that this was a serious matter. Soyab knew the story of the chief so he also laughed after he realized what he had just said. Nevertheless, he was very grateful for the offer since his dream was coming true and this showed him that the King had forgiven him and he would be able to see his wife. Soyab had been given one of the highest promotions available. He would receive more money, a place to stay at the palace, and he would be travelling a great deal with the King.

The Palace staff exchanged information with King Wisdom's staff. Emmanuel's mother was crying because it was the first time she would be away from Emmanuel for any length of time. But she was happy that her son would finally be doing something important with his life. She told this to the King. It was also difficult for the King to let Emmanuel go, but he wanted him to receive more education in Christ and he was determined that Emmanuel was going to be one of the great leaders of the ministry. Emmanuel was very happy for he had never dreamed of such travel and he was receiving the highest honor to go and learn from Princess Grace. The King invited Emmanuel's mother to stay at the palace while Emmanuel was gone so that she would not have to be alone. He also extended an open invitation to his staff for those who wanted to work for the Kingdom of God should come to the family room in the evening. He further warned them that some of them whom he had seen were very good at singing and praying and if they did not come, he would personally find them and bring them to the family room by force. Everyone laughed. He told them that he needed counselors, musicians, prayer worriers, ministers, and ushers. He told Rashidah that she would be writing the names of the people who were interested in joining the ministry work and their place of interest, as her work in God's Kingdom has also began. She was very happy that she would be doing something to help. He then told the butler to start preparing for hiring new palace staff since he was about to lose most of his staff to Jesus Christ. The King smiled and told everyone that it was the first time in his life that he felt good about losing people to someone else. Everyone laughed and King Wisdom congratulated King Yusuf on his success in introducing Jesus to his country. Everyone came forward to congratulate him. He asked everyone to pray for Princess Grace, the leader responsible for all that they had experienced. When they had finished praying, he asked them to pray for Pastor Eric and Sir James, God's two worriers who had travelled his country and introduced hundreds of millions of people to Christ. After that, they prayed for all their visitors and for all the people travelling. King Wisdom concluded the prayer by praying for all of the people who remained and for more workers for the Kingdom of God since King Yusuf needed much more than what he had. They ate their breakfast and began preparing so that immediately after lunch, they could leave. King Yusuf told his workers that those who were not busy should stay and continue with praises.

As the praise was going on outside the palace, they were also going on inside the palace. Lady Elisa taught them some of the songs she sang and they sang and danced. The celebration has started in earnest.

Just before they left, the palace staff brought out gifts for Pastor Eric, Sir James, Princess Grace, and Lady Elisa. Then the butler brought out a big gift for King Wisdom and his Queen. Even King Yusuf had not known that there were gifts for his visitors. He was surprised, yet pleased.

The two Captains brought out a gift for Pastor Eric and Princess Marisa and they told them it was an engagement gift.

Princess Marisa was very happy. She quickly moved to Pastor Eric's side and grabbed his hand.

Each Captain handed a gift to Pastor Eric and Sir James and saluted the two men. Then they went to Princess Grace and fell to their knees and thanked her for the knowledge she had imparted on them and the work she had started in their country; they stood up and saluted her. They gave her a gift. Princess Grace began to cry and she fell to her knees then hugged them. Pastor Eric and Sir Pastor James were touched by their honor. They told them that they were God's generals. Pastor Eric cried. Princess Yeti came forward and hugged him. King Yusuf thanked them for honoring his visitors and for the gifts.

Then King Yusuf came forward with a big box nobody had seen before. He presented it to Princess Grace and said, "My mother and my teacher, it is always a great pleasure learning from you and working with you. Words alone cannot express my gratitude regarding the light you brought to my country. No amount of gifts can pay you for what you have done for us, but may our God record all the works you have done in His book and reward you in a mighty way." He also saluted her.

The King and Queen's gifts were loaded into the trucks and ready to go to the airport. The rumor was that the box the King has presented to Princess Grace was full of Euros to support her in the work she was doing in the Kingdom of God. Some said it was a hundred million Euros, while others said it was two hundred and fifty million. Danny also gave ten million Euros each to Pastor Eric, Princess Grace, Sir James, Lady Elisa, the King and the Queen. King Yusuf thanked Danny for his gifts and told him to remain in the Palace after the visitors were gone as he had a lot to discuss with him. Danny was overjoyed.

The ceremony for their farewell began earlier than expected outside because the people had started gathering at the palace gates at ten in the morning to bid King Wisdom and his people farewell. When their convoy arrived, there were traditional dances taking place at the palace gates. The visitors stopped and watched the dancers. King Wisdom joined the dancing group. Even though he did not know the steps, he tried to dance and everyone appreciated his effort. The media was there and they took pictures of King Wisdom dancing. The ceremony was being shown live on television in King Wisdom's country (Netherlands) as well. Princess Grace went and prayed for all of them and blessed them. They got back into their cars and proceeded to the airport. The crowd at the palace gate was so happy and most of them took pictures. Sir James took a picture of King Wisdom dancing. The drivers drove slowly so that people could walk along next to the cars. Some people were crying because the visitors were leaving.

They spent two hours at the airport enjoying the celebrations. It had been so nicely organized that King Yusuf did not know how they had managed. Just before they got onto the plane, Lady Elisa sang the same song she had been singing when they'd arrived. By now, most people knew the song and they sang along with her. The crowd remained singing as the King and his people boarded the plane and took off to Netherlands. Many people waved banners reading, "Our King, we love you." And "You are our father!" Some said, "God Bless King Yusuf!" and "Long Live the Blessed King Yusuf!" King Yusuf was so touched because he had never seen that kind of love from his people before. It was very nice to be appreciated and to be wanted instead of feared. He arrived home and took the microphone and told his people that he loved them too and he was looking forward to working with them to make their country a better country in the name of Jesus Christ. The whole crowd gathered said, "Amen!"